One More River to Cross

Allen Futsch

DORRANCE
PUBLISHING CO
EST. 1920
PITTSBURGH, PENNSYLVANIA 15238

The contents of this work, including, but not limited to, the accuracy of events, people, and places depicted; opinions expressed; permission to use previously published materials included; and any advice given or actions advocated are solely the responsibility of the author, who assumes all liability for said work and indemnifies the publisher against any claims stemming from publication of the work.

Cover painting: Pieter Bruegel the Elder, *The Fall of Icarus*, the Royal Museum of Fine Arts, Belgium

Dorrance Publishing Co
585 Alpha Drive
Pittsburgh, PA 15238
Visit our website at *www.dorrancebookstore.com*

ISBN: 978-1-6393-7216-4
eISBN: 978-1-6393-7895-1

Singing wide river,
River of Jordan,
Wide river,
One more river to cross,
One more river to cross,
One more river to cross.

Marching Song
Infantry Officer Candidate School
US Army
Vietnam era

PREFACE

This is not a memoir. It's therapy. I wrote it at the suggestion of one of my PTSD counsellors. There is no "Eddie Brandt." He's fiction. Writing about him was easier than writing about myself. Also, there was no 5th battalion in the 173rd Airborne Brigade in Vietnam. Same reason. Everything else is true, as true to me as the face in the mirror in the morning. But when James Jones wrote The Thin Red Line, the novel based on his service as an infantryman in World War II, his last words were: "One day one of their number would write a book about all this, but none of them would believe it, because none of them would remember it that way."

PROLOGUE

Their science had met the basic challenge of space travel. Their ships could move at the speed of light. And so, they explored the universe looking for other intelligent life.

One of their probes entered our solar system between Mars and Earth. It registered the sun, rated it as a minor level IV body surrounded by dust and gas and otherwise empty. Seeing nothing else of interest, it moved on.

1950

It was the first day of school and he didn't want to go. He wasn't sure what school was, but he knew he wouldn't like it.

He liked exploring the woods behind the house, he and his dog. There was the foundation of an old barn that held brambles and wild flowers, the old gate to a field that was now overgrown, and the stone walls in the woods that now divided nothing. He didn't know anything about school, but he was sure it wasn't going to be anywhere near as interesting. He didn't want to go.

His mother dressed him in strange new clothes and he didn't like them: leather shoes, short pants, a white shirt, a tan coat. They made him look silly. He liked his blue jeans, his high-top sneakers, his striped jersey. They felt good. These new clothes didn't.

He stood outside the house at the front door. His mother had a camera. Just as she snapped the picture, he started crying and reached for the handle to go back inside. And that was the image of his first day at school.

These are the instincts that told us to run from sabertoothed tigers.

1952

It was early winter and they were playing outside, Eddie and Craig and Craig's little brother, Kit. The house up the road had a swimming pool, so of course that's where they went. They were looking at the water and, just like that, Kit fell in. Eddie looked at him as he slowly sank to the bottom, floating downward with an open mouth and a surprised look. Craig ran for home. The front door exploded open and his mother came out screaming. She sprinted to the pool. Eddie pointed to Kit lying quietly at the bottom. His mother dove down and pulled her child to the surface.

In no time there were people – firemen, policemen, medics. They revived Kit, who showed no ill effects from being underwater for several minutes. Eddie was scared…and then they made him a hero. The story was he saved Kit. The parents had a wooden medal made up. It was painted gold and inscribed with "for saving the life of our son Kit." The father was a manager at the local Ford plant and arranged a special tour just for Eddie.

And all the while Eddie said to himself he hadn't done anything, that all this fuss was for nothing. For the first time in his life, he realized that adults didn't always mean what they said. For the first time in his life, he realized that fuss could be made over nothing. For the first time in his life, he identified adult bullshit. For the first time in his life, he saw the "Big Lie."

1953

Eddie's father told him stories. He was the son of German immigrants. They lived on the eastside of New York City. As a young boy during World War I, he got beaten up by a bunch of the local kids for being a heinie and a square head. He looked each one of them up individually and beat the crap out of them all.

His father used to beat him. He grew quickly and was soon bigger than the old man. Then came the day when the old man went to hit him and he fought back. They broke all the furniture in the living room. The old man never hit him again.

As a teenager, he worked in a wire factory. On day one of the ginzos came at him with a knife and cut him. He reached for a hammer and hit him across the mouth spraying teeth and blood all over the floor.

Same place, he got into it with a big Pollack. He hit him and hit him and hit him, but the big son of a bitch wouldn't go down. Finally, the foreman broke it up. After that everyone left him alone.

He was in the reserves and got called up for the Korean War. One day he and his Korean driver were sniped at by guerrillas. The driver ducked down behind the console. With his left hand he steered the jeep down the road. When they got back to camp, he beat the shit out of the driver.

He did well in business, wore a suit and tie and made senior executive in a big company. He taught himself which fork to use and what wine went with what. When the great Northeast blackout hit, he was walking to the train station in a dark city. Someone grabbed him by the arm. He caught him right under the chin with his briefcase, stepped over him, and caught the train home.

These were the stories Eddie grew up with.

1956

The war. Although only nine months old when it ended, Eddie was formed by World War II. Almost without exception, the significant male figures in his youth were World War II vets: his father, his uncle, the fathers and uncles of his friends, his teachers, his coaches; he grew up with their stories. Iwo Jima and D-Day and the Battle of the Bulge were his tribal myths. Their pull was as strong as a shaman's song sung around a campfire ten thousand years ago. The message was the same: men go to war.

Growing up, stories of war were everywhere. They were in books; his fifth-grade teacher read to the class *Reach for the Sky*, the story of the legless fighter pilot, Douglas Bader. They were on television; *Victory at Sea*, *Combat*, *The Rat Patrol*, etc. And, of course, they were in the movies. War movies were a Hollywood staple and Eddie and his pals saw them all. There was *The Guns of Navarone*, *D-Day*, *The Victors*, *To Hell and Back*, *Anzio*, *Von Ryan's Express*, and so, and so, and so.

He had a sociology professor in college say, only half-jokingly, that the way to eliminate racism was to kill all the parents. Hmmm.

1957

At age twelve, Eddie was groped by a minister. He never told anyone.

1958

Eddie's father told him a story. Count Felix von Luckner, "the Sea Devil," was a German aristocrat who commanded a sailing commerce raider in World War I. He earned worldwide admiration, not just for his exploits, he captured fourteen Allied ships, but equally for his humane, even gentlemanly, treatment of the captured crews. No one ever died under von Luckner.

After the war, he toured the United States giving hundreds of talks. On one such occasion, Eddie's grandfather managed an introduction and somehow a bond was formed. The result was boozing, first socially and, in no time at all, on an epic scale. Thrilled to be getting shitfaced with a graf, grandpapa brought him home to meet the missus. She was not impressed, particularly when he started spending the nights flopped snoring and farting on the couch. After about a week of that shit, she put her foot down.

"Enough," said she.

"But he's a graf," said grandpapa.

"He's a bum," said she. "Get him out."

Of such stuff are heroes made.

1958

The road to hell is paved with good intentions. Eddie's father decided private school was the ticket for his boy, so he sent Eddie to Pudley Prep. Gothic buildings on a wooded hill overlooking a small town…it sure looked the part. As he walked through the main entrance, Eddie read the inscription carved there in stone:

"Enter here to be and find a friend."

The thing about Pudley was it was a second-rate school with first-rate aspirations. Institutions, like people, can have their noses pressed up against the window. Eddie broke the code on that one pretty quickly.

There was the bullying. He had just read *Lord of the Flies*, and goddammit, here it was. When the faculty withdrew, the monsters came out. A nice kid named Sandy had something of a flat face. He was "Push Face." Another named Perry had protruding lips. He was "Goose." And, of course, the Jewish kids were "kikes" and "hebes." One called Butch had a nervous breakdown. But the low point was a poor little turd named Dave. One day, Dave was walking along the basement corridor with Tommy, one of the seniors. Tommy pulled Dave into a storage room and buggered him in the ass. That one didn't make it into the brochure.

Not all the monsters were kids. True to private school form, there was staff faggotry. Mr. Hexter, one of the English teachers, led a bike tour through New England each summer. Everyone had a tentmate, including Mr. Hexter. You didn't want to share a tent with Hexter. Everyone knew that. Mr. Warren was the music teacher. You didn't want to be alone with Warren. Everyone knew that.

And then there was Mr. Valentine. Valentine ran the freshman dormitory. Valentine liked Eddie. He assigned Eddie the room next to his. He would come into Eddie's room after lights out and sit on the edge of the bed. He asked him about his day, his studies, how he felt, and if anything was bothering him. In no time at all what bothered Eddie was Valentine. How to get rid of this prick? He tried sullen. That didn't work. He tried smartass. No dice. Then, one day, he pinned a condom on Valentine's door: *Scumbag to scumbag, takes one to know one*, he thought. So, they put Eddie on suspension. When dear old Dad asked him what the hell was going on, Eddie told him if he didn't pull him out of Pudley he was going to be expelled.

The next week, Eddie switched to the public high school. So much for being and finding a friend.

1960

Eddie walked to high school. He had to go around some kind of a hush-hush facility. They called it a special care institution. It was a nut house. A seven-foot concrete wall sealed it off. One day, Eddie decided to cut through it. That would save some time...and, let's face it, he wanted to see what was there. Never seen a nut house. So, *boop*, over the wall, no sweaty da. Nice looking place. Big, old trees, gravel path. Pleasant walk, save time, nice.

The third time he cut through, some old guy started yelling at him. Naturally, Eddie told him to go fuck a duck. The old guy came uncorked, a flame shooting out of his ass and steam out of his ears.

"You little shit!" he yelled, lumbering after Eddie.

Zoom, Eddie was gone.

Same thing the next day and the next. Now things got interesting. This wall prick it seemed was developing a serious stay-the-fuck-out hard-on for Eddie. Well, now, let the games begin: Wall Prick and Indians. Eddie was the Indians. He varied his entry point. Sometimes, he even walked around, not cutting through at all. No patterns for Wall Prick, no siree. Keep him on his toes. Sometimes, he'd cross over and see Wall Prick in the distance. He'd give him a Three Stooges "nya nya," watch him put his fat ass into gear, wait until he got closer and then just rocket out of Dodge. Jesus, it was fun.

Then Wall Prick stopped showing up. Two, three, four days, then a week, no Wall Prick. After two weeks, Eddie realized Wall Prick was gone. Where was the fun in that? Game over. Eddie never cut through the nut house again.

1961

"*Street Without Joy*." It was a book about the French Indochina War, and Eddie read it. He was hooked. Indochina; it sounded so…exotic: La Guerre d'Indochine…la gair dan-do-sheen (Eddie was taking French in school). It sounded so…cool. It was in the Orient:

> Ship me somewhere east of Suez
> Where the best is like the worst
> Where there aren't no Ten Commandments
> And a man can raise a thirst
> For the temple bells are ringing
> And it's there that I would be,
> By the old Moulmein pagoda
> Lookin' lazy at the sea.

Cool.

It had babes right out of Terry and the Pirates, yeah, the Dragon Lady (did oriental pussy really go east to west?)

Cool.

It had the Foreign Legion.

Cool.

He saw the movie *China Gate*: A horny-fisted American demolition expert in the Foreign Legion in Indochina on a secret mission guided by a woody-inducing wet dream Eurasian babe.

Cool.

Jeezus, thought Eddie. Wouldn't it be cool to fight a war in an-do-sheen.

Ted and Eddie decided enough was enough. They were *going* to get laid. This weekend, goddammit. Saturday night they took the train into the city and the subway into the shitty area. Fortified with some cheap booze, they took to the streets. Watch out, women, some men were looking for some coochie. And just like that, a street hooker picked them up. It was chilly and she was wearing an overcoat, so they couldn't check out the goods. She was female, that much they felt certain. They followed her into some cruddy building, up some stairs to an even cruddier apartment. Latino music was playing, kids were crying, and a lot of Spanish was being spoken at all different volumes. This was some romantic shit, all right. They flipped a coin to see who went first. It was Eddie's honor. He followed overcoat into her apartment, into the bedroom. There was a kid's bike leaning against the wall. She was a little older than she looked outside. No matter, Eddie was on the main train to poontang city. He gave her the money. She took off the overcoat. She was kinda porky. No big deal, more cushion for the pushing. She hiked up her dress, sat down on the bed, and spread her legs.

"Venga, venga."

This was the first real live beaver he had ever seen. It was really hairy, and really, really big. It was like he was standing naked in front of the La Brea Tar Pit.

"Venga, venga."

His hard on, spurred on by visions of a Playmate centerfold, when confronted with the reality of Concita La Brea, immediately sounded the retreat. He could almost hear the pressure going down, like a tire with a nail in it.

"Venga, venga."

Eddie, with his innate flair for languages, began to reason with La Brea.

"Me gotto mucho problemo. Me havo biggo operation, snippo, snippo. No can venga, venga. You keepo dinero. Me adios pronto."

Adios, muchacha.

Out in the hallway.

"Jeez, Eddie, that was fast."

"Er, yeah, buddy. All yours."

Ted went in. A few minutes later, Ted came out. They hotfooted it outside. After a few blocks, Eddie turned to Ted.

"I couldn't do it."

Ted looked back.

"Me neither."

Then they both laughed like it was the funniest joke they had ever heard. On the train home, every time they looked at each other they laughed.

They had bragged to all their pals about the planned adventure. That Monday, despite a hundred questions, neither of them said a thing. And then a strange thing happened. The word spread about these two intrepid cocksmen. It had a life of its own. This was a lesson Eddie never forgot: the most effective way to brag is to say nothing at all.

1962

Eddie was accepted at the state agriculture school. Having no experience in agriculture, he was assigned to work on a farm that summer, way up on the Canadian border. Most of what he knew about farming was from Norman Rockwell, with a dash of Walt Disney. You know the stuff: A tidy little place surrounded by colorful flowers, overhanging shade trees, a pond with merry ducks, Elsie the cow with big brown eyes, apple-cheeked kids, and a floppy puppy frolicking in the front yard, Farmer Jones leaning on a hoe smiling, and Mother Jones putting a homemade pie on the window sill to cool.

Well, that was horseshit. The reality was a dumpy little house, a couple snot-nosed little kids, a fat, loud-mouthed farmer, his fat, overworked wife, and mud, lots and lots of mud…muddy yard, muddy barn, muddy cows, muddy dogs, muddy people.

Summertime meant harvesting the hay, and Eddie did some goddamn haying. Fat Fuck drove the tractor pulling the baler and a wagon. Eddie stood on the wagon, grabbing the bales with a hook as they got shat out of the baler. Then he stacked them: 3-3-3-2-1, 3-3-3-2-1, 3-3-3-2-1, and so on until the wagon was full. It was a hilly farm, okay when they were going uphill, a pain in the wazoo going down. Then Eddie had to keep the fucking bales from tumbling off the wagon. It was hot, grimy, exhausting labor, and boring to the edge of insanity. What might have been a minor plus, working outside in the fresh air, was completely negated by sucking in the diesel exhaust of the old John Deere tractor.

One day, another farm hand showed up. His name was Tripod. *At last*, thought Eddie, *someone to talk to*. Then he found out the reason for the name: Tripod could only say one word, "try."

"Morning, Tripod."

"Try."

"Nice day, huh?"

"Try."

"Up your ass with a meat hook."

"Try."

A whole summer with Fat Fuck and Tripod. Jesus.

Fat Fuck had a unique relationship with the English language. Standard profanity had apparently passed him by. "Jesus, asshole, Elmer" was his particular favorite.

Huh?

Fat Fuck was also not averse to passing on the distilled wisdom of three generations on the land: "If a man was smart, he'd get hisself a flat farm, cuz a hilly farm don't mean nothing but bruised tits and scraped tits."

Jesus.

That summer did help Eddie develop two lifetime ambitions. First, never to farm again. Second, to hunt down Norman Rockwell and kick him square in the balls. Jesus, asshole, Elmer.

1962

It was a land grant college so ROTC was mandatory. *Cool,* thought Eddie, *I get to wear a uniform.* And, in fact, they gave them uniforms. Of course they didn't fit, so they were instructed to go to the local tailor to get 'em cut to size. Right. Eddie had more important stuff than schlepping all the way to the tailor. Like getting shitfaced, for example. To pass muster at weekly drill, he hiked the too-long pants up to his armpits with suspenders. The jacket covered it, and what they didn't know wouldn't hurt 'em.

One night, in a booze-induced lapse of judgement, he entertained the boys by cutting off the ends of his army tie. Again, the jacket covered it; again, who's the wiser? And then the dismal fuckers went and held a belt check the next drill. They were not amused. It went all the way to the student colonel. He was not amused. *Well, fuck me in the ear,* thought Eddie. *It was a little funny.*

Then there were the weekly classroom sessions with Captain Schlemmer. Eddie thought he knew boring, but when introduced to army-boring a new personal standard was forever set. It looked so interesting in the syllabus – history, tactics, threat – *cool,* thought Eddie. He had, however, never experienced the alchemy of military instruction, that reverse Midas touch that ineluctably transformed everything it touched to brain cell draining boredom. "Four years of this shit," he speculated, "and I won't have enough gray matter left to tie my shoes." Eddie had no choice, he had to wicker together a defense.

In the grand tradition of Western civilization, he chose artwork: On the desk he drew a picture of Schlemmer blowing a sailor. The following week, he saw, to his vast amusement, someone had inked over his creation with a ballpoint pen. So, the gauntlet was thrown down. Never one to forego a challenge, Eddie swung into action. He sat at another desk. Then, faking heavy-duty note-taking, he drew a picture of Schlemmer taking it in the ass from the sailor. He could hardly wait for the next week. And, there it was, the puritanical pen fuck had scribbled over this one too. The game was afoot. Each week a new desk, a new editorial: Schlemmer blowing a dead dog, Schlemmer boffing a goat, Schlemmer getting boffed by a goat. Each week the Pen Fuck scribbled. Fuck army tactics, this was Eddie tactics. And, with that, a miracle occurred: ROTC actually became interesting. Jousting with Pen Fuck was a life's lesson for Eddie: If you tried hard enough, contrary to popular wisdom, you really could make chicken salad out of chicken shit. God bless you, Pen Fuck, wherever you may be.

1963

"Jesus Christ, son. You flunked out."

"Yeah, Pop. I kinda thought this might happen."

"Goddammit, boy."

"Yeah, Pop. I'm sorry."

"What in the hell happened?"

"Geez, Pop, I just don't like agriculture."

"Agriculture, your butt. Look at this report card: English – D. Chemistry – D. Biology – F. Orientation – F. Orientation – F? How in the hell do you fail Orientation?"

"I guess I don't orientate too well."

1963

Eddie drove a cab that summer. The dispatcher was Shorty. Shorty was, in fact, a very short guy. He had advanced diabetes resulting in the amputation of both legs, one above the knee, the other below. As the disease progressed, they would periodically cut off a little more, so Shorty kept getting shorter.

Eddie pulled the night shift and, in between fares, he and Shorty talked. He was a colorful guy. Although wheelchair-bound, Shorty was quick to point out in his younger days he had been "one of the toughest sonsabitches in town."

He had been a bantam weight boxer and claimed to have fought Panama Al Brown, the one-time world champion. Brown was an oddity, a six-foot tall bantam weight. "He was all arms," reminisced Shorty. "I couldn't hit that nigger."

He had been a gangster. In the thirties, Louis Pope was one of the major bootleggers in the county. He worked the liquor racket under the protection of Dutch Schultz. Shorty worked for him. Eddie asked him if he ever killed anyone. Shorty said quietly he had left a few for dead.

Off duty, Eddie liked to drive Shorty around town. They couldn't drive a block without at least one "Hey, Shorty. Whaddya say?" He was Italian and this was Eddie's introduction to Little Italy up close and aromatic.

One day, Shorty directed him to drive to the cemetery. Left, right, he was looking for a particular grave. They got to one. "Here, kid, stop here."

Here we go, thought Eddie, *the down and dirty, the inside poop on a mob hit.* It was the romantic in him. Shorty was staring. "Something special about this one, Shorty?"

"Oh yeah," he said closing his eyes. "I used to fuck cunt here."

Of such stuff are heroes made.

1963

And then there was Marta. She taught French at the community college where Eddie went to salvage his disastrous freshman year upstate. Marta was Austrian, a European in every sense of the word, educationally, culturally, and physically. The daughter of two physicians, she was raised in the classic Viennese upper-middleclass manner. She was the first truly cultured person in his life. That's not to say Eddie thought his parents were stupid. They weren't. His mother was a whiz at bridge and his father was a tough-minded corporate executive. Both, particularly his father, waved the banner of the American belief in education and self-improvement.

"Read Shakespeare, son," he said, "There's a whole education there."

"How come you don't read him, Pop?"

"Quiet ya little wisenheimer."

Culture wasn't an achievement badge Marta wore to impress other people. Culture was personal and private, a small group of trusted intimates, companions who never left her side, providing insight and perspective to her daily experience. Her inner life was like a discussion with really interesting people. Everything brought to mind a piece of music, a line of poetry, a character from a novel. As such, she was never alone.

She liked Eddie. He was good at French, and that helped. But there was a spark there that went beyond that. She lent him books to read and records to listen to, nothing to do with French. She would discuss them with him after school, and he began to understand the true utility of the arts. Life, as he was discovering, was a lonely journey along a dark, difficult path. Marta showed him how to make it a little less lonely and a little less dark.

Marta was not unattractive. By American standards she ten to fifteen pounds too heavy, big-titted, and big assed. But the more Eddie was around her, the more it worked. She was his introduction to and lifelong appreciation of the concept of "zaftig." Zaftig meant *juicy*, and she was definitely that. They never slept together, but for years the coulda-woulda-shoulda of it played hell with him. Oh, well.

1964-1967

Eddie learned to box. It was just YMCA stuff, but he didn't like it. Who likes getting hit? There was a lot of that at first. Yeah, he wore headgear, but hits are hits and headgear doesn't absorb all of it. Then he had to ditch all his natural responses to fighting: Don't tense up; you won't last two rounds; relax. Don't throw wide arm punches; throw 'em short from the back and shoulders, that's where the power is. Don't duck punches, slip 'em; saves energy and keeps your balance. Forget the haymakers; throw punches in bunches. Goddammit, there was a lot to learn. His coach was a seriously weird New York guinea named Benny who got hooked on boxing as a kid.

His mother wouldn't let him fight, so he snuck out to the gym on the sly, sparring with anyone he could. He boxed the little guys for speed and the big guys for power and paid the standard dues: Somebody mashed his nose in. With that puss, Benny could wear a tutu and still look like a fighter. Eddie wondered how he explained that to Mom.

When Eddie began to improve, Benny took an interest. Saturdays at the Y weren't enough. They started sparring during the week. There was a gym at the local insane asylum and Benny cut a deal to use it. After working out, he liked to relax by playing golf. The nuthouse had a par three course and Benny cut a deal to use that too. Eddie wasn't sure what they did could be called golf. Always keen to keep in shape, Benny didn't walk between shots, he ran. No problem when they were alone on the course. A little sticky when others were ahead of them. These roadblocks annoyed the piss out of Benny, who would literally dance on tiptoes in aggravation. Well, a man can take just so much. Benny would yell "fore!" drive one right down the middle and he and Eddie would double time down the fairway. Whatever dander dodging a whizzing golf ball might have raised, was quickly lowered when the obstructing party confronted bent-nosed Benny thundering down on them. "Playing through, goddammit, playing through!" It was, after all, a nut house, so who knew what to expect on the course. Benny and Eddie never had any trouble playing through.

Eddie went upstate to finish college. Like most schools, this one no longer offered boxing as a sport, so Eddie had to look off campus. In one of the town's shittier sections, he found a gym, a pro gym. *Well, it's not the YMCA, but why not?* Not the YMCA, indeed. Shitty ring, shitty gloves, shitty bags, shitty people...ah, the sweet science.

The owner was a guy named Irv. Summer or winter, indoors or out, Irv always wore a ratty overcoat. And Irv whistled, no tune, just a whistle, like a tea kettle come to boil. Eddie wondered if everyone in boxing was nuts. Sparring with pros, even second-rate ones, was a pisser. It was a crash course in getting thumbed, laced, butted, heeled, and rabbit punched. The YMCA was boxing; this was fighting.

Larry, an Indian off the local res, was one of the regulars. He and Eddie were the same weight, so they were paired up a lot. Larry went on a two-month bender and reappeared twenty pounds heavier. They were still paired up.

The star was a light heavy named Horse, a truly tough motherfucker. One time, he hit Eddie in the liver and folded him up like a cheap suitcase. Horse cleaned up the local talent and got a shot at Bob Foster, the world champion. Foster knocked him out in the third round.

What Eddie really liked about boxing was the total lack of fantasy. Karate dicks might think they could whip anyone. Boxers knew better. Eddie knew on his best day and their worst, there were some fuckers he just could not beat. That lesson in natural pecking order stayed with him for the rest of his life.

1964-1967

Vietnam slowly raised its ugly head. Eddie watched it move from the middle of the paper to front page above the fold. Sometime in his junior year, he realized this was going to be his war. From then on, he never had a doubt. He wanted to quit school and sign up, but his father wouldn't have any of that. So, he followed it from the sidelines. He saw the news report of the Buddhist monk setting himself on fire. He watched the film of American troops coming ashore in 1965. He read the first-hand reports of the first battles. Then one of the other students, a Navy veteran, announced in the campus paper he was dropping out to join the Army. He did just that, and periodically the paper published his letters describing his ineluctable journey to combat. He went to the 101st Airborne Division and was wounded in action. Eddie was fascinated.

At the beginning of his last semester, Eddie went to the local Army recruiter. He told him he was graduating in June and as soon as possible he wanted to join up, get commissioned, and go to Vietnam. It was the easiest sell that guy ever made. Still, they went through the formalities. Eddie filled out some forms and then had to sit before a panel of officers.

"What are your top three branch preferences?" asked one.

"Infantry, Armor, Artillery," said Eddie.

"Jeesus, one, two, three," said another.

Eddie thought this was a process to select first-rate officer material. Later, he realized it was no more than a body hunt. There was no way they were going to turn down a "one, two, three" dumbo.

After the panel, one of the officers, one with several rows of ribbons on his chest, put his hand on Eddie's shoulder. "Do you know what you're doing, son?" This was the first of several times someone asked him that question.

Eddie graduated that June. Five days later, he was in the Army.

1967

Eddie took the train into the city and walked two blocks to the Induction Center. No mistaking it, the place was jammed, hundreds of young men, the war was hot. Looking back on it, he didn't remember much, just a lot of pissed off sergeants doing a lot of yelling. He did recall standing around naked for a long time, but in the weeks to come he got used to that. Inducting that many bodies took most of the day and then in the afternoon they herded them all together into a big room.

A pissed off sergeant read off a list of names. "Fort Polk, Louisiana! Move! Move! Move!"

A pissed off sergeant moved them out.

Another list of names. "Fort Benning, Georgia! Move! Move! Move!"

Another pissed off sergeant.

And so it went until the room was almost empty. Pissed off sergeant number one began collecting his paperwork.

Eddie and one other kid looked at each other. They were the only ones left.

"Excuse me, Sergeant," said Eddie.

"What do you two fuckin guys want?"

"What about us?"

"Who the fuck are you?"

"I'm Brandt," said Eddie

"I'm Beckendorf," said the other.

He went through his paperwork. "Oh, yeah. Fort Dix, New Jersey," and recollected his paperwork.

"Excuse me, Sergeant," said Eddie again.

"Now what?"

"How do we get there?"

"Ya go to the fuckin bus depot and take the fuckin Fort Dix bus. Any other fuckin questions?"

At the fuckin bus depot, they were told the fuckin Fort Dix bus didn't leave for another two fuckin hours.

His new buddy looked at Eddie and said, "Let's get a drink." So he and Brokendork (Eddie was never good with names) hit a joint across the street.

"What'll it be?" asked the barkeep.

"I'll take an ouzo," said Brokendork. He was something of a horseshit merchant, as Eddie soon learned.

"Make that two," said Eddie nonchalantly. He didn't have a clue what ouzo was.

After an hour and a half of slamming down the ouzos, Eddie and his, by now, best buddy Brokendork were hammered. *This Army is all right*, they thought as they strolled over to the bus depot.

They got to Fort Dix, got off the bus with everyone else, and in two minutes were alone on the platform—no pissed off sergeants, no other recruits, just Eddie and Brokendork.

"Now what do we do?"

"No problem, good buddy," said Eddie with a clear sign of leadership potential. "We find basic training."

So, that's just what they did, going from place to place trying to find basic training.

Finally, after dark, they saw a large brick building filled with a lot of lights and a lot of yelling. They cautiously opened the door.

"Who are you fuckin guys?"

"I'm Brandt; he's Brokendork."

"Where the fuck ya been?"

It wasn't like this in the movies.

1967

Perhaps the single most enduring legend of military myth is the drill instructor. He is the apotheosis of the warrior ethos, the father, mother, big brother, the devil, angel, role model, the mystic mean fucker that transforms fat-assed civilian shit stains into fearsome combat killing machines. Eddie's DI was Platoon Sergeant Mervin. Like so many of the Vietnam era NCOs, Mervin was a semiliterate shit-kicker from some duck-fuck Southern shit pile that made the Army a great career move. He was just back from a combat tour with the First Infantry Division.

Hot damn, thought Eddie, *the real deal.*

The first thing Mervin did was call the roll. This was not a task Eddie had thought particularly challenging, but then he had only been in the Army for one day. Halfway through, Mervin stopped, squinted his eyes, and wrinkled his nose like a dog sniffing a particularly rank bunghole. After a long pause:

"Rupacut."

No answer.

"Rupacut!"

Silence.

"Rupacut, goddammit!"

Still no answer.

Thoroughly browned off, Mervin moved from trainee to trainee, checking nametags against the roster. When he got to Private Rupprecht, he stopped. Nametag to roster, roster to nametag, then, just to be sure, nametag to roster once more. "Goddammit, Rupacut, sound the fuck off when I call your name!"

This was Eddie's introduction to NCO literacy. To be fair, Mervin did get the first and last letters right. It was just all that shit in between that tripped him up…too many goddamn letters. So, it was Rupacut, end of fuckin story.

The next thing Mervin did was to assign a platoon guide. No sweat there, he just picked the biggest guy: "Large and in charge," as they say. Then squad leaders.

"Which one of you boys is goin' to OCS?"

Violating the ages-old Army adage of "don't volunteer for nothin'," Eddie raised his hand. So did Rupacut. *Good leadership experience*, they thought. By that first night, they realized how wrong that was.

Right before evening chow, Mervin called them all together.

"Boys, I just come back from Veetnam and I ain't had no round-eye pussy for twelve mons. I got some ketchin' up to do."

Back in the barracks after chow, no Mervin. Eddie and the Ruper waited. No Mervin. They waited some more. No Mervin. So, they told their squads to crap out and hit the sack.

The next day for morning formation every platoon but theirs was wearing web gear. Mervin was pissed.

"Goddammit, y'all are squad leaders. It's yer job to see the men's wearing the right shit."

"But, Sergeant…" Big mistake! It was the first and one of the most important Army lessons: Never make excuses.

And so it went. At 1800 every day, Mervin would change into his cunt-huntin' duds and disappear into town. Eddie, the Ruper, and the other squad leaders would see what the other platoons were doing and passed some version of it on to their men. It sort of worked. In the morning, Mervin, his ashes successfully hauled, would tidy things up.

Sparked by God knows what, Mervin would periodically tell the platoon a story:

"When ah was jes a young private, ah was put on KP one day. The mess sergeant was a big, fat fuck. Ah took one look at him and jes knew we was goin to git in it. Ah knew he was too big fer me to whip fair, so ah made me a plan. Sho nuff, the fat fuck come after me, but I was ready. Real quick like ah ducked under'm and grabbed hold of his nuts and started asqueezin. He was beatin' on mah back, 'Leggo mah nuts! Leggo mah nuts!' Ah kept squeezing them nuts. 'Leggo mah nuts! Leggo mah nuts!' An ah kept squeezing them nuts. Then he jes fell over stone cold out."

Eddie and the Ruper looked at each other. If there was a teaching point there, they missed it. It wasn't like this in the movies.

Eddie had a New York accent. This was not a plus when in the clutches of the Southern-heavy Army NCO corps.

"Where you from, boy?"

"Louisiana, Sergeant!"

"Buuulllsheeet! Yer frum New York. Yew know what, boy? Ah hate *fuckinyankees. Fuckinyankee* is one word in mah book, cuz there ain't no otha kind. And yew know what ah really hate, boy?"

"No, Sergeant!"

"Ah really hate New York fuckinyankees!"

Eddie didn't think he was talking baseball here. So, his survival instincts kicked in and he lost his accent like a bird shitting on takeoff. He never got it back.

During the breaks on the ranges, the shitters in the latrines were always packed. Stress and Army chow made almost everyone constipated. One day, Eddie was part of a full house grunting and squeezing out their rock-hard little trainee turdlets. With a *bang*, the door slammed open and a big NCO stood there. Seeing that all the crappers were in use, he marched over to the nearest one and sailed the occupying trainee into the middle of the room. Then he dropped his drawers, fired off a shit exploding like an artillery salvo, and, wasting no time with wiping, pulled up has drawers and marched out. The whole thing couldn't have lasted more than twenty seconds. It was the most impressive thing Eddie saw since joining up.

One day, when they fell out for first formation, there was a Newark City police car in the parking lot and a couple of Newark City police. After some big humma humma with the company commander, they called a name. A trainee stepped forward. The cops handcuffed him and the company never saw him again.

There was a black kid named Simmons. He had a pregnant girlfriend back home in Trenton. One day, Simmons was absent from formation. Someone had hit his girl, she called Simmons, he went home, beat the shit out of the guy, and then came back.

"Simmons," said the first sergeant, "did you ever think of making the Army a career?"

There was a white kid named Fredricks. One night when Eddie was the charge of quarters, the phone rang at midnight. It was the company commander. "Brandt, get Private Fredericks in my office, now!"

Eddie rousted Fredricks out of the sack. He started to put on his fatigues. "No time for that shit," said Eddie. "The Big Dog wants to see you right fuckin now."

As they double-timed to the office, Fredricks explained he joined the Army to get away from his money-grubbing ex and that, most likely, she had tracked him down. Shivering in his skivvies, he pounded on the old man's door:

"Sir, Private Fredricks reports!"

"Get in here, Private!"

Eddie couldn't make out the words, just the volume. It started loud, went to semi-loud, and then not loud at all. After about fifteen minutes, the door opened and the company commander strolled out with his hand on Fredricks' shoulder.

"Not to worry, Fredricks, we'll take care of that twat."

That was the end of shit from the ex.

There was a kid with tears in his eyes after a phone call with his mother. He had said "fuck" three times. Eddie had no problem with profanity. He had, in fact, been an enthusiastic practitioner for as long as he could remember. Army profanity was something else altogether. In civilian life, it was used periodically as an intensifier, as an outpouring of extreme emotion, or as just plain "colorful" language. In the Army, there was nothing periodic about it. It was as pervasive as a regional accent. So, "pass the fuckin butter, please," a harelip inducer in almost any other setting, in the Army was simply a buddy trying to be polite. As Eddie soon realized, Army swearing wasn't really profanity, it was dialect: "Pass the fuckin butter," was deep Army, every bit as much as "y'all" was deep South. He knew if he were ever to attempt a description of his Army experience, he would have to do it in dialect.

There was a kid named Schneider. Army wisdom isn't wide, but it is deep. The standard label for its usual seventeen-year-old trainee was "young, dumb, and full of come." That was really all you needed to know about Schneider. He was in Eddie's squad and didn't feel Eddie had the right to tell him what to do. Eddie laid it out in words of one syllable, but Schneider didn't buy it. Then, one day, he called Eddie a cocksucker in front of the squad. There was another time-tested Army adage: "When you're dealing with stupid people, you have to deal on a stupid level." Eddie hadn't heard that one yet, but there were times when the logic of the situation was so compelling you 'didn't need the words. He took Schneider out behind the barracks and beat the snot out of him. It was the first time he had ever used his boxing skills outside the gym. It was a magic touch. No more shit from Schneider. "Goddamn," mused

Eddie, "something that actually works." He imagined Coach Bennie with his bent nose giving him a proud wink. Good on ya, Bennie.

There was a kid named Bud. He was in the Army only because of the Secretary of Defense, Robert S. McNamara. McNamara, a numbers puke extraordinaire, was put off by how many draftees were failing to meet the minimum score on the Army intelligence test, hence, exempted from military service. This was boogering up his win-the-war manpower projections. It was a simple systems analysis fix: Lower the minimum score. The unstated, but obvious, result would be that these low scorers wouldn't qualify for anything but infantrymen: More cannon fodder for the defense dollar, fuck the dumbos. To create the illusion of fairness, the Army ran a 100,000 man "pilot" program, better known as "McNamara's 100,000." Bud was one of them. Even in the lowest common denominator 'sixties Army, Bud was a slow mover. The Army issue belt was about forty inches long, one end with a brass tip, the other with no tip. You fitted it to your waist so the brass tip extended from the brass belt buckle, then you cut off the excess from the end with no tip. The first formation Bud fell out with the no tip end sticking out of his belt buckle.

"Hey, Bud. Ya got the wrong end of your belt sticking out."

"Gee, thanks."

He undid his belt, no brass tip. Bud had cut off the wrong end.

And then there was best buddy Brokendork. Brokendork was smart, athletic, and was breezing through basic hardly raising a sweat. One day on a field exercise, some dickhead poked him in the ribs with his M-14. Brokendork grabbed the muzzle, dickhead twisted the rifle, and Brokendork dislocated his shoulder. After a short stay in the hospital, he pulled light duty in company headquarters and a week later was given a medical discharge from the Army. Eddie pondered this for years. As a result of nothing more than a momentary loss of muscular control, Brokendork's life changed profoundly. The path he and Eddie had shared from the induction center was split in an instant. For Brokendork, there would be no Vietnam, no combat, no wounding, no PTSD. And no reason for it. Why, wondered Eddie, was Brokendork spared all that while he wasn't? Much later, he came to understand this was the meaning of "shit happens" and nothing more than that.

They spent a week on hand-to-hand fighting techniques. The Army had bought into something called "The O'Neill Method of Close Combat" and that was the basic lesson plan. It consisted of a lot of poking and kicking, accompanied by a lot of yelling and grunting: "Eeeuup!" poke. "Eeeuup!" poke. "Eeeuup!" poke.

"This stuff ain't goin' to work," was the consensus.

Mervin provided his professional input:

"Boys, don be tryin' this shit in town. They whip yo ass."

Thereafter, anytime the company was presented anything particularly worthless, they would look at each other and go, "Eeeuup!" poke.

Eddie started to notice an odd thread running through the training. There was the official classroom presentation...protecting Vietnam...containing the spread of Communism...Geneva Convention...all tight and tidy. Then there was the unofficial version you got chatting with the instructors on the breaks.

"That whole fuckin' shit-hole country ain't worth the life of a single GI. Kill 'em all an' let God sort 'em out."

He heard that over and over and over.

Eddie began to see the Army like an old, Victorian house, from the street a showpiece. Inside was the front parlor all neat and clean. That's where the visitors went, that's where they saw the public face showing them what a decent place it was. Then there was the back room, not so neat, not so clean. That's where the people who lived there spent their time, that's where they did the dirty work of really running the house. Front parlor, back room. Illusion and reality.

The last day of basic training, Mervin called them together to read out their branch assignments. There really was an army logic to it. All those like Eddie who had enlisted for something specific got it. So, he and the Ruper were going to Infantry Advanced Individual Training, Ft. Dix, then Infantry OCS. All the big guys went to Military Police School. Those who scored well on the aptitude tests went to clerk school. And the rest, the small dumb shits, infantry AIT, Ft. Polk, Louisiana, the pipeline for infantry replacement, Vietnam. There was a Puerto Rican kid named Ruiz who cleared the minimum height requirement by maybe an inch. His English was a hair above the "no comprendo" level. So, with the inevitability of sunset, the Big Green Dick sent him to Polk. *The Army Times* was the service weekly aimed at providing soldiers with items of interest. The main item of interest was the casualty list, the roster of those killed in action the past week. It was the first thing everyone turned to. A few months later, Eddie saw Ruiz's name there. For the rest of his life, whenever someone talked about a poor dumb fuck, he thought of Ruiz. Via con Dios, hermano.

1967

Just about everyone in infantry AIT, Ft. Dix, agreed that combat skills acquired in basic were minimal. The care, cleaning, and firing of the M-14 were fine and dandy. The only problem was the Army in Vietnam was using M-16s. Minor detail, they'd get 16s in AIT. They didn't. They'd learn jungle tactics. They didn't. They'd learn helicopter assault procedures. They didn't. In his mind, Eddie was still hopeful his country wouldn't send him into combat poorly trained. But in his gut the worm of doubt was beginning to grow. Wormy had lots to feed on in Ft. Dix

It began like basic.

"Who's going to OCS?"

Eddie and the Ruper weren't buying that shit again. But the slow learners did, and they became the squad leaders for the cycle. It was another bit of wisdom Eddie had added to his ever-expanding army survival guide: whenever possible, fly under the radar. Let the gung-ho fuckers step up; Rear Rank Rudy didn't get the glory, but he didn't get the headaches either.

As one might expect from the name "Infantry Advanced Individual Training," the program paraded all the weapons in an infantry battalion. It began with the small stuff, the .45 caliber pistol, and progressed to the large, the 4.2-inch mortar. "Training" was stretching it a bit; it was really just familiarization. They fired some of it, but most was simply demonstrated. A few were borderline weird, the automatic M-14, for example. The standard M-14 was semiautomatic, one round for every pull of the trigger. To provide extra firepower, each squad had one M-14A2, the full auto version, pull the trigger and it fired automatic until the trigger was released. One minor problem, it climbed, you couldn't keep it centered on the target. For some reason the program called for the whole company to fire for qualification. No one made it.

"Yep," reflected the range NCO philosophically, "we ain't had nobody qualify on this fucker since I been here." And then with classic Army logic,

"But, no sweat, y'all get M-16's in Veetnam." The fact that they didn't have M-16's in preparing for Vietnam was never addressed.

Another odd duck was the ENTAC, a French-built wire-guided anti-tank missile. The operator fired it and then controlled its flight to the target using a joy stick. Guaranteed 95% first round hit capability. Maybe in France, but not in Ft. Dix. They selected a trainee to fire it and he missed the target by a good ten feet. "Yep," reflected another range NCO philosophically, "we ain't had nobody hit that fucker since I been here. But, no sweat, the gooks ain't got no tanks."

The company first sergeant could have had top billing in a horror movie. He was endlessly tall, rail thin, and had a puss with so little flesh on it it looked like a death's head. On top of that, he was a mean bastard. He just scared the shit out of everyone. One night, Eddie was pulling charge of quarters with one of the drill corporals, a muscle-boy who liked to take his shirt off. In the slow hours past midnight, they actually talked. At some point, Eddie mentioned what a scary fucker the first shirt was.

The corporal looked around to make sure they were alone. "You don't know half of it," he whispered. "Right after I got here, the prick hit on me."

Well, shit in my hat, thought Eddie, *looks like blood wasn't the only thing Dracula was sucking.*

One day early in the cycle, Eddie was doing pushups for some minor rule infraction when the by now familiar voice of a Southern shitkicker rasped in his ear.

"Ahm forty-two years old, trainee, an ah ken do more pooshups than you can."

Eddie felt the sour breath and saw the hairless haircut of the career NCO. That was his introduction to Platoon Sergeant Koon.

Koon was so far over the top he was almost funny. "Ahm related to every Koon in West Virginia." (Snicker, what a fuckin' moron.)

He hated civilians. Rumor was he barely tolerated his wife for being one. (Chuckle, what a fuckin' moron.)

Everything reminded Koon of combat. One day, a trainee fell out with the camouflage cover of his helmet hanging down in back.

"Thas jes like one of them German helmets. Ah cut a man's throat wearin' one jes like it." (Yuk, yuk, what a fuckin' putz)

In line to turn in his rifle one day, Eddie made the mistake of leaning on it.

"What in tha fuck are yew doin' with that weapon, boy?"

"Nothing, Sergeant."

"Thas a rifle, not a goddam leanin' post!"

"Yes, Sergeant."

"Yew know how ta use that weapon, boy?"

"Yes, Sergeant."

"That a fact? Well. Les jes see about that. Yew see that field over yonder?"

"Yes, Sergeant."

"Yew take yer rifle with one round a ammunition and stand on that side. Ah'll take a bayonet an stand on this side. An then ah'll kill ya. Whaddya say, trainee?" (Har de har har, what a fuckin' yutz.)

Then there was graduation day, Class A uniforms. Eddie and the rest of the platoon fell out sporting their lonely little National Defense Service Medal. Then Koon arrived. Up until then, they had only seen him in fatigues, a hard-ridden, beer-bellied, dragon-breathed, foul-mouthed old futz. Eddie had dismissed him as just another bull-shittin' old NCO. Koon in Class A's was something altogether different. Above his left pocket row after row of ribbons rose in multicolored splendor, liberally sprinkled with V-devices (for valor), arrowheads (for invasions), and oak leaf clusters (for multiple awards). Like a plinth for a public monument, they terminated in the ultimate tribute to infantry combat, a Combat Infantryman Badge with two stars. That meant Koon had seen action in three wars: As a boy in World War II, a young man in Korea, and salty old fucker in Vietnam. There wasn't a drop of glamour in him. If you put his picture on a recruiting poster, everyone would join the Navy. But, standing there in full regalia, this oafish old lout achieved something as close to military grace as Eddie would ever see. Koon was the point of the sword whenever and wherever his country drew it. He was 11 Bravo, no airborne, no ranger, no special forces, none of that profiling elite forces crapola, just straight leg infantry, period. Sure, those fancy pantsies looked good on parade, but when you needed someone to do the shitty work of close and continuous infantry combat, Koon was the one you wanted. Eddie almost admired him.

The dark undertone from basic continued in AIT: "That whole fuckin' shit-hole country ain't worth the life of a single GI. Kill 'em all and let God sort 'em out." Again, over and over and over.

Eddie had expected the Army to be an education in matters military. What he had not expected was an equal and, in many ways, more profound education in the American character. Years later, he heard the comedian George Carlin nail it:

"The human race is a freak show and if you're an American you have a front row seat."

Before the Army, Eddie had little knowledge of, nor interest in, the South. In those odd moments when it did cross his mind, he dismissed it as kind of a backward place filled with slow moving mouth-breathers who talked funny. And he particularly didn't give a rat's bazaza about the Civil War…ancient history as far as he was concerned, and no connection whatsoever with him. His family wasn't even in the country at the time; they were busy getting fucked over as part of the central European peasantry. Then in basic and AIT he got his introduction to Southerners up close and in the worst possible way: Southern NCOs in charge. It became increasingly clear to Eddie that, for many of them, time had stopped somewhere around 1865. It was like the war had just ended and losing it was really pissing them off.

Eddie knew nothing about PTSD then, but later in life he came to understand it as not simply a personal disability, but a disorder that could affect an entire region, like the South. True, drawing conclusions from a population sample as narrow as the Army NCO corps might lead to skewed conclusions, but as an operating principle it was a useful tool. While over the years Eddie developed friendships with Southerners he respected and admired, his point of departure was always based on his Army experience: They were all a little nutty. In his view, the South was the creaky attic in the American house; that's where you stashed crazy old Uncle Elmo to keep him from scaring the neighbors.

The next stop in Eddie's training was Infantry Officer Candidate School, Ft. Benning, Georgia. He took Interstate 95 south, his first trip below the Mason-Dixon Line. Crossing the border into South Carolina he saw a billboard with a fully robed Klansman riding a rearing white horse. Big letters across the top announced, "Welcome to Klan Country." Eddie knew Vietnam was going to be strange. He had no idea the weirdness would start in the US.

1967

Eddie signed into OCS. The company needed 220 bodies to start the program, so he and the rest of the prospective candidates had to wait until they hit the magic number. It was called a "holding company" and was situated in an OCS barracks surrounded on both sides by OCS companies in full blast. It was the eye of the storm. OCS raged around them while they watched wide-eyed from their frail position of temporary immunity. Basic and AIT had their trying moments, but nothing like this. They had been yelled at, but not like this. They had been harassed, but not like this. This was unremitting fury. The instrument of that fury was the tactical officer, the "Tacs." The Tacs seemed psychotic in their anger. Eddie had never seen people so pissed off. It was non-stop, in your face screaming at candidates frozen in glassy-eyed attention or knocking out pushups or double-timing around the barracks. That went on without letup for a week. Three people in Eddie's group quit before the program even started.

They hit their number, were sorted into six platoons, and were marched over to their designated barracks. Whether by design or happenstance, it was night time. They stood in formation in the dark waiting. The barracks were lit. Then the doors slammed open and dark forms from hell descended upon them: their Tacs. The screaming started.

OCS was twenty-six weeks long, and after a while Eddie learned to zone out the abuse. That was one reason he survived. But he didn't know how to do that when it started. Still basically a civilian at heart, Eddie took it personally at first. A raging asshole yelling so close his spit splattered on his face, Eddie took that personally.

Unlike the NCO cadre of basic and AIT, combat veterans to a man, none of the Tacs had been to Vietnam. Indeed, most of them were recent OCS graduates with less than two years in the Army. The rationale for this astonishing fact was that the Infantry School felt men with experience in the real Army might not buy in to the harassment. No danger of that when the only thing the Tacs knew was OCS. Later, an old timer told Eddie everything in the Army had a purpose. It might be a stupid purpose, but purpose nonetheless. Bingo OCS.

Eddie's Tac was a tall, pear-shaped putz from Bumfuck, Nebraska. He wasn't just a recent graduate of the program, he had been commissioned the day before Eddie's class started. His name was Grayson. He was all of twenty years old, the latest in the disheartening parade of uninspiring leaders that seemed to stretch depressingly to the horizon.

Eddie thought basic was neigh on worthless. Ditto AIT. But that was route-step Ft. Dix. This wasn't just Infantry OCS, it was Ft. Fucking Benning, home of jump school, ranger school…home of the infantry. Yessiree, shit was going to done right here. Harassment, not a problem. Let them pound the crap out of him, that's how you temper steel, right? And Eddie really wanted to be tempered. He was going to war, to lead troops in combat, and he wanted to be ready. Bring it the fuck on!

The first disillusion was the monomaniacal concentration on appearances. There was personal appearance. They had been issued three pairs of fatigues in basic. Not enough! Each candidate was given a clothing allowance of $200, directed to buy nine more, get them tailored, and take them to the post dry cleaners for a "military starch." Military starch meant you could hold the fatigue pants at the waist and the legs were so stiff they would stick up straight up. Donning a fresh set was called "breaking starch." You couldn't just slip them on like normal fatigues, you had to pull the arms and legs apart, making sure the starch was completely broken. Incompletely broken starch resulted in, God forbid, "fins," a near capital offense incurring fifty pushups at a minimum. They wore the blue Infantry School patch on their left shoulder and repeated heavy laundering caused its edges to turn white. Applying a blue magic marker corrected that felony. A black one kept the name tag and U.S. Army tag kosher. Once dressed, you were checked by a buddy for "ropes," threads that came loose at the seams. A lighter burned them off. That was breaking starch, and you did it two to three times a day (can't be seen in a dirty uniform). Boots; once again standard Army issue was taboo. Two sets of Corcoran jump boots were required. They spit shined so much better. Finally, the plastic helmet liner; just shining them up was unacceptable. They took them to an autobody shop in town for a high-grade baked-on automotive sheen. The finishing touch for the company on the march was a color guard, replete with swords and guide on. Eddie had to admit they looked impressive. What that had to do with jungle warfare he hadn't a clue.

Then there was the barracks. They spent hours, hours every day cleaning, polishing, waxing the fucking barracks. The floor was their particular nemesis. It was linoleum and they spit shined it, just like their boots. They used something called "Butcher's wax," a tin of warm water, and a rag wrapped tightly around the index and middle fingers. Then around and around and around, polishing one square at a time, until you could look at the floor and see the ceiling. And not just the rooms, but the hallways as well; hours, every day. To keep from dorking up this masterpiece, the hallways had two narrow strips of rubber matting, one for candidates going one way, the other for those coming the other. The strips were so narrow it required a weird pigeon-toed mincing to keep centered. Meeting a candidate coming the other way required further gymnastics, groping along the wall as each leaned away to avoid running into one another. Entering the rooms was equally athletic, tippy-toeing along the edges and then bouncing onto the bedframe. For six months, Eddie never walked on the floor.

The latrine was its own monument to absurdity. The crappers and urinals were polished to a near incandescent shine, and then all but one unofficially placed off limits, shitting and pissing subordinated to inspection-ready gloss. The single concession to reality was to exempt the sinks and showers from these restrictions. Whether needed or not, candidates were required to shave every day, so the sinks were fully engaged each morning. Showers were another matter. With the iron law of triage for men with a lot to do and not enough time to do it, something had to give. The obvious first casualty was the daily shower. So, unless they were really grody, candidates bagged the shower. The result was classic Army: Candidates from a distance looked great; up close, a little gamey.

For the first eight weeks of the program, the company would return from training to trashed rooms and enraged Tacs: "The barracks are not up to standard." It was the "Arbeit Macht Frei" of Infantry OCS.

In an earlier cycle, some candidate with a woeful lack of understanding of Army ways, wrote a letter to his congressman complaining that, because of all this, he wasn't getting his regulation eight hours of sleep. A "congressional" came down to the Infantry School demanding they address this problem. Once again, the result was classic Army: Lights in the barracks were turned off at 2200 hours and turned back on at 0600. The candidates did all the same shit, but now they did it in the dark. Another dickhead complained to a congressman about the expense of tailoring his fatigues, generating another congressional. Not a problem, responded the Infantry School, and published official guidelines of pantleg width for each fatigue pant size. So, in a textbook case of unintended consequences, candidates had to get their fatigues "gusseted," inserting a triangle of material to extend the pantlegs to the newly required standards. No clothing allowance for this one; candidates paid for it out of their own pockets. Civilian control of the military.

The jewel in the crown of these absurdities was OCS mess hall procedure. The first hurdle was just getting into the fuckin' place. Candidates formed a line on the walk to the entrance. "Line" doesn't capture it; it was more like a malignant centipede. While waiting to move forward, each candidate had to stand at rock-hard parade rest, exactly one arm's length behind the candidate in front. Couldn't move forward from the position of parade rest, could only move forward from the position of attention. Couldn't snap to attention on your own, could only snap to when the candidate in front did so, hence the dance of the centipede: As the lead candidate changed position, it rolled down the line with insect-like precision. So, just for fun, one of the Tacs would run the lead candidate through a series of commands:

"ATTENSHUN! PARADE REST! ATTENSHUN! PARADE REST! Etc. Etc." The changing positions rolling down the line like a slinky toy. Like a wolf pack of U-boats, the other Tacs would patrol the line looking for victims. Hunting was always good:

"TOO SLOW, SHITBIRD! GIMME TWENTY!"

And the offending candidate would fall out of line and, in cadence, knock out the corrective pushups:

"ONE, SIR! TWO, SIR! THREE, SIR! ...SIR, CANDIDATE SHITBIRD REQUESTS PERMISSION TO RECOVER!"

"RECOVER, SHITBIRD, END OF THE LINE!"

And Candidate Shitbird would double-time to the end of the line. The fun didn't stop there. When Shitbird finally arrived at the mess hall entrance, he faced another test of military competence:

"SIR, CANDIDATE SHITBIRD REQUESTS PERMISSION TO ENTER!"

"I CAN'T HEAR YOU, SHITBIRD! GIMME TWENTY!"

"ONE, SIR! TWO, SIR! THREE, SIR! ...SIR, CANDIDATE SHITBIRD REQUESTS PERMISSION TO RECOVER!"

"RECOVER, SHITBIRD, END OF THE LINE!"

Once in the mess hall, outside fun was replaced by inside fun. Moving "with a purpose," the candidate mirrored the walls of the mess hall with Olympic race-walking speed to the beginning of the chow line...if he managed to avoid the inside wolf pack:

"TOO SLOW, SHITBIRD! OUTSIDE AND GIMME TWENTY!"

In the chow line, the candidate (with a purpose) picked up tray, knife, fork, spoon, plastic cup, and chow. The mess hall was a series of four-man tables. On exiting the chow line, the candidate identified the closest table with a vacancy and (with a purpose) navigated there directly. Once there, following OCS procedure, he set up his meal: Edge of the tray aligned exactly with edge of the table, fork, tynes down, resting ninety degrees on the left side of the tray, spoon, inverted, resting ninety degrees on the right, knife, cutting edge inward, forty-five degrees on the far right corner, cup just touching the same corner. This done, if the four-man requirement was not met, all present at the table waited at parade rest. Last to arrive, having set up his meal, snapped to attention, the other three likewise, and with his best command voice ordered:

"TAKE SEATS!"

With gymnastic agility, the four bounded around the chair to place the back third of their butts on the front third of the seat. All this was performed under the periscopic scrutiny of the wolf pack, all too often followed by the all too familiar, "TOO SLOW! TRY IT AGAIN!" Three or four attempts usually did the trick.

Actually, eating the chow was its own ritual: Pick up fork with left-hand, pick-up knife with right, look down at tray, identify chow to cut, cut chow, replace knife, switch fork to right hand, move chow to mouth by the most direct route, replace fork, direct eyes at opposite candidate, chew, swallow, repeat. And, for the sake of all that is holy, DON'T fuckin chew until the fuckin' fork has been replaced on the fuckin' tray and you have locked on to the fuckin' eyes of the fuckin' opposite candidate. Violation of any of these rules triggered the inevitable: "OUT SIDE! GIMME TWENTY!" The inevitable spilling of chow on fatigues triggered the other inevitable: "YOU GROSS DISGUSTING SHITBIRD! UPSTAIRS AND BREAK STARCH!"

The final inevitable was not enough time. When the Tacs determined that things were running late, they announced, "PIG PRIVILEGES!" Using both hands the candidates crammed in the remaining chow, and that meant ALL the chow. For the sake of all that is holy, don't hand in a tray with any uneaten fuckin' chow.

That shit went on for twelve weeks. It was collective harassment, directed at the company in general. At the same time there was individual harassment or "counselling," directed at a single candidate. There was a variety of counselling techniques, the most popular being grass drill. Training aids for grass drill were minimal: Grass and a whistle. Personnel requirements were equally few: A Tac for supervision and guidance and a candidate for correction and improvement. Rules were simplicity itself: One tweet on the whistle; the candidate double-timed in place. Two tweets, pushups. Three, sit ups. The drill started slowly: Tweet........................ ....Tweet-tweet...Tweet-tweet-tweet. Then the pace increased: Tweet...........Tweet-tweet........... Tweet-tweet-tweet. Intervals between tweets continued to shorten until it was pretty much just, tweet-tweet-tweet-tweet-tweet-tweet, resulting in the candidate flopping around on the ground like a landed fish. After about ten minutes of this, he was usually well counselled.

For the purists, counselling was running laps. This was generally done around the barracks, but Eddie's company was across the street from the 250-foot jump school towers that were surrounded by a mile-and-a-third track. "Two laps airborne!" was additional corrective action often applied. During mortar instruction, they were issued large, circular plotting boards, originally intended to plot mortar fire, but in OCS more commonly used for "Plotting Board Exercise," the candidate holding the fucker at arm's length until his arms danced with fire. Counselling could also occur indoors, the preferred technique here being "the Green Chair." The term "chair" was something of a misnomer. The counselled candidate simply stood back flat against the wall and lowered himself into a seating position sans chair. A few minutes of that and his knees danced with fire. Maintaining a tenuous connection with its big brother, West Point, OCS also offered needy candidates the opportunity to walk tours, one tour being an hour of marching at right shoulder arms back and forth across the parade field. Eddie did 'em all on a regular basis.

Harassment was the purview of the Tacs. Once the company was turned over to the Infantry School instructors it stopped, sort of. The big challenge in classroom instruction wasn't the material, it was staying awake. Unless the instructor was particularly engaging, not generally the norm, sleep-deprived candidates tended to doze off. The OCS remedy was simple: If the guy next to you was falling asleep, you whacked him in the ribs. The result was that classes often sounded like jungle drums sending urgent messages. The other result was lots of sore ribs.

Eddie was quickly disabused of his hope for immediate and intensive field exercises. To his astonishment, the company didn't start tactical training until week twelve, almost halfway through the program. So, his concern about the future began to metastasize into full blown, asshole tightening fear. When the fuck was he going to learn this shit? Equally, how the fuck was he going to learn it? The Tacs helped to fuel that fire.

"Brandt, you ignorant piece of shit! You're going to get your whole platoon in Vietnam killed!"

That was the chorus he heard day after day and he couldn't help but begin to believe it.

More gasoline on the fire was the candidate chain of command. There were six slots in the chain, three at the platoon level: squad leader, platoon sergeant, and platoon leader, and three at the company level: first sergeant, executive officer, and company commander. They rotated every three days. In theory, every candidate was supposed to fill each slot at least once. That worked at the platoon level slots, the little three, and everyone did get a go at each. But, for the big three, the company level slots, there just wasn't the time. Only a select few could serve there.

In another classic case of inverted objectives, OCS determined what should have been a privilege became instead a punishment. The big three were targets. If you got assigned to one of them, they were trying to bounce you out of the program. For three days, the Tacs hounded, harassed, and humiliated the big three with unremitting fury. This went on cycle after cycle, resulting in the most ironic inversion of all: OCS, rather than teaching candidates to desire and seek leadership, taught them to fear and avoid it. Leadership just scared the shit out of them.

Everything was evaluated, particularly performance in positions of leadership. To be sure, the Tacs did their evaluation. To create the illusion of fairness, the candidates evaluated each other in something called a "Spot Leadership Report." They were disabused of its fairness with the submission of the first one:

"Candidate Bazatz performed well as platoon leader..." drew a thunderous "BULLSHIT!" from enraged Tacs. "If he knew how to be a platoon leader he wouldn't be here! Do 'em again!"

So, the leadership reports became bayonet sheets, with candidates tossing and goring each other with abandon. After seven weeks, the Tacs smugly announced they had enough dirt to bounce anyone they wanted out of the program; just another depressing layer in the tightly packed OCS turd-burger.

Everyone had to stay in the program for the first seven weeks. Thereafter, anyone could leave simply by voluntarily resigning. This was called, "turning in a quit letter." From the first week on, a growing number had decided on this option, however survival instinct rightly directed that they keep this from public knowledge.

Every day at morning formation, the Tacs would snarl: "Who's quitting?" For four weeks, no response. Then, to the astonishment of all, in week five a hand went up...Lenny. Like watching someone step in front of a freight train, the company gasped at the sure knowledge of the terrifying consequences.

Geez, Lenny, thought Eddie, *bad move.*

Even the Tacs were momentarily thrown for a loss at such self-destructive behavior. Not for long. "MARTIN! GET UP HERE! NOW!"

Dumb bunny Lenny dutifully double-timed to the company front. That was just about the last time anyone saw Lenny in the upright position. For the next two weeks, each morning formation started the same way:

"MARTIN! GET UP HERE! NOW!"

No one actually counted the immense number of push-ups, sit-ups, and laps Lenny did in those two weeks, but if not a record for OCS, it was for certain a personal best for Lenny. Mercifully, week seven arrived, Lenny handed in his quit letter, and disappeared forever from everyone's lives. Some thirty others also turned in their letters.

The thirty odd classmates who decided to hand in quit letters felt sure their degrees would guarantee them safe jobs in non-combat slots. So, went the reasoning, someone with a degree in accounting would, of course, get assigned to the Finance Branch. Surprise, surprise, the army made them all scout dog handlers. This was not just a combat job, but a really dangerous one; the handler and his dog walked ahead of the rifle platoon. Too late, the distraught quitters realized taking an infantry commission would have been a lot safer. It wasn't called "The Big Green Dick" for nothing. Years later, Eddie came to understand this was not the Army being vindictive, it was just another instance of the iron "Law of Army Numbers." Numbers, not animus, powered the big machine, particularly under the aegis of Secretary of Defense, Robert S. McNamara, numbers nosepicker extraordinaire: "If you can't quantify it, it doesn't exist."

Somewhere in the bowels of the Pentagon, an early generation computer had spit out a manpower projection report. Somewhere in the inner rings of the Pentagon, a low-level Army bureaucrat sitting in a cubicle looked at the bottom line of that report and made a note that one of the many anticipated shortfalls was scout dog handlers, and passed it on. Somewhere in the middle rings of the pentagon, some mid-level army bureaucrat sharing an office compiled the various reports, one of which listed thirty bodies being freed up from Infantry OCS. Somewhere in the outer rings of the pentagon, a poohbah in a single office made the match, and *boom*, thirty men were set in motion towards harm's way, some of them to be killed in action: "The Law of Army Numbers." When Eddie reflected on this, he realized it was the soulless anonymity of it all that was truly frightening.

There was something unique about Eddie's group. OCS had in the past been the vehicle for promising NCOs to get a commission. Vietnam's voracious need for lieutenants called for expanding that pipeline. Accordingly, the Army opened OCS to college graduates with no prior military experience, the odd logic being four years of college was somehow equivalent to the same amount of time in the ranks. College men could enlist for OCS, accepting both a commission and a two-year commitment upon graduation. An added attraction was, should the individual fail to complete the program, he would assume an enlisted commitment of only two years, rather than the three normally incurred by those who joined the army voluntarily. This was called "The College Op Program," and Eddie's class was the test case.

The perceived wisdom concerning College Ops was, while they might not do as well as the prior service companies tactically, they were sure to lead the brigade in academics. Imagine the surprise when Eddie's class ranked near the bottom in classwork. How was this possible? How could college educated candidates do poorly on written tests? Eddie knew the answer to that one, the classes bored the piss out of them.

Once again, they reviewed the organic weaponry of a rifle company. Once again, they reviewed the weaponry in support of a rifle company. New and even more boring ground was broken when they worked their way through the entire manual for drill and ceremony. Additional lows were reached when they were presented with the proper procedures for filling out the forms attendant on managing a rifle company. But absolute zero was achieved with the class on how to seat officers and their wives at a formal dinner.

Well, kiss my ass, thought Eddie, *I really am going to die in Vietnam.*

1968

Friendship between candidates and Tacs was not possible. The Tacs were there to beat the crap out of their charges and that was a gulf too wide to breach. Even so, the separation between Eddie and Grayson was an abyss of Mercator proportions. Eddie was a college graduate, older, and quite frankly, smarter. Grayson had a year of college and, while not stupid, was woefully average, an ordinary schmo who in peacetime would have schlumped his way through life causing a few ripples, but basically not affecting too much of anything. Unfortunately, this was a wartime army, and ordinary people placed in positions of extraordinary responsibility affected a lot. Plumbing Grayson's shallow depths took no great insight on Eddie's part. All you had to do was look. Grayson was a fat boy waiting to happen. As a candidate, low chow intake coupled with high caloric burn kept him thinned down. That changed when he became a Tac. The chow intake doubled while the caloric burn halved. The all to obvious result was Grayson began to pork up. Big problem: His fatigues were tailored to skinny Grayson. Somewhere around the fifth week they just flat didn't fit fat Grayson. But field jackets weren't tailored, so fat boy just wore that, indoors and out. Nice. No role model there.

Week twelve arrived and Eddie and the boys finally went to the field. Notwithstanding the myriad shortfalls in just about all previous tactical training, hopes were high this time it would be done right. Benning was, after all, "The Home of the Infantry." This was the hallowed ground of "The Queen of Battle;" every range was named after a hero killed in action. Unfortunately, the Queen was not omnipotent. In the weird little principality of OCS the jesters ruled and chaos reigned. As with leadership slots in the rear, those in the field were perverted from learning opportunities to punishment details. Once again, candidates targeted to get bounced were put in charge of the exercises, with the predictable result that things, by and large, did not go well. Couple that with the candidates' universal lack of military experience, "not going well" all too often became just plain old familiar fucked up. Take Ranger Week.

Ranger Week was a seven-day field exercise calling for platoon-sized elements to operate independently to conduct raids, ambushes, and reconnaissance patrols. The school support brigade was tasked with adding realism by acting as aggressors. As neither Eddie nor anyone else in his platoon had really mastered map reading, they generally either arrived at their targets late, or missed them altogether. For the entire week, they never made contact with the aggressors.

Periodically, the incompetence of the class hit historic levels, the Leadership Reaction Course, for example. Broken down into six-man teams, they were presented with a series of challenges and tasks. A typical scenario required the team to use wooden planks or ropes as bridges to get themselves and their equipment across a water obstacle. Each team had six problems, each problem calling for a new leader. Eddie's team missed them all. They almost got one. It required tying a litter to a cable strung over a water obstacle and then moving a wounded man on the litter across the water. Simple, except that no one knew how to tie knots. Exactly in the middle of the obstacle, the knots broke, and everyone went into the water. On their debrief, a somewhat nonplussed instructor told them he had never had a team fail all six of the tasks.

Every now and then, Eddie was sent up to main post to collect something for the platoon. He always detoured to the post library. The library had a listening room with stereos, head phones, and a collection of LPs. Most of the records were country, some were rock, but a few were classical. Needing to get as far away from OCS as possible, Eddie went for the classical. The aptly titled "The Classical Symphony" by Prokofiev did the trick. For the first time he began to understand what Marta, his mentor from school days, had tried to tell him. The arts really could make life's hard journey a little less lonely and a little less dark. He listened to the symphony as often as he could. It would remain a special favorite for the rest of his life. Music like this would play when the world ended.

They were conducting a field exercise and Eddie was the designated platoon leader. He managed to slip-slide through the admin portion without any fatal mistakes. The tactical part, not so lucky. They were moving out towards the objective when the aggressors sprung an ambush, hitting them with an avalanche of blank rifle fire. Eddie had no idea what to do. He did, however, know what not to do…just sit there and do nothing. In desperation, he moved from man to man, not really organizing anything, just moving. The rest of the exercise was a blur as he prepared for a flame thrower debrief from the lane grader.

"Good work, Candidate. Outstanding hands-on leadership."

Years later, in business, he heard it called "management by moving around." Show up, stay calm, pretend you know what you're doing. He never forgot it.

As the program toddled along to its feared conclusion of mass infantry commissions, Eddie and the boys were increasingly beset with a growing sense of impending doom. They were superb in appearance, magnificent on the march, and maintained an impeccable barracks. They just didn't know dick about leading an infantry platoon. They all knew the second lieutenant's prayer: "Please, God, don't let me fuck this up." How could they not? Fucking up was all they ever saw. Like condemned prisoners, they watched the weeks and days evaporate before graduation, after which there would be no turning back. Eddie had never seen so many people scared pissy-eyed green. And then the miracle occurred. Somewhere around week sixteen, they filed into Infantry Hall to receive an unscheduled presentation. Even the Tacs didn't know what for. A pudgy little major wearing Adjutant General insignia took the podium.

"Men, the Army has an immediate need for 200 Military Intelligence lieutenants. All of you are welcome to apply. Anyone who passes the background check will be commissioned MI."

Momentarily stunned, the class then exploded into cheers, manic laughter, and back slapping. Safe! No fucking infantry! Safe! No fucking rifle platoon! Safe! Safe! Safe! It was the most exquisite example of deus ex machina Eddie would ever see. And the unlikely deus was the little pork chop major. On the march back to the barracks, the company's singing rocked the area.

Two days later, all the MI aspirants reported into one of the classrooms to fill out the DD Form 398 Statement of Personal History, the first step in the background check. Facing the class was a bored-looking senior NCO. He passed out the 398s and took his seat behind a small desk and read the *Army Times*. For the first time in their military careers, no one minded filling out an Army form.

About ten minutes in, the NCO said, "Put down your pens and listen to me."

All did so.

"I've been in the Army twenty-two years, and you know what I'm proud of? THIS!" he said pointing to the CIB on his fatigues. "Now, go ahead and fill out yer fuckin' forms," and went back to reading his paper.

Jeez, thought everyone, *what an asshole*, and resumed filling out their forms.

Everyone but Eddie. He looked at his classmates, he looked at the NCO. He looked at the 398. *What the hell am I doing?* he thought. All the stories from his father. All the stories from others. All the books, movies, and TV. And he was going to spend the war sitting behind a desk? Not testosterone heavy, brass balled, stiff pecker Eddie. Fuck that. He stood up, walked to the front of NCO's desk, wadded up the 398, threw it in the trash can, and marched out of the classroom.

Jeez, thought everyone, *what an asshole*, and resumed filling out their forms.

"What now, smart guy?" That was the question. Where was the answer? Eddie reviewed his situation. It was now clear OCS was not going to give him the training needed to lead a rifle platoon in combat with competence. It was also clear self-respect made worming out to MI a no go. In school, he had read about existential questions. Now he had one face to face: How could he walk out of this mess (assuming his survival, an outcome with a rapidly decreasing probability) with his head held high? How do you spit shine your boots when you're knee deep in bullshit? The answer came in the unlikely vehicle of Fat-boy Grayson.

Tension between the two had long ago risen above the standard Tac-candidate kabuki dance. Eddie didn't just not respect him, he found the fat prick repulsive, the porky embodiment of OCS in all its phony preaching. Grayson was pushing Eddie's horseshit meter dangerously close to the red zone. Then, one night, in the midst of Grayson-directed laps for an infraction of some inane rule, the needle was buried. Eddie ran slower and slower…and then he stopped. A golden path opened before him, a yellow brick road to salvation. In a flash, he saw how to get out of OCS with honor. He couldn't hand in a letter, that would carry the stigma of "quitter." He couldn't get paneled out, that would carry the stigma of "couldn't cut it." He would get thrown out for insubordination. He would be able to look anyone in the eye and say, "OCS? Yeah, I told 'em what they could do with their fuckin' push-ups, and they threw me the fuck out." It had the simplicity and elegance of genius. He went back into the barracks with a spring in his step. Without asking permission, he walked into Grayson's office. Fatboy looked up in surprise.

"Finish your laps, Brandt?"

"Sir, Candidate Brandt, no, sir!" (Eddie had to walk a fine line here. He wanted to be just insubordinate enough to get kicked out, not to go to the stockade.)

"What? Why not?"

"Sir, Candidate Brandt, I'm not running any more laps, sir."

Fatso blinked, literally and emotionally. Where the hell was this in his scanty playbook? With all the speed his bulk would allow, he waddled around his desk and hovered over Eddie. "GET DOWN, BRANDT! GET DOWN AND START KNOCKING THEM OUT!"

"Sir, Candidate Brandt, no, sir."

"I SAID GET DOWN!"

"Sir, Candidate Brandt, I'm not doing any more push-ups, sir."

"GET DOWN! GET DOWN! GET DOWN!" Panic was starting. Fatboy's tiny trick bag was empty. Repetition was all he had left. "GET DOWN! GET DOWN! GET DOWN!"

Hearing the uproar, the company Executive Officer, First Lieutenant Lent appeared in the door. More seasoned than Grayson, Lent walked slowly over to Eddie.

"What's the problem, Candidate?" Voice calm, controlled, authoritative.

"Sir, Candidate Brandt, no problem, sir."

"Are you sick, Candidate?"

"Sir, Candidate Brandt, no, sir."

"Feeling poorly?"

"Sir, Candidate Brandt, I feel fine, sir." That was an understatement. In fact, Eddie hadn't felt this good in months.

"Just don't want to do any more push-ups, is that it?"

"Sir, Candidate Brandt, yes, sir."

Lent looked hard at Eddie. "Come with me, Brandt."

Eddie followed him into his office. *This is it*, he thought, *the big banana*. Boom, boom, boom, and this time tomorrow he'd be in holding company, Private Brandt. He could hardly keep from dancing. Then, the incomprehensible happened, nothing.

Lent spent half an hour pontificating about the benefits and advantages of officer service, its attendant rewards, its many satisfactions. He concluded with, “I’m going to keep an eye on you, Brandt,” and dismissed him.

Thunderstruck, Eddie staggered up to his room. This was way too much to process. A couple of bewildered “fuck me’s” was all he could muster. Men plan, gods laugh. No shit.

Eighteen months later, when Eddie returned to the Infantry School as an instructor, he figured out what had really happened. He discovered that the main driver in OCS was numbers, not training, not proficiency, numbers, fucking numbers. Manpower projections calculated that each Infantry OCS class had to generate 120 lieutenants. So, with a starting headcount of 220, meant a hundred bodies were expendable. Harassment and panels were the winnowing instruments. Brutally applied at the beginning of each cycle, as the program progressed and the headcount got closer to the magic 120, they by necessity had to ease up. Coming in under 120 was a career killer for the company commander, and that just wasn’t an option. Eddie’s rebellion, coming so late in the cycle, must have threatened the magic 120. And so, his small gesture of independence was defeated not by laughing gods, but by something even more powerful, the Iron Law of Army Numbers.

Eddie needed a new plan. If outright rebellion wouldn’t work, then it would have to be covert operations. Vietnam was an unconventional war, right? So, his private war with the Army would be unconventional. The symmetry appealed to the romantic in him. Yes sir, he would play act compliance with the horseshit, but in the secrecy of his inner self, he wouldn’t buy any of it. They could make him go to their fuckin’ party, but they couldn’t make him dance. Commando Eddie, that’s the ticket.

In week eighteen, they became senior candidates. It was called “turning blue,” light blue being the infantry color. The uniform changed, blue helmet liners instead of black, and white scarfs with the OCS logo. The rules changed, walking instead of running, relaxed mess hall procedures, no harassment from the Tacs. Their authority changed. Junior and intermediate candidates were required to salute them and address them as “sir.” Finally, senior candidates could, and indeed were required to, harass the intermediates and juniors.

The pinnacle of senior harassment was “Blue Monday.” A senior class snuck up to a junior barracks and when the wakeup bell sounded, tore in. With a roar Atilla the Hun's victims would have recognized, Eddie's class proceeded to Blue Monday the shit out of the helpless fuckers. Eddie had his plan. He raced up to the third floor, ran down to the last room, ducked inside, and shut the door. Three scared little mice looked at him.

"Make your bunks." Quiet, but firm. They made their bunks.

"Get dressed." They got dressed.

"Take a seat." They took a seat.

Periodically, Eddie's classmates would try to get in.

"Got it covered, boys." They moved on. After fifteen minutes, the blue tornado ran itself out. Without a word, Eddie left the room. Suck on that one, OCS. It was one of the proudest moments of his military career.

As with so many things in the Army, OCS sort of dribbled out at the end. Like a tired old dog, it laid down and went to sleep. The last week of the program they were given "off post privileges." In English, that meant they could rent an apartment in town. Eddie, the Ruper, and Fredericks got one right outside the main gate. Harassment was gone, fieldwork was over, and classes were minimal. Often released in the early afternoon, they would drive to the motel. They didn't have any civilian clothes, so they sat around in their skivvies drinking beer and watching TV. Eddie never thought he would say it, but OCS at this point was boring.

One last spark in the program was the issuance of orders. Earlier, they had been given the chance to request assignments. Eddie had put down airborne, ranger, 82nd Airborne Division. Of course, that didn't happen. They weren't called "dream sheets" for nothing. Shortly before graduation, Martin Luther King was assassinated and riots broke out in cities across the nation. Parts of the capitol went up in flames. In response, that small number to receive infantry commissions were sent to the 6th Armored Cavalry Regiment, Ft. Meade, Maryland. Eddie's first assignment as an officer was no airborne, no ranger, not even his branch, infantry. It was riot control for Washington, D.C. It was often said the Army was its own worst enemy. That one got Eddie's vote.

The final act in their OCS saga was graduation. All those who passed the background check were, indeed, commissioned in MI. Another got Finance, the simple reason being that halfway through the program it was discovered that he was almost legally blind. The rest, some dozen of them, Eddie included, were infantry.

It was an Army tradition; newly commissioned lieutenants gave a dollar to the first enlisted man to salute them. As they all filed out of Infantry Hall, the first sergeant was standing there, saluting and collecting a dollar from each. He snapped a salute at Eddie. "Afternoon, sir," and held his hand out.

Eddie returned the salute. "Afternoon, First Sergeant," and kept on walking.

"Ain't you forgettin' something, Lieutenant?"

"Not a fucking thing, First Sergeant."

Half a block later, a young private saluted Eddie. "Afternoon, sir."

Eddie returned the salute. "Just a minute there, Private," and handed him a dollar. Eddie felt great.

Notwithstanding the company's piss-poor performance in both the classroom and the field, their test case for the College Op Program was deemed successful, and it was implemented into army practice. Later, the company scored another historic first: It was the only Infantry OCS class in the Vietnam era to suffer no graduates killed in action. Most of its twelve infantry officers were wounded, but all survived the war. Ironically, those who quit the program were not so lucky. Eddie was to see many of their names in the *Army Times* casualty lists. Two Tacs didn't make it either. Fatboy Grayson did, however, but in typical Fatboy Grayson style. Somehow, he avoided Vietnam, thereby saving untold American lives. Years later, Eddie heard he wound up selling life insurance in Hawaii. Woody Allen couldn't have written it any better.

And so, those close partners in so much pain and fear split to the four winds, most of them never to meet again.

1968

The 6th Cav was basically a holding company. Half the troops were just back from Vietnam and were riding out their time for discharge. The other half were waiting to be fed into the war as replacements. Very few were trained armored cavalrymen. Undeterred by this fact, regimental leadership determined that all were at least going to look like cavalrymen. The cavalry color was yellow, so everyone was required to wear fruity-looking yellow scarves. Officers under some of the nuttier commanders also had to wear Stetsons and spurs. One of the few amusements in the regiment was to watch the spur-wearers hit the dirt after catching them on something.

Completely ignorant of anything relating to the cavalry, Eddie had to pick up the jargon. Companies and battalions were now troops and squadrons. The motor pool was now motor stables. He was waiting for "follow me" to be replaced by "hiyo silver."

The 6th was the only tactical unit on post, so it drew all the shit details. The first one was daily police call. Ft. Meade was divided into three sectors with one squadron assigned to each. Every day began with squadrons in their respective sectors on line picking up trash. Seeing men with CIBs picking up cigarette butts seemed to Eddie a new low in Army horseshit. Next came guard duty. Regimental guard was to be expected. But then there was post guard and, Ft. Meade being First Army Headquarters, First Army guard. Eddie felt like every other week he was pulling fucking guard. Finally, there was the unit's primary mission, riot control. That consisted of him putting the platoon into different formations, bayonetted weapons to the front, and then counting cadence with a bullhorn: "Hut! Hut! Hut! Hut!" He thought he was going to go crazy.

Officer Personnel Operations (OPO) was just down the road in Northern Virginia. It handled officer assignments.

After an agonizing month in the 6th Cav, Eddie drove down there. "I'm not even in my branch," he protested, "Give me an infantry slot, please."

"Do you have a platoon?"

"Yes."

"Well then, consider yourself lucky. A lot of lieutenants don't."

"How come I don't feel lucky?"

Once they actually did have a field exercise. It was a little constricted because the post commander's wife didn't want those nasty armored vehicles tearing up the pretty shrubs, so the troops were ordered to stay on the roads. As an infantry officer, Eddie was tasked with aggressing against the cav units. *A little canned*, he thought, *but what the hell, field work!* Relying on foggy concepts from training, supplemented by a hurried review of field manuals, Eddie set up an ambush along one of the roads. Thanks to the commander's wife, he knew the tracks would come this way. Okey, dokey. Claymore mines here, machine guns there, riflemen dispersed… Ready to rock and roll. Eddie looked down the road. There they were, turning the bend, coming closer, fifty meters to the kill zone, and… "Pop! Whoosh!" White smoke poured out behind him, giving away his whole position. The tracks stopped, turned around and left.

"Whaa? Hanh?" Eddie turned around and saw every junior officer's nightmare, Private Cook. Cook was big and fat and congenitally dirty. He could shower, shave, get a haircut, put on clean fatigues, and still look like pure shit. And there he was, standing next to a belching smoke canister, pull ring still in his big, fat, grubby finger.

"Cook!" choked Eddie. "Cook! Why in the fuck did you pop that canister?"

"I never seen one before, Lieutenant."

Incandescent with rage, Eddie was about to choke the living shit out of this human turd, when he saw a jeep coming down the road. The troop commander. *Fuck me*, thought Eddie.

"You fucked up, Lieutenant."

"Yes, sir."

"What happened?"

"No excuse, sir."

A second jeep came down the road. The squadron commander. *Fuck me to tears*, thought Eddie.

"You fucked up, Lieutenant."

"Yes, sir."

"What happened?"

"No excuse, sir."

A third Jeep came down the road. The regimental commander. *Fuck me to death*, thought Eddie.

"You fucked up, Lieutenant."

"Yes, sir."

"What happened?"

"No excuse, sir."

It wasn't like this in the goddamn movies.

Annual qualification on the M-60 machine gun came due and who else but Infantry Eddie in charge. *No sweat*, he thought, *just follow the checklist*. Coordinate with Range Control, reserve the range, check. Coordinate with the Ammunition Supply Point, lock in ammo, check. Coordinate with the First Sergeant, assign range control NCOs, check. Coordinate with Arms Room, lock in guns, check. Coordinate with Motor Stables, lay on transportation, check. Tight and tidy, ready Teddie.

Qualification day: Secure range, check. Pick up guns and ammo, check. Deploy range control, check. Pick up troops, check. 0900 commence qualification, check. Piece of cake. Then it started to fall apart. No one was qualifying. Rounds were all over the targets. The officers got down behind the guns. They couldn't qualify. The squadron commander got down. He couldn't qualify. As a mystified Eddie stood by bewildered, the regimental sergeant major strolled up. The regimental sergeant major, done it all, seen it all, in the army the proverbial "since Christ was a corporal."

"How's it going, Lieutenant?"

"Goddamn if I know, Sergeant Major."

"How'd you get this range, Lieutenant?"

"Through Range Control, Sergeant Major."

"Asked for the machinegun qualification range, Lieutenant?"

"That's right, Sergeant Major."

"Uh huh. What's the required range distance for machine gun qualification, Lieutenant?"

"A thousand inches, Sergeant Major."

"And what's this one, Lieutenant?"

"Fifty meters, Sergeant Major."

"What's that in inches, Lieutenant?"

"A thousand inches, Sergeant Major."

"More like two thousand, Lieutenant. They gave you the wrong range."

Dumb with fear, Eddie could only stand there in agonized silence. No wonder no one could qualify. The fucking range was twice as long as it should be.

"Jesus, Sergeant Major. What do I do now?"

"Well, let's see if anyone catches it."

For the next two hours, Eddie shit razor blades. The sergeant major looked on serenely. Finally, the squadron commander pulled Eddie aside. *Here it comes*, he thought, closing his eyes in anticipation of a world class corn-holing.

"Piss-poor marksmanship, Lieutenant, really piss-poor. These men need more training."

"Yes, sir, more training," he mumbled.

The sergeant major left without a word, whistling contentedly.

Ralph Poteet was a semi-literate Cajun from Hammond, Louisiana. Another old time NCO, Poteet had escaped a no-chance, no-hope, no-way life in the Bayous to eat, sleep, and breathe the US Army. He was Eddie's platoon sergeant.

One day, when they were running the men through riot control formations, Eddie got a call from his troop commander.

"Straight from higher, Lieutenant. No more scarves. Take 'em off."

These were the yellow cavalry scarves, universally disliked as uncomfortable, fruity looking, and just something else to keep clean.

Eddie called the platoon together. "Take the scarves off."

Poteet pulled him aside.

"You shore about that, Lootenan?"

"Yep, just got the word from the old man. No more scarves."

Poteet addressed the platoon. "Okay, men, take 'em off...but y'all be ready ta put 'em back on."

Eddie looked at him. What was this shit? An hour later, another call from the troop commander: put 'em back on. Once again, Poteet came off as the savvy, old NCO and Eddie as the dumb-as-dirt second lieutenant. Goddammit, it was frustrating. On any standardized test ever devised, Eddie would not just score higher than Poteet, he would probably score twice as high. But the fact of life was, on anything Army-related, Poteet would always get it right while

Eddie bounced between sometimes and not at all. And he knew why. Poteet hadn't simply seen these things before, he had seen them many, many times, so many times he didn't need to think, he just let his reflexes do the work. This "scarves off, scarves on" drill, no reasoning needed, just an automatic "be ready ta put 'em back on." It wasn't a matter of brain power, it was a function of time, pure and simple. Poteet had been doing this stuff for twenty-five years and there were no surprises left. What was also pure and simple to Eddie was he didn't have that kind of time. He would never lead troops as well as semi-literate, ninth grade educated, Louisiana shitkicker Poteet. Goddammit, it was frustrating.

First Lieutenant Julio Almendez, Big Al, reported into the regiment not too long after Eddie. Just back from Vietnam, Big Al was from New York City, Puerto Rican, a combat tested officer, and not old enough to vote. He and Eddie clicked. Almost every night they pulled out of Meade to the Baltimore-Washington Expressway. Then, big decision; left to go to the joints in DC, right for the ones in Baltimore. No matter, Big Al and Eddie were launching, babes take cover. Eddie thought Al was a total pisser. Neither particularly tall nor remotely handsome, Al had "the Gift." He got more nooky by mistake than Eddie ever got on purpose.

Take Captain Constanza. One of the few female officers at Ft. Meade, Captain Constanza was under constant siege by every would-be swordsman on post. Their universal lack of success was a thing of legend. One day at lunch in the club, she was, as usual, dining alone in the corner. Eddie gave Al the run down and pointed her out. Al smiled at him, got up, went over, smiled at her, and sat down. Two days later, her perfect record was broken. "Yep," mused Eddie, "a total pisser."

Big Al was in a quandary. He had survived Vietnam, but what now to do with the rest of his life? He often talked of what a charge he got out of combat, but Eddie knew that was bullshit. He spoke of staying in the Army, but that would have meant another trip across the pond, and Al wanted no part of that again. He had gotten used to the prestige of being an officer, but as a twenty-year-old without college, he didn't see any achievable equivalent in civilian life. It was, as Eddie would himself later encounter, the combat veteran's dilemma: now what? Al thought the answer was flight school. Sure, flying a helicopter was dangerous, but it was a clean rack, hot chow, and no humping a fuckin' rucksack. Al took the flight exam. For two weeks thereafter, Eddie listened to the much anticipated and soon-to-be-received joys of chopper piloting. Then Al got his test results; he had failed. Adios Flight School. Adios Army career. Once again, and with much fewer options this time, Big Al faced the fearsome "Now What?"

Months later in Vietnam, Eddie ran into a pal from the 6th Cav. Right after Eddie left, Big Al ran his car into an abutment on the BW Expressway. An accident? Suicide by abutment? Quien sabe?

Eddie continued his monthly pilgrimage to OPO. "Please, please, PLEASE," he pleaded, "get me out of here." Every time he saw a different major. The third one shook his head and told him there was no way they were going to give him a transfer, but if he wanted a sure fire out, plus additional training in the bargain, volunteer for Vietnam. It took Eddie all of five seconds. "What the hell? I'm going anyway. Why not?" He filled out the form on the spot, requesting airborne, ranger, Vietnam. A month later, he got his options: jump school and Jungle School in Panama, or just ranger. He took the first. A month after that, he got his orders.

And its 1,2,3 what are we fightin' for?
Don't ask me I don't give a damn,
The next stop is Vietnam,
And its 5,6,7 open up the pearly gates.
Well there ain't no time to wonder why...
WHOOPEE we're all gunna die.
- Country Joe and the Fish

1968-1969

Jump school, Ft. Benning one more time, only now as an officer, only now with fewer illusions. How many times had Eddie seen the movie version of it? Paratroopers in the making, lean, mean, and horny-fisted, running eight, nine, ten miles, singing all the way. Watch out, bad guys, America's finest are coming at you and they are some tough motherfuckers. *We'll see*, thought Eddie. Sure enough, almost immediately, the illusions began to fall away in the face of a much less impressive reality. Perhaps at one time they did run ten miles in jump school, but not in 1968; three miles, maybe, but not an inch more. Even so, guys fell out, wheezing and puking. No jump wings for them. Wrong! After midday chow they were all back in formation.

Then there was the swing landing trainer, a device that simulated the oscillating motion of a paratrooper under canopy as a means for practicing parachute landing falls (PLFs). Eddie happened to be standing behind the instructor recording performance. The student jumped off the platform, swung down to the ground, did a PLF, and reported to the instructor. Eddie couldn't help but notice the instructor marked successful completion for not one practice jump, but three. "Next!" Later, upon reflection, he realized this was another manifestation of the Iron Law of Army Numbers. The Army needed so many jump qualified personnel, and by God it was going to get them. More than once in his active-duty career, Eddie heard a senior NCO bemoaning the fact that the war was destroying the Army, and that only with peacetime could they get back to real soldiering. It was like saying that actually fighting fires hurt performance, that the real fire department was back in the station house.

The jungle in Panama was a scary place. For once, it really was like the movies. There were massive trees with roots as tall as a man snaking across the ground. There were hidden birds with an eerie "ooh-ooh-aah-aah" call. There were fearsome insects and animals whose sole purpose seemed to be biting human beings. There was black palm, a malignant plant that grew sharp and brittle, that at the slightest touch broke off into your hand and had to be dug out. Eddie read somewhere that over 5,000 men died digging the canal. He could see why. This was a scary place.

The post commander was an ancient colonel who, it was purported, had so much metal in him, he made lensatic compasses twitch. Marching to class the first day, they passed the corpse of a gigantic snake, at least a foot thick in the body, except for the tire tracks that killed it. Part of the "Welcome to Jungle School Orientation" was a tour of the post zoo, a heads up for what they might encounter out there. At one cage the assistant instructor reluctantly put on a suit of thick padding and a face mask. Eddie and the boys looked inside the cage trying to determine the source of this anxiety. All they saw was a small door. An entry that size couldn't let in anything much. The nervous AI nodded, the door slid open, and a cat, not much bigger than a house pet, jumped out. It looked around calmly, and then it saw the AI. With a roar even the most pissed off pet couldn't make, it was on him, biting and clawing and tearing the stuffing out of his protective gear. The AI, swatting and punching, lasted about five seconds before he dove through the exit. The class was told that though small, this little fucker had no fear and would attack anything. If the purpose of this administrative part of the course was to scare the piss out of everyone, it achieved its goal.

On day two, a Marine Battalion Landing Team came ashore to go through the course. Eddie and the boys were standing under the trees as the landing craft approached the beach. They hit the shore and the ramps went down. Eddie had heard the term "raggedy assed Marines." This was the first time he actually saw them. No two wore the same uniform. Some had jungle fatigues, some had stateside fatigues. Some had jungle boots, some had leather ones. All had their names written on the back of their fatigues, again, no two alike; some in big letters, some small, some straight across, some slanted. They poured out of the landing craft and swarmed up to Eddie's group.

"Hey, buddy, got any extra socks? Fatigues? Boots? Skivvies?"

The post commander had offered them one of the barracks. The battalion commander refused.

"Marines sleep in the open."

After hitting up the Army, the Marines went to the nearest tree and promptly fell asleep. Semper fucking Fi.

The highlight of the course was an escape and evasion (E & E) exercise. The class was broken down into five-man teams, given a compass, dropped off in the jungle, and instructed to "e and e" to the coast. Aggressors patrolled the roads picking up any team foolish enough to use them. Additional incentive to stay off the roads was a simulated POW camp notorious for its rough handling of captured students. The ranking man on Eddie's team was a Special Forces captain. As they went into the jungle, the captain, manning the compass, manned it carefully: stop, take a reading, move; stop, take a reading, move. Half an hour later, they had gone about 300 meters. The team, though not yet full up jungle experts, knew they were going too slowly.

"I don't want to spend the night in this fuckin' jungle." That was the consensus. The team revolted.

"Well," sniffed the captain in a huff, "if anyone thinks he can do better, here's the compass."

Eddie took it and, without a word, set off at a half run. Every so often, he glanced at the compass, but basically it was just to keep the direction from being a total wild-assed guess. "You go east, you hit the ocean." Eddie sure hoped that was the case. They careened through jungle, rock cliffs, and swamps. It kept on getting darker. Then at twilight, just as Eddie was beginning to feel he had really dorked it up, they broke out onto a beach…the ocean! They were the second team in, and, much more important, no night in the fuckin' jungle. It taught him a big lesson, applicable in almost any human endeavor, military or civilian: a half-assed plan executed quickly and vigorously is always better than a perfect one doled out in dribs and drabs.

January-March, 1969

After a short leave, Eddie was on his way. In uniform, he flagged down a cab to the airport.

"Been to Vietnam, soldier?"

"Going there right now."

They pulled up to the terminal.

"What do I owe you?"

"Not a thing, buddy. Good luck."

Eddie was touched. He picked up his ticket and walked to the gate.

"Excuse me, Lieutenant," from a pleasant looking middle-aged woman. "Have you been to Vietnam?"

"No, ma'am, I'm on my way there right now."

"God bless you, son. Please be careful."

Now he was really touched. It the first time since he joined the Army that someone other than family gave a shit about what he was doing.

Oakland was jammed. People coming from Vietnam, people going to Vietnam. Eddie found his flight and boarded. Every seat on the plane was taken, and it was a big plane. Going off to war in a commercial jet with civilian stewardesses seemed a little weird to Eddie, but by this time everything about Vietnam was weird. As luck would have it, seated across the aisle was an OCS classmate, Sutherland. Sutherland, one of the MI pukes, was a tiny guy, so small his feet barely touched the floor. *Well, holy fuckaroo,* thought Eddie, *I'm going to war with a midget.* Where the hell was John Wayne when you needed him? If things stopped being weird, the shock would probably kill him.

Hours later, they landed in Hawaii. Restricted to the terminal, they futzed around for a few more hours and then got on another plane. Next stop, Wake Island. Eddie recalled a movie that dramatized the World War II battle with its famous message of defiance from the doomed American garrison: "Send us more Japs." He bought that as a boy, but after eighteen months in uniform his horseshit meter dinged Lima Charlie, loud and clear. Indeed, the few Americans who survived the disaster dismissed it as crude wartime propaganda. Eddie mused on the possibility of his involvement in historic battles, the probability of his survival, and the almost certain generation of army aggrandizing horseshit. Would he be one of those crusty old vets setting the record straight? He certainly hoped so.

Eddie orbited in and out of sleep. When the announcement was made to prepare for landing, he looked out the window. All he could see was water. The wheels came down. They went lower, still water. When it seemed that they were going to crash into the Pacific Ocean, the plane landed on Wake Island. They got off with about an hour to kill for refueling. This time they weren't restricted to the terminal. Why bother? There wasn't much there. To be generous, Wake was a little sparse. They re-planed and then an announcement was made.

"Anyone seen Private X?" They all looked at each other. Again, "Private X?" Nothing. Some MPs got on, huddled with the crew, left, and the plane took off.

"Goddamn!" marveled Eddie. "Some dumb shit actually went AWOL on Wake Island." How would he hide out? Disguise himself as a gooney bird? Where would he go? Dog paddle into the lagoon? For once, John Wayne said something useful: "Life's tough. It's tougher if you're stupid."

They had a new crew and Eddie noticed the stews were older. He found out later the airlines had hazardous duty pay for flights to Vietnam; the closer you got, the more you got. It was seniority, plain and simple; the older stews got first choice, so the closer to Vietnam, the older the babes. It was a small matter, but it seemed in retrospect enormously informative, about Vietnam in particular, and war in general: it was a money-maker for the old fuckers.

They landed at Clark Field in the Philippines. It was night time and they got the by now familiar directive, "Don't go nowhere." Then the final leg, Vietnam. No sleeping on this one. Not much talking either. Hours later, "We have passed over the territorial waters of the Republic of Vietnam." Nothing. Minutes later, "We have passed over the territorial land mass of the Republic of Vietnam." Again nothing. Again night time.

Eddie looked out the window. Lots of lights up ahead. Lights? In a war zone? Lights, indeed. This was Ben Hoa, one of the busiest airports in the world. The only noticeable concession to armed conflict was a precipitous descent. The whole place was ablaze with light. The plane taxied around for a while and then stopped. They sat there. Now what? Low crawl into a fire fight? Hand-to-hand on the tarmac? The cabin door popped open and someone came aboard and sprayed something around the exit.

Then a mean looking MP came forward and halfway between a sneer and a scowl said, "Welcome to Vietnam. Get off the airplane."

They picked up their duffel bags and filed off. There wasn't any firefight, but goddammit, it was impressive. It wasn't just the lights, there was stuff, stuff everywhere, huge mounds of it, palletized and wrapped in cargo netting, waiting to go somewhere. Forklifts whizzed around, picking up stuff here, moving stuff there.

Eddie dimly recalled the words of a supply officer in an otherwise forgettable class, "Amateurs talk tactics, professionals talk logistics." This was Eddie's introduction to what the American Army did better than any other in the world: stuff…getting it, moving it, pissing it away. The "American Way of War" was stuff. What he was seeing here was the final step in the worldwide pipeline, stuff just before it got delivered to its end user who would shoot it, eat it, wear it, or, in that quintessentially American manner, throw it the fuck away. As he looked over at the men shuffling in silence to some unknown place, Eddie couldn't help but see them as another pipeline of stuff, impersonal, indistinguishable, replaceable stuff. He realized he was in that pipeline: lieutenant, infantry, airborne, one each. He hoped the end user would not piss him away too.

They were herded over to a line of Army buses, same as the state-side ones, but with wire mesh on the windows as a grenade shield. An MP jeep with a mounted fifty caliber machine gun took the lead, another brought up the rear. They left brightly lit Ben Hoa, and motored into dark, shadowy, spooky Vietnam. There had been heavy fighting here and what little they could see was mostly wreckage.

Great, thought Eddie, *still in khaki uniforms, unarmed, driving through hostile territory with a handful of MPs for protection. What do I do if we get hit, throw my fuckin' duffle bag at 'em?* Could it get any more depressing? Yes, indeedy.

They arrived at their destination without incident, Long Binh, the Army's Vietnam in-processing center. It was still dark, but at this point Eddie had no idea what time it was. They began the transformation from stateside to in-country army. First, they presented a copy of their orders. That was followed by a trip to the clothing issue point where they received a basic Vietnam clothing issue: jungle fatigues, jungle boots, socks, OD skivvies, jungle sweater, poncho liner, etc. Then there was the exchange of US currency for Military Payment Certificates, or MPC. Possession of US money was a military offense, but just about everyone held on to a quarter or a fifty-cent piece for good luck. This was followed by filling out a seemingly endless series of Army forms. Finally, there were a few lectures about something and they were in-processed. It was still dark and Eddie still didn't know what time it was.

The last move for the night was to the temporary barracks, officers to one, enlisted to another. Eddie staggered in lugging his stuff. He was wearing his brand-new, bright green jungle fatigues, so new you could still see the folds made when they were shipped from the factory. He dumped everything next to an empty bunk and sat down, suddenly tired. There was someone stretched out in skivvies in the adjacent bunk. A khaki uniform with two rows of ribbons hung off the bed frame. This guy was going home.

"Just get here, Lieutenant?"

"Yeah."

"Well, I got less hours left than you got months."

Eddie reviewed his options: smack the prick, tell him to go fuck himself, ignore him. But it was just another case of Army insensitivity, bunking the guys just arriving in-country with those going home the next day. Eddie lay down and went to sleep. A man can only have so much fun.

Every day, at 1000 hours, they posted the assignments on the bulletin board:

1st Cav

xxxx

xxxx

4th Infantry Division

xxxx

xxxx

101st Airborne Division

xxxx

xxxx

...and so on. First day, half his plane load got their assignments and disappeared. Nothing for Eddie. There was a dismal little club nearby. He split his time between there, sipping strange tasting Coca-Cola's, and crapped out on his bunk. Second day, the rest of his plane load assigned and disappeared. No Eddie; club, bunk, club, bunk, da da, da da, da da. Third day, guys who arrived after Eddie, assigned and disappeared. No Eddie, club-bunk kabuki dance. Had the Big Green Dick missed him? Were his orders wadded up in the innards of a mimeograph machine?

Fourth Day:

173rd Airborne Brigade

Brandt, Edward L, 2LT.

That was it. No other names. He was at a loss for words. The Death Brigade, The Herd...first Army unit in Vietnam, only mass tactical combat jump of the war, fought in Dak To, biggest battle of the war. He stared at the board. Then all he could say was, "Jesus asshole Elmer."

The Herd was headquartered in An Khe. Eddie hopped a C-130. There were lots of other people on the plane, but it looked like he was the only replacement (the spanking new, bright green fatigues were the giveaway). Of course, there was no one there to meet him. He got directions to Brigade HQ from someone, picked up his duffle bag, and started walking. There was an infantry platoon sprawled out in the shade, waiting to go somewhere. Eddie had to walk right by them, these grunts in their faded fatigues. They gave him the silent once over. Bright green fatigues = cherry lieutenant. It was not a friendly encounter. Jesus, he felt lonely.

What the hell was that smell? It was human shit mixed with fuel and set on fire. That was the army answer to no sewer system. Like so many army answers, it solved one problem, only to create another: turds went away; the odor never did. It stayed with Eddie for the rest of his life.

At HQ Eddie reported in to S1, personnel. A captain in an OD tee shirt gave him a five-minute overview of the Brigade situation, and gave him a new set of orders. All replacements had to attend a week-long course of instruction at the 173rd Jungle School there at An Khe. This was, in theory, where they would be introduced to the Brigade SOPs (standard operating procedures). That was his next stop.

"Sir?"

"Yeah?"

"Where do I go after that?"

"Look at your orders, Lieutenant."

Eddie looked. F/5/503. He was going to Fox Company, 5th Battalion, 503rd Infantry (airborne). That was the final destination of his eighteen-month pipeline to combat.

A young NCO drove him over to the school. They didn't speak. He reported in, presented a copy of his orders, and was directed to the officers' barracks. Two young lieutenants were already there. They greeted him warmly. Friendly faces at last. They were all second lieutenants and they knew the course ended with an actual combat patrol. Which of them would lead it? They compared dates of rank. Eddie was junior by a few days. The OCS lesson of dodging responsibility was still an unhealed wound. Safe! Eddie was safe. One of these other poor turds would lead the patrol.

An unintended benefit of the week's instruction, almost certainly not part of the official lesson plan, was acclimating newbie stomachs and colons to the food, the microbes, and the air of Vietnam. It involved diarrhea of the most urgent and painful sort. For a good part of the week, Eddie and the boys shit their brains out.

By now, a veteran Army course attendee, Eddie approached 173rd Jungle School with modest expectations. Even that lowest of bars was barely met.

"Men, this is the Pistol, Caliber, .45, Automatic, M1911A1…" "

Jesus, not again. How many fuckin' times was he going to be informed of the fuckin' weapons organic to a fuckin' rifle company?

And so it went for a week. They threw the odd grenade, blew a few claymore mines, and zeroed their M-16s (yes! M-16s at last!) In the midst of floating down this slow-moving river, Eddie did pick up a gem:

"Now men, in order to avoid *confusement*…" Army NCO English at its finest. Avoid confusement. *Love to*, mused Eddie, *please show me how*. Confusement followed him like a hound dog after an escapee from a chain gang.

Day 6, combat patrol with overnight ambush. Eddie bopped into the classroom smugly secure in the knowledge that the Big Green Dick wasn't aimed at him.

"Patrol Leader, Lieutenant Brandt."

Wait just a fuckin' second, there boys. There's clearly been some confusement here. Doing as best he could to hide the turd in his new fatigue pants, Eddie approached the NCO in charge.

"Excuse me, Sergeant, but you do know I'm not the ranking officer here, right?"

"Tha's affirm, sir. But y'all's infantry and them's artillery. Infantry runs the patrol."

Ah, Queen of Battle, the gift that keeps on giving.

The cadre helped him organize the class into a combat patrol. The eighty or so enlisted were broken down into two sections, each led by one of the artillery lieutenants. School NCOs were sprinkled here and there. The school commandant paired up with Patrol Leader Eddie. Live ammunition was issued and loaded into magazines. They mounted into trucks and drove out of the An Khe main gate…Indian Country. After a few clicks (kilometers), they dismounted and spread out. They were on patrol.

Periodically, the commandant would tell Eddie to tighten it up. Then periodically, he would tell him to spread it out. And so it went for a few hours. They passed through a small village. An ancient gook sitting in the traditional Vietnamese crouch watched them go by. Then, just as Eddie was starting to feel like he might be able to do this, two shots were fired: Pop! Pop! They were in contact! He grabbed the hand set from his radio telephone operator (RTO). He called the lieutenants. No commo.

"Lieutenant, turn them around, get them on line, and sweep the fuckin' area, NOW!"

Guidance from the Commandant. A lot of yelling later, the patrol swept back through the village. There in the dirt where Luke the gook had been crouched were two expended rounds. They were like two tiny little exclamation points: "Welcome to Vietnam, GI! Fuck you!" He had probably been doing this his whole life, as a kid against the Japanese, a man against the French, and now as an old papa san against the Americans. How do you fight that? There was nothing to fight, no command structure, no organizational structure, no logistical chain, just a solitary old bird with a rusty rifle and a box of ancient ammo. And, every so often, he probably hit someone. He could do this forever.

Following this "combat," they resumed the mission. At dusk, with the help of the cadre, they set up an ambush. Eight noncombat but sleepless hours later, they turned around and went back to An Khe. It was official, they were trained up and ready to deploy to the field.

5th Batt was operating out of a fire base in the Central Highlands. The nearest town was a place called Tuy Hoa, so Eddie hopped a 130 there, then in a UH-1H (Huey) choppered out to the fire base. Hueys flew with doors open, so Eddie had a good look at the ground below. It seemed like he was going back in time. Tuy Hoa was built up, then came a grid of rice paddies, then small villages, then nothing, no roads, no trails, nothing but green as far as he could see. He felt like he was leaving civilization farther and farther behind. This was the highlands, so the green jungle undulated like an evil sea serpent slithering through a malevolent lagoon. In the distance he saw a brown spot. It was a mountain top with the vegetation blasted away. It stood out like a chancre sore. It was the 5th Batt fire base.

The fire base consisted of a battery of six 105 mm howitzers protected by concertina wire and a detachment of infantry in fighting positions. 5th Batt was conducting joint operations with the Korean Tiger Division, so half the perimeter was American, half Korean. A bunch of dugouts in the middle was headquarters. That's where Eddie went. He reported to the battalion executive officer (XO). The XO confirmed he was going to Fox Company and would fly out on the resupply next morning. Until then, find a hole and relax. He found one, dumped his shit, and decided to have a look around. Korean troops were notorious for their toughness and their brutality. Unconstrained by such Western foolishness as the Geneva Convention, they were there to kill people, which they did indiscriminately and with regularity. The Vietnamese, friendly and enemy, gave them a wide berth. When a Korean patrol approached a village, all the villagers ran away and hid. VC and NVA also avoided them whenever they could, preferring instead to engage the less fearsome Americans. Eddie had heard all this as far away as Ft. Benning. As he walked around, he came across a Korean NCO inspecting a squad. Bap! Down went one of the troops. He scrambled to his feet, back to rigid attention. Bam! Down went another. And so it went. Yep, tough motherfuckers. At one of the Korean fighting positions, he saw troops eating chow out of what looked like an American can of C-rations. Smiling, they offered him some. Eddie smiled in return and took a mouthful. Not American Cs at all, Korean, and the infamous kimchi. Diplomatically, he swallowed the shit, smiled again, and moved on. A few yards on, he came to a Korean latrine. He knew without a doubt that it was Korean, because it smelled exactly like kimchi.

Eddie was trying to relax in his hole when a tall, lean captain stopped by.

"Going to Fox Company, Lieutenant?"

"Yes, sir," said Eddie, getting to his feet.

"Relax, so am I. Joe Reddington," he said, putting out his hand. "I'm the new CO."

They chatted for about half an hour. Reddington was lowkey, easygoing, and here on his second tour.

"See you tomorrow."

Eddie watched him go. *Seems like a good shit*, thought Eddie. *Maybe this won't be so bad after all.*

That night, the Koreans stretched a blanket between two poles and watched a movie. It seemed like they were daring the gooks to hit them. They didn't.

Next morning, after a C-ration breakfast of coffee and poundcake, Eddie walked over to the helipad. Captain Reddington was there.

"Morning, Lieutenant."

"Morning, sir."

"Good day for it."

"Yes, sir."

They chatted some more. Eddie was starting to feel good about this. Then an NCO came over.

"Captain Reddington, the major wants to see you ASAP."

Reddington left. A few minutes later he was back.

"Everything okay, sir?"

"My father died. I'm going home."

He picked up his shit, walked off, and Eddie never saw him again.

The helipad was broken down by company. There was stuff and personnel for Alfa Company, stuff and personnel for Bravo, Charlie, and Delta Companies, and stuff and Eddie for Fox. Alfa resupply went out, then Bravo. The NCO running the helipad came over to Eddie.

"Hey, Lieutenant. Those guys going out to Alfa? They got hit on the LZ. One of 'em's dead. Thought you should know."

He found out later that was bullshit. Welcome to the field, Lieutenant.

The bird for Fox came in. They loaded the stuff and then pointed at Eddie. He climbed on and they took off. He didn't know what to expect. He saw a rough clearing in the middle of a big green nothing. They came in, hovered at about six feet, threw the supplies out, and the crew chief pointed at Eddie. He climbed out onto the skids. They were still hovering. "Fuck it," he said and jumped. He hit hard and his rucksack flipped him onto his back. With what little dignity remained, he collected his rifle and got to his feet. A soldier, bare to the waist, stood there, looking, expressionless.

"Where's the CP?"

Without a word, the soldier pointed. Eddie went that way. A few meters off the clearing he saw a cluster of radios and people: the CP.

"Carl Raymond, welcome to Fox Company."

Should he salute? Nah. They sat. 1LT Raymond was the temporary CO. A few days earlier, Fox Company was in a nasty little fight. The CO was killed and one of the platoon leaders was wounded. Eddie was his replacement. His platoon would link up in the morning for resupply and for him.

Raymond gave Eddie a little background on the company and on his approach to leadership.

"Take this resupply. They sent out marmite cans with hot chow cooked up in the rear. Gives the boonies rats a decent meal instead of Cs and LRRPs. But two of the platoons are out on ambush and we had to turn in the marmite cans on the bird you came in on…so, no hot chow for those guys. So, I told the guys here, no hot chow for them, no hot chow for you. There was a little bitchin', but when they have time to think about it, they'll see it's only fair. Those are the things you have to think about when you're in charge."

Sounded okay to Eddie. A few days later, he found out when Raymond wasn't looking, they ate the hot chow anyway.

Next morning, the other two platoons linked up. Second platoon was Eddie's. The platoon sergeant was an E-6 by the name of Wells. He introduced himself and Eddie's RTO. The platoon picked up their resupply, and fifteen minutes they all moved out. They moved along a trail and after about a click it split into two smaller trails. Raymond directed Eddie to take his platoon on one; he and the rest of the company would take the other. Eddie was now on his own. He vaguely recalled being told in training never to walk the trails. Oh, well. The trail got smaller and smaller and then there was no trail. Wells told the lead squad to start "bustin' jungle." Two guys dropped their rucksacks, took machetes, and started cutting down the vegetation. Everyone else faced left or right, weapons at the ready. After about ten minutes, the jungle busters were exhausted and Wells replaced them with two more. And so it went. With the heat, ten minutes was about all anyone could handle doing that shit. In an hour, they had gone about seventy-five meters. Now Eddie understood why you walked the trails in Vietnam. The one benefit of bustin' jungle was, unless you ran into gooks bustin' jungle exactly the other way, the chances of making contact were pretty close to zero. They quit around dusk, set up a perimeter, set up a guard rotation, and heated Cs or LRRPs for dinner. That was the end of Eddie's Day 1 in charge.

As he sipped his shitty coffee, Eddie sorted through the many impressions of that first day. Foremost was the astonishing realization of how different everything was to what he had been taught. And not just walking trails; just about every fucking thing was different. First, there was the headcount. According to doctrine, an infantry platoon was forty-two men; he had twenty-three. According to doctrine, an infantry platoon had three rifle squads and a weapons squad; he had two, each one with a machine gun. Then, there was the uniform. Stateside fatigues were the cotton utilities, shirt tucked into pants; Vietnam, rip-stop jungle fatigues, shirt worn outside the pants. Stateside, leather boots; Vietnam, jungle boots. Then the biggest and nastiest surprise of all, the basic combat load. Stateside, they were issued ass packs; Vietnam, rucksacks. You could carry a lot of stuff in an ass pack. You carried an unbelievable amount of stuff in a rucksack. It started with the war fighting stuff: fifteen to twenty magazines of M-16 ammunition. Throw in a can of machinegun ammo, two or three fragmentation grenades, a couple of smoke grenades, a claymore mine, some trip flares, and some empty sandbags. Then there was the personal stuff: water, four to five canteens; food, a couple of boxes of Cs and one or two add-water LRRPs. Top it all off with a poncho, a poncho liner, a jungle sweater, and some socks, and you were weighing in at a load of somewhere around eighty to eighty-five pounds. Machine gunners, RTOs, and medics carried even more. Years later, Eddie read a study done by the German army on the maximum weight an infantryman could carry and still maintain his combat effectiveness; one third of his body weight. More than that and effectiveness declined markedly. Eddie figured that after shedding stateside pudge, most grunts in Vietnam ran 150 – 165 lbs., making the maximum load fifty-five lbs. He couldn't help but wonder how many of the 58,000 names on the Vietnam Veterans Memorial were caused by overloaded grunts being just too goddamn tired to function properly.

They wandered around for a few days, linked up, and were lifted out to a MACV compound in Tuy Hoa for a short stand down. There he got to know his fellow platoon leaders. 2LT Don Crane was a kid from Pittsburgh. Before the Army he had been a pipefitter making, as he boasted, "big dust." He scored high enough on his tests to go to OCS, did enough to graduate, and *boomo*, landed in Vietnam as an airborne rifle platoon leader. The men in his platoon determined in a few weeks what the Infantry School had failed to discover in six months; Crane had minimal leadership skills. This not so uncommon situation was not always a show stopper. A good platoon sergeant and a compliant lieutenant could wicker together a leadership approach that made things work. Not so with Crane, he was going to run the show his way. The unfortunate result was a classic case of "Shitty Lieutenant." After a few months, he was relieved of duty, posted back to a do-nothing job in the rear, got sick, and was sent home. No John Wayne movie there.

2LT Roger Parker was a variation of a similar theme, the major difference being that Rog was a thoroughly decent guy. He came from someplace in Kansas he claimed was the exact geographic midpoint of the US. Rog was in many ways the exact human midpoint of the young American male population of the 1960s. Tall, skinny, with a goofy smile, in a more innocent time he would have spent his adolescence fixing up old cars, and his adulthood selling farm equipment to his neighbors. The Big Green Dick re-routed that gentle path. Like a part of a school of fish in a hatchery, Rog swam anonymously in the middle, being inexorably moved along for release into a hostile and unforgiving environment. He had no thought of making the army a career, and yet, he was enormously proud of his journey.

"Yep, OCS, Jump School, leading an airborne platoon in combat," he mused, "that's some heavy shit."

Eddie had to admit it was, especially the combat part. Too bad Rog wasn't very good at it.

"What's the most dangerous thing in Vietnam?" went one of the war's enduring jokes. "A second lieutenant with a map." Case in point, Rog. For the life of him (and those he led), he could not read a map. Being in the middle of the heavily wooded Central Highlands where you couldn't see terrain features didn't make it any easier. Rog devised the unfortunate work-around of climbing a tree "to get a better look." Dorky, uncoordinated Rog thrashing around in a tree was not an inspiring sight. His platoon irrevocably deemed him a numb-nut, case closed.

From the MACV compound, they were released into town for R&R.

"Everything off the main drag is off limits. The bus will pick you up at 1500 hours."

Dropped off in Central Tuy Hoa, Eddie and Rog flagged down a cycle rickshaw and grandly announced their objective to the driver: "Number one boom, boom!" The driver zipped off the main drag, threading his way through a rat maze of side streets. Eddie and Rog shared a bottle of strange tasting whiskey and in no time were merrily singing, blissfully shitfaced. The driver stopped, pointed at a crappy looking building and proudly announced, "number one boom boom." They tossed some MPC at him, told him to stick around, and rolled in. They were greeted by an overly made up, gold toothed mamasan.

"GI numba one!"

"Number one boom boom, mamasan!"

She led them into another room. Rog was singing. Two young Vietnamese men were sitting there. They were wearing shorts, sandals, and floppy shirts. They had close cropped hair. They had muscular legs. They were not in uniform. They were not friendly. Rog was still singing. Eddie sobered up in a flash. Eddie and the gooks looked at each other. Rog waved at them. They didn't wave back. They didn't smile. They were not friendly. Mamasan said something in Vietnamese and herded them out of the room. Eddie was about to grab Rog and make a run for the door when the girls came in, took hold, and steered them into the back. It was not number one boom boom.

Back at the MACV compound it was beer and hamburgers. Someone had bought a Vietnamese dress for his sister. Several beers later, he was wearing it on his head. Many beers later, someone else threatened to beat the shit out of Sergeant Wells. The next day, they went swimming in the South China Sea. The battalion commander showed up and they threw him in the water. He took it for a manly demonstration of wartime camaraderie. The troops took it for what it was: they didn't like the prick. The next day, fully refreshed, they flew out to the fire base.

It was Charlie Company's rotation to perimeter security and they took up the defensive positions. The new CO was waiting for them and he relieved LT Raymond. His name was George F. Charles. Captain Charles had ten years in the Army, most of it enlisted. He had spent five of those years as a buck sergeant on the Far East Drill Team. When Vietnam heated up, he put in for OCS and was commissioned. From a distance, Charles looked the part. He was tall, slim, and walked like he had a cleaning rod up his ass…right off the recruiting posters, a trim, squared away looking infantry officer. The closer you got, the more the picture changed. When he took off his helmet, you saw his eyes were a little too close together and a little uneven, one slightly higher than the other. Same with his ears, not quite aligned. And his nose was a little too big. As Eddie got to know him, he realized Charles was the Army writ small. He looked great on the parade ground, where it was all drill and ceremony by the numbers. In the field where it took real leadership, not so great. Like so many wartime officers, Charles wasn't stupid, he was just deeply ordinary. While the Army hyped the officer corps as the big green version of the priesthood…a calling, a vocation, a sacred trust…in reality, it was for so many a straightforward exercise in personal advancement. Charles got his commission not to join the select brotherhood of leaders, he got it because he wasn't making rank fast enough as an E-5. Also, the perks as an officer were better. So was the uniform. So was the pay.

Perimeter security was easy duty, a chance to relax and catch up on sleep. Not under Captain Charles.

"I don't like it, Lieutenant."

"What's that, sir?"

"The men, lying around."

"Sir?"

"Let's have some training."

"What kind of training, sir?"

"Weapons training, Lieutenant. Let's set up training on individual weapons."

Not a bad idea, thought Eddie. Troops always like firing their weapons, particularly when no one's firing back at them. He had a detail collect wooden ammo boxes from the artillery and place them at 50, 100, 150, and 200 meters outside the wire. The riflemen, grenadiers, and gunners merrily blazed away.

"How far away is the enemy in the average firefight, Lieutenant?"

"I'd say somewhere around fifty meters, sir."

"Right. So why do we have targets here out to 200 meters?"

Eddie didn't have an answer for that one.

"And the M-79, the grenadiers. How do they engage the target if there's vegetation in the way?"

"Sir?"

"High angle firing, Lieutenant. Fire the M-79 like a mortar."

"How's that, sir?"

"Simple, Lieutenant. Rest the butt of the weapon on the ground, place your boot in the sling and pull the weapon upright until it forms a triangle with the sling, determine the angle for the various ranges, and mark them off on the sling. Thereafter, when you're in contact, if you need to engage an enemy at fifty meters, you just set up for high angle firing using the fifty-meter tic mark and you're zeroed in."

Eddie had never heard that one, but it did sound logical. They set it up. They held the M-79 at about a forty-five-degree angle from the ground. The round impacted at around 300 meters.

"Too far. Bring it in."

Sixty degrees…200 meters.

"Still too far. Bring it in closer."

Eighty degrees …a hundred meters.

"Closer."

"Captain, that's almost straight up."

"Closer!"

Bloop! Boom! Three guys went down, hit, one with a sucking chest wound.

"Fuck!"

"Shit!"

"Medic! Medic!" Doc came on the run.

Captain Charles sat, stunned, speechless.

The battalion S-3, a mean looking major with a nasty scar on his cheek, came stalking over. He looked at Doc working on the wounded.

"What the hell happened here, Charles?"

Captain Charles mumbled something, barely coherent as he saw his sad little career swirling down the crapper.

The Sergeant Wells spoke up. "Sir, I think it was incoming."

Everyone looked at him in amazement.

The major barked at him. "Incoming?"

"Yes, sir. I'm pretty sure it came from over there," said Wells, pointing at the tree line. "Why don't you let me take out a patrol and check it out?"

The major glared at him.

Wells collected a few troops, saddled up, and filed outside the wire, into the tree line. The major took it all in.

A few minutes later, Wells and co. came back through the perimeter. "Here you go, sir. Just like I said, incoming," he said, handing the major an expended M-79 shell casing. The major took it and waved it under Wells' nose.

"That's bullshit, Sergeant. I'm going to check the lot number on this, and if it's one of ours, you're going to jail!" He looked at the shell casing. Wells had scraped off the lot number. The major stared at him hard, then stalked off. They medevacked the wounded to the rear. Then Eddie pulled Wells aside.

"Sergeant Wells, what the hell was that?"

"Well, Lieutenant, it's like this. If it's incoming, they get a purple heart. If it ain't, they don't get shit."

Infantry logic. Eddie couldn't argue with it. Later, when Charles revealed his true colors, Eddie realized he should have scorched the prick. When the gods give you a gift, you reject it at your own peril. Oh, well.

A few days later, they gave Eddie a hard stripe E-7 to replace E-6 Wells as the platoon sergeant. Bear, as he was known, had spent years running Tower Week in Jump School. This was his first tour in Vietnam. He knew less about the war than Eddie. The company was airlifted back to An Khe. A major air assault was in the works.

Intelligence reports indicated a heavy concentration of gooks on a hilltop in the highlands. The concept of operations was simple: Blast the shit out of it and then send in Charlie Company. This was Eddie's first one and he was both scared and excited; probably more excited than scared. Here was the truly American revolution to warfare, the air assault. It was the modern-day version of the cavalry charge, UH-1H helicopters replacing horses. No one did it better than the US Army, in fact, no one else did it at all. Tally fuckin ho!

The choppers flew into the helipad, rotors whop-whop-whopping. The troops, broken down into sticks, climbed aboard. Eddie's platoon was going in first, so he would be in the lead bird. For some reason, it was further down the line, so it broke out and moved to the front of the column. Eddie looked at the company as he moved by. It was like trooping the line. Everyone was waving and yelling. The noise of the rotors drowned out everything, so he couldn't make out what they were saying. Maybe they were telling him to go get fucked, but he like to think they weren't. Anyway, it really was exciting. Then they took off, 2LT Edward Brandt in the lead.

Artillery was already working over the hill and what had been green was rapidly becoming black. Fox Company circled in the air. Then the jets roared in blasting with bombs and burning with napalm. Eddie watched fascinated. Just how many gooks were down there to call for all this ordnance? Well, he'd find out shortly. Then Fox Company uncoiled and went in. Just off the deck, the door gunners opened. The choppers hovered, the crew chiefs pointed, and Fox Company jumped out. Eddie and his platoon ran about fifty meters and got down. The choppers left. Silence. No contact. No gooks. Just a black, smokey mess. They got into column formation and moved off the empty hill, Eddie's platoon up front, walking a trail as always. They had a scout dog team attached. They were walking point.

It was the highlands, so it was up and down. Hilly and hot, in no time at the rucksacks ground everyone into pack animal autopilot. Trudge…trudge… trudge…follow the guy ahead…trudge…trudge…trudge…I need some fuckin water…trudge…trudge…trudge…when can we take a fuckin break. All day long, no contact. At dusk they set up a defensive perimeter. There was a steep hill on one side of the trail.

"Lieutenant, take your platoon and set up security on top of that hill."

Eddie took a look. *For Christ's sake*, he thought, *that's not a hill. It's a fuckin' cliff. No one's coming that way.*

"I mean now, Lieutenant."

They dropped their rucks and started up. It wasn't patrolling, it was mountain climbing. They slung their weapons and pulled themselves up bush by bush. After an hour, they weren't just about halfway. It was getting dark.

"Fuck this," concluded Eddie. Charles could go fuck himself. He ordered a halt. "Set up for the night." Way too steep to form a perimeter, everyone tied themselves to a bush and hunkered down for a shitty night. At day break they slid back down to the rest of the company. After a quick C-rat coffee and roll, they moved out.

Around noon, they set out security and halted for a break. Eddie was eating his cheese and crackers when one of the security elements came in on a run.

"They're all over the fuckin' hill!"

Eddie grabbed his rifle and followed him back to his position, just in time to see the last man in a VC patrol turning the corner on a trail on the adjacent hill. Captain Charles arrived and Eddie reported.

"Why didn't you shoot him?" Was this guy for real?

They saddled up and moved out. Sparked by the gook sighting, Eddie fought off the rucksack stupor to examine the surroundings. He noticed steps cut into the trail when it went uphill. He saw sluices cut from bamboo when it went down. This was not empty jungle. They were definitely not alone. Then they came across a mountain pool, surrounded by rocks and fed by a small waterfall. Triple canopy vegetation made it invisible from the air. They halted and searched. Caches of food and ammunition were quickly discovered. They had stumbled into a VC base camp. They set up and continued the search. Then the dog team leader came up to Eddie.

"We got to go in, sir."

"Say again?"

"It's the dog. He can only do forty-eight hours. Then he has to rest. It's regulation."

"The dog needs a rest?"

"Yes, sir."

"Well, shit in my hat."

Charles ordered Eddie to recon the trail. The platoon saddled up, leaving rucks behind. They moved cautiously along the trail. It went up, down, and sideways, contouring the hill. A chopper flew overhead, then there was a long burst of automatic fire. Eddie crawled forward.

"Gooks, sir. Up there." The point man pointed to a rise in the trail. The RTO crawled up to Eddie.

"The old man's on the horn, sir." He held out the hand set.

Eddie looked at it like it was a poisonous snake.

"Six, this is Alfa, over."

"What the hell is going on, Alfa?"

"Contact, Six. Alfa, out." Enough of that stupid shit. Now what? Everyone opened up.

"Hey, Lieutenant, why don't you send someone around that ridge line to the right?" Maneuver right, yeah, Jesus. He sent three right. Firing broke out, M-16 and AK-47. Then silence. Eddie and the platoon moved up the trail. He heard a strange sound. They got closer. Bagpipes! He heard fuckin' bagpipes! What the hell? They got to the top of the hill. It wasn't bagpipes, it was wounded gooks moaning, three of them, badly shot up.

"Kill 'em," said Eddie. The point man shot one in the head. Kill 'em all, let God sort 'em out. The gook's forehead popped open and his brain slid into the dirt. Someone moved past Eddie and bent over the bodies.

"Here ya go, LT," holding out a severed ear.

Eddie declined.

The element from the right flank came in.

"Got 'em just as they was comin' around to get us, Lieutenant. Two of the little fuckers."

Eddie called it in. Five confirmed enemy KIAs, four AKs and an RPG included. The patrol headed back.

Charles gave him some shit for terminating the commo. "You don't terminate. I do." He called it in to battalion. He was a happy captain.

Later, as he debriefed the patrol, Eddie put it all together. Just as they were coming up the trail to the enemy position the helicopter flew over. The gook holding the RPG looked up at it. The point man didn't and caught him and his pals with a full burst. That chance flyover probably saved Eddie's life. If not for that momentary distraction, the RPG man would have fired his rocket into the lead element of the patrol, certainly killing the point, and almost certainly Eddie as well. Same with the flanking movement. Sent out a few seconds later, the flanking Americans, not the two flanking gooks, would be lying in the dirt. It wasn't talent, it wasn't expertise, it was luck. It was random. That's what really scared Eddie, the soulless happenstance of this deadly little encounter. There was no reason or larger meaning for any of it. It was all arbitrary. To be sure, good, solid training helped, but he knew that wasn't part of his personal equation, not unless you could kill gooks by spit shinning floors. He now knew, for the American infantryman in Vietnam, survival had all the tactics and strategy of a game of roulette: the wheel spun, the ball rolled, and who knew what number would come up. And Eddie was the ball.

Wasting those five VC was a big deal in the company. Eddie and his platoon walked tall. Years later, he read stories about tearful vets bemoaning the people they had killed. That sure as hell wasn't how it went down at the time. The highest praise a grunt could get was, "he killed a lot of gooks." Eddie bought into it. He wore the boonie hat he took from one of the dead gooks. It still had brains and blood on it.

"You're cool, sir."

Yeah, Eddie bought into it. It never occurred to him at the time that ordering the killing of the wounded gook would make him a war criminal to some people. But, as he reflected later, those short peckers had never been shot at, so fuck 'em. Besides, the dark chorus of "kill 'em all and let God sort 'em out," and "that whole country ain't worth the life of a single GI," told to him a hundred times by dozens of NCOs in the eighteen months before his deployment, that was the real preparation for Vietnam. And good preparation it was. Eddie never had any regrets.

And so it went. Patrolling, extracted, inserted, patrolling, extracted, perimeter security…boom-de-boom-de-boom. There was no story to it. There was no grand saga of landing on D-Day and sweeping triumphantly eastward to linking up with the Red Army and final, unequivocal victory. It was episodic, a series of disconnected events, characterized by hardship, discomfort, fatigue, sickness, boredom, and, every so often, terror. There was no geographic continuity either. They bounced around II Corps, from Tuy Hoa to An Khe to Quin Nhon to Bong Son. There was one constant, however, anger. No matter where they went or what they did, Charlie Company was always pissed off. This was not civilian pissed off, upset because you had a bad day or a long commute. This was Vietnam Pissed Off, pissed off to the max and pissed off all the time. This was Infantry Pissed Off: everyone was always getting a better shake. The other platoons in the company were getting over, second platoon was getting fucked. The other companies in the battalion were getting over, Charlie Company was getting fucked. The other battalions in the brigade were getting over, fourth batt was getting fucked. The other units in the war were getting over, the Herd was getting fucked. The Air Force and the Navy were getting over, the Army was getting fucked. It was, Eddie came to understand, one of the distinguishing marks of the true infantryman; he always had been, always was, and always would be fucked, fucked, fucked. It was just one more thing that war movies never got right.

Like any isolated group, the American infantryman in Vietnam developed his own special jargon. Eddie learned the US was not "the States" or "home," it was "the world." It was a brilliant piece of insight; Vietnam and all its weirdness was so far removed from home that it wasn't even on the same planet. All Vietnamese, friendly or enemy, were gooks or dinks or zipper heads. Enemy combatants were either VC (Viet Cong) or NVA (North Vietnamese Army). The armed forces of the South were ARVNs (Army of the Republic of Vietnam), universally dismissed as Marvin the ARVN or friendly VC. All US personnel with safe jobs in the rear were always referred to with acid contempt (and not very well-hidden envy) as *flatpeters*. Infantrymen were *grunts*, about as unheroic a label as ever applied to a nation's fighting men. Career soldiers were *lifers* and *ticket punchers*. Vietnamese village women were *mamasans*, the men *papasans*, the kids *babysans*. Fucking was *boom boom*. Food was *chop chop*. And, a holdover from the time of getting hosed by the French, *boocoo* was a lot. One of the most useful bits came from the Vietnamese language itself, *sin loi*. Roughly translated, it meant something like "sorry about that." To the GIs, it simply meant "tough shit." Bad stuff happened; sin loi. Good stuff happened; sin loi. Anything in Vietnam; sin loi. It was all part of the Sin Loi Program, and for grunts the program was everywhere.

"Sin Loi, Malloy." That was the GI take on the war in Vietnam.

There may not have been a big story, but there were little ones. There was the time they were extracted to go to the rear. The platoon was broken down into sticks with an NCO in charge of each. The slicks came in, the platoon loaded on, Eddie looked to the NCOs, got a thumbs up from all, they took off. Back at An Khe he made a headcount...one short. He called the roster; the missing man was identified. A slick and a gunship went back out to the PZ. When they landed, the missing troop came on the run, insane with terror. He had fallen asleep and awoke to find himself all alone, alone in Indian Country. That half hour pushed him over the edge. He was sent to an evacuation hospital and disappeared from Charlie Company forever. His squad leader was relieved, demoted, and sent to another battalion. Sin Loi.

They were getting ready for another air assault. Everyone was saddling up. One of the privates, a young kid, came up to Eddie, smiling and jiving.

"I ain't feelin' too good, LT. I don't think I can go on this one."

"Everybody goes. Put your shit on."

He walked off. A few minutes later, he was back, no smile this time.

"I ain't going."

"I said, put your shit on. You're going."

"No, I ain't."

That sent the kid to jail. Eddie never heard another word about it.

There were a few great troops in the platoon, a few horrible ones, and most were just so-so. Paine was one of the bad ones. He and Eddie locked horns from the start. Paine was drafted out of the ghetto and went to jump school for the extra money. He didn't like the Army, he didn't like Vietnam, and he really didn't like Eddie. Eddie knew this, but tried to play his part as an officer anyway. He counselled Paine, pointing out if he didn't get with the program, he was headed for a court martial, a federal conviction that would be on his record for life.

Paine looked at Eddie for a few long seconds, and then said, "What do I give a fuck about my record?" When Eddie first encountered Paine, he was an E-4. When they parted ways, he was an E-1. Well, Paine's civilian endeavors most likely wouldn't require an honorable discharge.

Then there was poor old Rog. The company was split up by platoons and Rog was operating on his own. Towards the end of the day, he selected an ambush site for the night and set up half the platoon. He then directed the other half to move off about a click and set up another. Off they went. Rog did a quick recon, discovered that there was a stream nearby, and determined that would be a better spot for an ambush. He relocated his men to cover the stream. It slipped his mind to inform his other element of the new ambush position. They too discovered the stream and sent a detail to refill canteens. The gunner in Rog's group saw movement, opened with a full burst, and killed SP4 Cookson, one of his good buddies. Somehow Rog was neither relieved of command nor assassinated by his men.

Eddie got to the field during the period of "search and destroy," one of the few army labels that actually meant what it said; they looked for stuff and when they found it, they destroyed it. The Herd was patrolling the Central Highlands, a hilly place sparsely inhabited by Montagnards, a tribal group one step up from hunter-gatherers. Every so often, Eddie's platoon would come across one of their villages. It would always be deserted. They may have been primitive, but they knew bad news when they saw it. Although the Yards were not officially classified as enemy, the rules of engagement applied the odd logic that if a search uncovered any American equipment, the village was, ipso facto, enemy, and would be, again ipso facto, torched. "American equipment" was, to say the least, loosely defined.

"Lookee here, LT." A plastic C-Ration spoon.

"Burn this fucker down."

Destroying these harmless little villages didn't bother Eddie, then or ever. Sin Loi.

Eddie had to admit the Army had done a superb job of making day-to-day living in the jungle unchallenging. He had entered military service with no woodsman skills, and, his official designation as "Jungle Expert" notwithstanding, still had none. He didn't need any. He didn't need to track and kill animals or identify and root out edible plants. Every three days a resupply chopper dumped off C-rations, LRRPs, and water. Add heat, hot sauce, and a little imagination and the stuff wasn't too bad, except for the ham and eggs, everyone hated that shit. True, the lack of variety quickly became a problem, but that was the reason for the hot sauce. You could make a fairly accurate guess as to how much time someone had been in-country by how much of the stuff he dumped on his food. He didn't need to know how to start a fire. None of this rubbing sticks together, just tear off a hunk of C-4 plastic explosive and strike a match (included in C-Rats). Its hot flame would boil a canteen cup of water in no time flat. He didn't need to know how to find potable water. Just fill up from a stream, add some iodine pills to kill any harmful varmints, add some Kool-Aid to kill the cruddy taste, and good to go. He also didn't need to know how to build a shelter. Bedding down for the night was simple, just wrap up in your poncho liner. Chilly? Put on your jungle sweater. Raining? Rig a hooch with your poncho. Yep, city-boy Eddie could live in the jungle indefinitely; unless you cut off his re-supply. Then he'd be dead in a week.

There were some other things he did to adjust to field operations. A drive on rag was paramount. It was non-regulation, non-issue, and Eddie found to be absolutely essential. It was nothing more than a square piece of light fabric, folded into a triangle, and tied around the neck. It prevented a painful sunburn, and, when wetted, cooled him off. No mention of that in training. Nail clippers were another secret. Under heavy and continuous humping, untrimmed toenails acted like razor blades, slashing the shit out of adjacent toes. No mention of that either. As he acclimated, Eddie found certain standard items of clothing superfluous, skivvy shorts, for example. They tended to bunch up and rub him raw in the crotch. Plus, they were just something else to dry out when he got wet. They had to go. So did socks. After his feet toughened up, adios socks. Who knows, he thought, if he stayed in the field long enough, he might end up completely naked.

They got resupplied by chopper every three days. In addition to food, water, ammo, and replacements, they also got a sack full of clean jungle fatigues; you took off the stuff you had been wearing for three days, rummaged through the clean stuff until you found a pair that fit, put 'em on, and good to go for another three days. Actually, as Eddie discovered, clean was a relative term, he was clean only for a few hours. Then sweat and dirt combined to create a gross black crud. The crud started at the shirt cuffs and pant knees. Then, as if it had a life of its own, over the next three days the malignant shit spread.

Years later, as a civilian, Eddie was walking through the park in town, when he got panhandled by a bum. He couldn't help but notice the bum's clothes. That's right, black crud. He gave the bum five dollars.

One time, the company was getting extracted to go from someplace to some other place. Eddie and his platoon arrived at the designated PZ first. He set up security and waited for the other platoons to link up. He heard them five minutes before he saw them: *crash*, *thud*, *bam*, "Fuck!" Then they broke out into the clearing.

Christ, thought Eddie, *these guys would be easy to fight.* Reflecting on it later, a truly terrifying idea popped into his head. Was it just possible that Army training was piss-poor not by incompetence, but by design? Had some bloodless fuck in the Pentagon, applying systems analysis techniques, concluded a draftee Army had neither the time nor the human raw material to turn ordinary civilians into competent jungle fighters? Had further analysis also determined that the Army's real military advantage was not its infantry, but its artillery, its gunships, its tactical air support? What the American Army did really well was not outfight the enemy man to man, but blow the shit out of him, machine to gook. If you accepted these as fact, the resolution was both logical and macabre: dangle the half-assed trained infantry out there; if the gooks took the bait and engaged, call in fire support and blow the shit out of them. Eddie wondered, *Was it possible that an American Army could be so cynical?*

Could his country really use him as the worm on the hook? Was his world really this dark? Welcome to the Sin Loi Program, GI.

One day as a morale booster, the mess sergeant sent out to the field two mermite cans of homemade vanilla ice cream. What a great guy. The company lined up and got a canteen cup each.

"What's this shit?"

"What's this fuckin' stuff?"

"What the fuck is this?"

He had forgotten to add sugar. It was cold, white, tasteless shit. The bitching hit seismic levels. Everyone went back for seconds. When they loaded the marmite cans onto the chopper, there wasn't enough tasteless shit left to feed an ant.

Eddie began and ended his day the same way.

"Ah, fuck," opening his eyes after a shitty night.

"Ah, fuck," closing his eyes after a shitty day.

Eddie's first impression of Captain Charles did not improve with familiarity. There was the time the company had picked up a bunch of villagers. The Vietnamese National Police came out to conduct interrogations. They had an American with them. He wore no rank, just a "US" on each collar. His mysterious presence indicated American sanction of what was about to happen. "Interrogation" was a polite way of putting it. They basically beat the shit out the detainees. When they were particularly interested in someone, they held him down, put a towel over his face, and poured water into it until he started to drown. Years later, this procedure would be called "water boarding." Back then, they called it "the water treatment." Same shit, different generation. Eddie felt sure Charles would intervene. He did indeed. Apparently, not happy with the responses given by one of the female detainees, Charles leaned over and punched her in the mouth. If the villagers weren't VC supporters before interrogation, they most certainly were after. Truth be told, Eddie didn't care one way or another about these gooks. But the sight of Charles slugging a woman was disturbing. Eddie had no clue as to why Americans were in Vietnam, but he was certain it didn't justify this kind of shit. He thought back to the statue in front of Infantry Hall at Ft. Benning. Titled "Follow Me," it was the iconic picture of an infantry officer waving his troops on into battle, and the image was reproduced on all Infantry School publications. That was the myth they sold in OCS. In his more sardonic moments, Eddie thought a more realistic depiction would be Charles beating the crap out of this little Vietnamese woman. Follow that, Lieutenant.

One of the hallmarks of military leadership is the concept of "setting the example." Down through the millennia, armies have used it as a means of shaping young, impressionable adolescents into competent fighting men. The catalyst for this transformation has always been the company commander. The lieutenants help, but the captain make it happen. He is the role model, not just for the enlisted men, but for the junior officers as well.

The inner compass of Captain Charles did not point in that direction. His driver was pursuit of the main chance. He had it all figured and made no secret of it. Around a fire in the CP one day, he announced to all present this was the last time he would ever have to command troops. He'd do his stint here in the field, finish up his tour running the Herd Jungle School, then back to Benning for the Infantry Officer Advanced Course. Finally, he'd go to college on the Bootstrap Program, and then, bingo-bango, his twenty years completed, a comfortable retirement. Years later, in business, Eddie heard the term "empty suit," referring to someone who, in spite of a position of authority, is, in reality, a) completely ineffectual, b) incompetent, and/or c) unremarkable. Check, check, check for Charles. Eddie knew he was a dickhead. In retrospect, he realized he was nothing more than a set of empty fatigues.

The XO completed his tour and rotated home. Charles, taking note Eddie was the only college educated officer in the company, concluded he would be the best choice to knock out acceptable paperwork. *Two months in the field; not quite Homeric, but what the hell,* Eddie thought, *it gets me away from Non-Charging Charlie.* So, in the rear with the beer.

April-May, 1969

The rear was, in many ways, even more of an eye-opener than the field. Eddie was astounded by how many people were there. In the field, his platoon was consistently understrength, sometimes a low as 50%. In the rear, people were everywhere. It was a supply depot for flatpeters. Granted, this was a base camp, the place where the administrative and logistical requirements of the field units were met, but goddamn, how many bodies did it take to support the grunts? Years later, he read about something called "The Tooth to Tail Ratio," the number of rear echelon troops (the tail) it takes to support one grunt (the tooth). In Vietnam, the ratio was, depending on your source, anywhere from 1:10 to 1:12. That meant at the peak American troop level in 1969, some 540,000 personnel, no more than 40,000 to 50,000 were actually combatants. The other half million or so were punching typewriters, running mimeograph machines, or stacking toilet paper. That's a big tail. Eddie saw it in An Khe. Then there were the civilian contractors. Somewhere the decision had been made to provide the troops, excluding, of course, the grunts in the field, with as many state-side comforts as possible. Hence in An Khe, and by extrapolation, Eddie reasoned, in all the other base camps, there was a slew of fast-food joints that would have done justice to a mid-sized American town: the franchise outlets for fried chicken, hamburgers, pizza, and donuts. Then there was the club system, the ubiquitous source of cheap liquor, rigged slot machines, and second-rate live bands. The dirty little secret, seldom if ever covered by the press, was that the vast majority of troops in country lived pretty damn well. The big danger for them wasn't the VC or the NVA, but cholesterol and boredom.

Another surprise was seeing so many senior NCOs, E-7s, E-8s, and E-9s, the historic "backbone of the Army." To be fair, many of them had gone to the field on their first tour early in the war. But, by 1969, the midpoint of the war, they were coming back for a second tour. As one of them confided to Eddie, "The first time it was duty and patriotism. This time, it's for me."

For many, arriving at Bien Hoa initiated a phone call to a sergeant major buddy, a favor called in, and a safe job in the rear resulted. Addressing this dearth of field NCOs, the Army initiated a twelve-week NCO Candidate (NCOC) course. AIT graduates with acceptable test scores were run through this mini-OCS. Upon successful completion, they were promoted to sergeant E-5. Those graduating in the top 10% were given staff sergeant E-6. They were derisively known as "shake and bakes." By '69 it was not uncommon to see an infantry platoon with an OCS platoon leader, a shake and bake E-6 platoon sergeant, and two shake and bake E-5 squad leaders. Not one had more than eighteen months in uniform. Sin Loi, Malloy.

Then there were the Vietnamese women, the mamasans. At 0800 every day, the main gate opened and a gang of 'em was herded in. Mamasans did all the grunt work. They did KP, shined boots, washed and ironed fatigues, cleaned hooches, picked up trash, and were not averse to negotiating a quick boom boom, a furtive sucky-sucky, or a fast dope deal. GIs "supervised," which meant GIs didn't do shit. Eddie was quick to pick up on that program, and in no time at all, he didn't do shit either. Most of the company admin was done by the first sergeant, in this case a prissy E-8 named Pensy.

Top Pensy had about a hundred years in the Army, and was universally disliked by the Charlie Company rank and file. He was that seemingly unlikely combination of soldier and schoolmarm all too common in senior NCOs. There was the Army way of doing things and that was that, thank you, ma'am. Pensy was of average size, but there was something a little off about his appearance. While not fat, he had shoulders a little too narrow and an ass a skosh too wide. He had a CIB, but that normal one-upper didn't work in a company where everyone else had one too. This lack of automatic deference really pissed him off. He spoke with slightly lopsided lips as if he had never fully recovered from a serious butt-stroke to the mouth. It made everything he said sound like a scolding for poorly done homework. When Eddie reviewed his mental stock of war movies, there was not a Top Pensy to be found.

Eddie had other disconnects with this rear echelon world; people had jobs he had never heard of. Staff Sergeant Brenner, for example, ran "the beer and soda point." His mission was to guide in CH-47 shit hooks carrying sling loads of beer and soda, and then to make sure that each company received its allotted share. Apparently, there was an entrepreneurial element to this, as one night

Brenner bought drinks for the entire NCO club. Can't do that on E-6 pay. Another sui generis slot was held by sui generis 1LT Gentry. While almost all lieutenants faced a steep learning curve, Gentry's was a sheer wall that, after a few of his near disastrous attempts, it was clear to all he was genetically unable to climb. After his being almost immediately relieved from leading a platoon, it also became clear that was genetically unable to do almost anything. So, they created the position of "Arms Room Officer." As there was already an Arms Room NCO, Gentry was kept well out of harm's way. But that did mean he had lots of free time. Not a problem. When the 1st Air Cavalry Division initially set up the base camp, leaders with a good understanding of young soldiers also set up Sin City. Located in the small town of An Khe itself, Sin City was an even smaller town of bars and whore houses, surrounded by a high wall with a main entrance guarded by a lone ARVN. Each joint in Sin City had a theme. Some establishments catered to lovers of country music, some to Motown and soul, and some to rock. Patrons of one never went to another. Periodically, the medics checked the booze and the girls, so liquor poisoning and VD were kept under control. Sin City operated every day, opening for business at 1000 and closing at 1700. Every day at 0955, 1LT Gentry was front and center, main gate. Whatever his other genetic shortcomings, Gentry could fuck, and he did so several times daily. While most troops drew only a partial pay, sending the bulk of it home, Gentry took the works, merrily pissing it away in Sin City. He probably did more damage to the Vietnamese gene pool than Agent Orange.

A few days after Eddie rotated to the rear, An Khe was hit with a sapper attack. It was, of course, night time. He was sleeping in his hooch when a series of explosions jarred him awake. He low crawled to the door, pushed it open, and peered out. All around him he heard, "clunk, clunk, clunk," the sound of M-16 bolts locking a round into the chamber. Then there was firing, here, there, starting to grow. He was unarmed.

"Fuck this."

He jammed his mattress and rack up against the door and hunkered down. Then he heard some loud firing. Cautiously, he looked out the window. A truck with quad 50 caliber machine guns had backed up to the foot of the little mountain in the center of the base camp. It was bouncing rounds off its rock face.

"Fuck that."

He hunkered down again. He stayed that way for the rest of the night. The next morning, they sorted out what had happened. VC sappers had crawled through the rolls of concertina barbed wire, gone directly to the chopper pilot hooch, tossed in their satchel charges, and crawled back through the wire. They left behind a bunch of dead and wounded pilots. The target of this attack was no accident. The gooks hated pilots. Its precision was also no accident. They knew exactly where to go. Someone with knowledge of the base gave them the information they needed. Eddie figured it was the mamasans. Each morning they still kept coming in. He also wondered how the sappers got through the concertina. One day at the helipad, an incoming chopper blew his hat into the wire.

"No sweat, Lieutenant," said one of the RTOs.

He pointed to one of the Vietnamese kids always hanging around. The kid slipped through the wire, picked up Eddie's hat, and slipped back out. Eddie couldn't have waked the distance any faster. So much for security.

One day, when reviewing the daily distribution of paperwork, Eddie came across a set of orders awarding the latest group in Charlie Company the Combat Infantryman Badge. Reading down the list, he saw his name. There was no ceremony, no drumroll, no official induction to that most select fraternity. It was just a piece of paper in a stack of other papers, routine stuff. The perfunctory nature of it all really didn't surprise him, for by this time, with almost two years in uniform, Eddie had most of the surprise squeezed out of him. What did surprise him, however, was the intense pride he felt. He immediately went to the PX, bought a CIB, and had the mamasans sew it on. He walked out with his newly adorned fatigue shirt. It felt like the CIB stood out two feet and flashed with neon. Goddammit, he was proud. Eddie had to hand it to the Big Green Dick, it understood insecure young guys.

To kill the boredom, Eddie decided to see the sights. In ordinary circumstance, that would mean absorbing the local culture. In wartime Vietnam, it meant seeing other army installations. Travel was easy. Just breeze down to the helipad, chat up the pilots, find out who was going where, pick one, ask if he minded giving him a lift, and hop on. He heard that his buddy Ruper was assigned to I Field Force Headquarters in Nha Trang. He asked Sergeant Brenner if he wanted to take a trip, and off they went. They got there and bummed a ride into town. They ambled around a bit. It was just a gook town, nothing much of interest. Then an MP jeep pulled up in front of them. Two hard looking MPs got out. They looked at Eddie, then Brenner, then back to Eddie.

"Let's see your pass, sir."

"I'm an officer. I don't need a pass."

"Let's see your ID, sir."

"Don't have one, lost it in the field."

"Get in the Jeep…sir."

Well, goddamn, Eddie chuckled to himself, *I'm getting arrested. This should be fun.* They got to the MP station and were escorted inside and delivered to the desk of a pudgy, starched and pressed, spit-shined MP E-7. After a quick humma-humma with the jeep dicks, pork rind gave Eddie the "you in big trouble" glare.

"Whacha doin' in Nha Trang…Lieutenant?"

"Sightseeing."

"Ya know, Nha Trang's off limits to the 173rd, right…Lieutenant?"

"Nope, that's news to me."

"No ID?"

"Lost it in the field."

"How about dog tags? Got them…Lieutenant?"

"Sure," said Eddie, fished them out and handed them over.

"Watcha say yer name was…Lieutenant?"

"Brandt, Edward L."

"Zat so? It says here Simpson, Hurley D."

Eddie started laughing. He turned to Brenner. "Jesus, I got Hurley's dog tags. Must have got 'em mixed up somehow."

"Well now…Lieutenant…sir…how do you figure that happened…sir?"

Now fun stopped and Eddie was getting royally pissed. Senior NCO yer butt, he wasn't about to take this kind of shit from a fat, chair-borne flatpeter.

"Well…Sergeant, if you got out from behind that desk and went to the field every now and then, you'd know that things get mixed up."

Fat boy looked at Eddie's CIB, looked at his rank, and looked at him. He felt pretty sure Eddie was lying, but there was just enough doubt that the careerist in him called for caution.

"Got anyone who can vouch for you…sir?"

"Sure do. Lieutenant Richard D. Rupprecht, I Field Force Headquarters. Give him call."

Fat Boy's doubts rose a few more notches. Reluctantly, he picked up the phone, got to I Field Force, and in a few minutes, got the Ruper. A short conversation later, he hung up.

"Lieutenant Rupprecht will be here in a few minutes. Why doncha wait out there, sir."

The Ruper arrived, exchanged words with fatso, and out they went, free men again.

"Jesus, Eddie."

"Hiya, Ruper. Nice town ya got here."

Brenner split to get his ashes hauled. Eddie and the Ruper went to his office. Eddie had no idea what I Field Force Headquarters did, in fact, he had never even heard of I Field Force itself. What he saw was lots of maps on the wall filled with lots of multi-colored push pins, and lots of people looking at them.

"What do you do here, Ruper?"

"Well, when they're planning an operation, I brief higher on enemy activity in the area according to the latest intel reports."

"Do they listen to you?"

"Sometimes, yes, sometimes, no. One time, they had an op already laid on. They asked me who was in the area. When I said, 'a lot of monkeys,' they got pissed."

"So, they cancelled, right?"

"Oh, hell no. It went off as planned."

"Tough titty for the monkeys, huh?"

"Oh, yeah."

Ruper introduced Eddie to some of his co-workers. One of them took particular interest.

"You're in the 173rd?"

"That's right."

"That's my area! Mind if I ask you a few questions?"

"Fire away."

For the next half hour, he grilled Eddie about the Herd's operations.

"That helpful?"

"Sure was. Thanks."

"You know, you could just go out there periodically and get the straight poop."

He looked at Eddie like an adult who has just been asked a silly question by a child. Clearly, Eddie was unaware of the Prime Directive that guided all Flatpeterdom: stay the fuck away from the field.

The next day, Eddie picked up Brenner. It seems what began as an honest effort to rack up a little innocent boom boom, ended up with a shitfaced Brenner tearing up the joint. Fortunately, he dodged out before the MPs arrived. A second encounter with Sergeant Pork Rind would not have gone ne'er so well as the first. They hopped a ride back to Ahn Khe.

Eddie was wandering Qui Nhon with Sergeant Crow. For no particular reason, they went into one of the small shops. A somewhat attractive mamasan came out from the back and gave them a "What do you want here, GI? Make it fast and then beat it," smile. It was all the usual second-rate shit.

"Why don't you go on along, sir. I'm just goin' to take a closer look here."

Eddie went on along.

That afternoon back at the base, he ran into Crow. Just to make conversation, not really caring one way or another, he said, "Find anything interesting?"

Crow smiled, reached into his pocket, pulled out a pair of red panties, and twirled them around his finger.

"That's a roger dodger, sir."

"How much did that cost you?"

"Not a thing, sir, not a thing."

So much for winning the hearts and minds.

One day, driving by the helipad, Eddie saw a lonely lieutenant standing there. The dark green jungle fatigues and confused look announced lima Charlie, new guy.

What the hell? he thought, remembering not so long ago when he was a new guy. He pulled over. "Need a ride?"

New guy hopped in. They chatted. Yep, same old same old, squeezed along the pipeline, not a friendly face to be found.

"How about some lunch?"

"I'm supposed to report in."

"They can wait."

Eddie took him to the mess tent. His name was Brooks and he was not the typical cookie-cutter second lieutenant. He was that rarest of birds in country, an ivy league graduate. He was also a little older, having spent time in the Middle East as a teacher. After the standard "where you from" stuff, Eddie had an experience almost unheard of in Vietnam, a conversation about something other than the war, the army, a dumb son-of-a-bitch, or pussy. Another rarity, the word "fuck" wasn't used once. They talked about things Eddie hadn't addressed in almost two years, books, movies, history. He realized how much he missed that. Brooks was a truly nice guy.

After lunch, Eddie took him to HQ and then to Jungle School. They continued their talks when he picked Brooks up after training. Then they sent him to the field. Two days later Eddie got word that 2LT Brooks was dead, killed by a booby trap. Two days in the field. Goddammit to hell.

Eddie had to go out to the company for something. They were sharing a perimeter with some ARVNs. While he was there, they got hit. After the firing was over, a group the ARVNs came up to the CP, chattering like monkeys, pointing at their part of the perimeter. Captain Charles and the HQ element went over to see what the fuss was all about. It was a dead ARVN. Problem was, he was shot in the back of the head, not the front facing the enemy. The even bigger problem was right behind him was an American position. It was pretty obvious Marvin the ARVN was shot by a GI, unintentional to be sure, but dead as hell all the same. A spooked E-6, Staff Sergeant Rojas, still sitting in the position in question, was nervously fidgeting with his M-16. The ARVNs angrily pointed from him to their dead buddy. No translation was needed. Captain Charles made a command decision.

"Lieutenant Brandt, unfuck this." His work there done, he moved out with his best parade ground stride.

While Eddie had no use for Rojas, the grim chorus from a hundred war stories rang in his ear: "The whole country ain't worth the life of a single GI." For a lifer like Rojas, the Army was his life. So, without a moment's hesitation, Eddie fudged the After Action Report. He wrote that a poncho had been strung between the dead ARVNs position and the center of the perimeter. Further, upon close examination, a bullet hole was discovered in the poncho. Finally, upon even closer examination, when the bullet hole was lined up with the dead ARVN, the line of fire clearly came, not from SSG Rojas, but from another ARVN position. Conclusion, one ARVN had shot and killed another. When the battalion XO read the report, he looked at Eddie.

"Good job, Lieutenant." Case closed, lifer Rojas off the hook. Nobody was fooled for a second.

One day, Rog got hit. In a nasty little firefight, the gooks rolled a grenade in on his position. He took fragments in his right hand and in the butt. It was the perfect wound, not fatal, not crippling, just bad enough to get him back to the world. They packed him off to Camp Zama, Japan, and everyone thought 1LT Parker was history. A month later he was back.

"Rog, buddy, what are you doing here?"

Like the rest of the company, Eddie was astounded. The pecker checkers in Zama had asked Rog the routine question, pro forma for those not too badly hit: "Do you want to go home or go back?" They had probably already checked the box for home, when Rog chose to go back. God bless the poor dumb shit, he felt that he really hadn't done his share. In addition, he was now a bona fide badass. The wound to his right hand left it permanently crooked, not disabled, just crooked. So, when Rog saluted, it wasn't the "fingers extended and joined" version as required by regulations. It was "fingers combat bent and field fucked up." It was just plain salty, and Rog loved it. He'd throw a salute at a mamasan. There was a minor problem; his slot had been filled by a replacement. So, Rog flew out to field to talk to Non-Charging Charles. That done, he was walking back from the helipad. There was a fire mission going on, the battalion mortars supporting an element in contact. One of the rounds misfired, fell short, and went off next to Rog. It tore off his right arm, the one with the salty salute, ironically, the one with the wound that could have been his ticket back to the world. It was as if the angry gods were telling him if he wasn't going to use the gift he was given, then they'd take it back. He bled to death before the medics got to him. Crane didn't make it either. His exit was a lot less dramatic; he just got sick. It was enough; they sent him home. Eddie was now the last one.

One of the NCOs was Sergeant Mint. Mint was a hard stripe E-5 who had done time in the bush and somehow wangled a flatpeter job in the rear. Eddie was never quite sure what that job was, but he saw Mint almost every day. They developed a good working relationship. At least, that's what Eddie thought. Then one night, he was walking by Mint's hooch and heard him sounding off, loud and pissed off. He had been drinking. Eddie got closer.

"That fuckin' Brandt ain't shit!"

That stopped Eddie. The rant went on. Eddie listened for a while and then turned and went back to his hooch. Lying in his rack, he sorted through what he had just heard. To be honest, it hurt. He and Mint weren't ever asshole buddies, but he had thought they were friendly. The fact Mint clearly didn't like him was an eye-opener and another lesson learned about how leadership really functioned: officers and enlisted could work together, but they could never be friends. From that moment, whenever he was in charge, whether it was the army or business, he always maintained distance between himself and his subordinates. It just made things easier.

Another time out with the company, another fight. The whole perimeter opened rock and roll, full auto. When the officers and NCOs finally got everyone calmed down, Eddie had a sobering thought. If the gooks were serious, instead of just the usual hit and run, all they had to do was fire a few rounds, wait until the company pissed away most of their ammo, and then hit them with the real assault. It brought to mind a legendary quote from Casey Stengel, first manager of the notoriously inept NY Mets. After watching the team make a spectacularly egregious foul up, Stengel moaned in frustration, "Can't anyone here play this game?" Eddie had read it in a bestselling account presenting the team's remarkable tale of ineptitude, mediocrity, and abject failure. He made a note to get the book when he was back in the world.

Eddie went in to town for a steam bath, popularly known as a steam and cream. He was talking to the mamasan. She was giving him the hard eye, that is, harder than usual.

"You gotty gir fren, rootenna?"

"No, mamasan, me no gotty gir fren."

Mamasan left and Eddie started to get undressed. A minute later, mamasan was back. With her was a young girl. In a country of flat chested women, it was hard for a round eye to figure female age. Even so, this one couldn't have been more than fourteen.

"You likee babysan, rootenna?"

"Yeah, sure. Babysan okay."

"Babysan numba one, rootenna."

"If you say so, mamasan."

Mamasan left. Babysan stayed. Eddie undressed and hit the steam bath. Babysan was still there when he got out. He took a shower and got dressed. Babysan smiled at him. Mamasan came back.

"Babysan numba one, rootenna. You numba one."

Eddie looked closer. Jesus, maybe thirteen.

"You come next time, rootenna. You get married."

"Sure, mamasan. Numba one good time."

Eddie never went back.

Then there was the time the company was setting up a new static position. There was a clump of bamboo that had to be cleared. One of the new lieutenants was tasked. Eddie was helping. They tried hacking it down with machetes. It didn't budge. Eddie called in for chain saws. That didn't work either. Then a combination of ropes, machetes, and chainsaws. Zilch. By chance, Eddie happened to overhear SP4 Pape mutter to someone,

"The two of 'em together wouldn't make a good EM."

Eddie called a halt to the work. He gathered everyone around. "Specialist Pape will now take charge of the detail. Pape, front and center."

Pape reluctantly came forward.

"All yours, Specialist. Carry on."

The work was just as fucked up, with the added bit of everyone giving Pape the razoo. Eddie had made another enemy.

Eddie was flying out to the company on re-supply. They were flying at a couple hundred feet, doors open as usual. Passing over a rice paddy, they saw a bunch of mamasans bent over doing something in the paddy. They were all stripped to the waist. No big deal. Then all at once they all saw it, a mamasan with titties. The pilot pulled a high-G turn. They went back for a closer look. Good god almighty, it wasn't just titties, it was big titties, big beautiful, sweaty, swaying titties. The pilots, the gunners, the crew chief, and Eddie, everybody was cheering. Those who had been in titless Vietnam the longest cheered the loudest. The clueless mamasan looked up at the crazy round eyes. After circling for about ten minutes, the pilots remembered why they were airborne, and reluctantly peeled off to bring supplies to the company. The nameless mamasan was the talk of the base for days.

One day, Eddie was called into the office of some warrant officer in charge of something to do with battalion property.

"Yer books is all fucked up, Lieutenant."

"How's that, chief?"

"Ya got a lotta stuff with serial numbers that ain't supposed to be here."

"Like what?"

"Like rifles. They's about twenty that don't match the inventory."

"So?"

Eddie had been in country long enough to know that missing stuff was usually just written off as combat loss.

"So, let me take anuther look."

A few days later, Charles ordered him to fly out to the company for an important sit down. Eddie went out with the re-supply."

"Lieutenant, the company inventory is all fucked up."

"Yes, sir."

"I want you to sign a statement of charges for all the missing shit."

Eddie blinked. "Say again, sir?"

"The missing shit. I want you to sign for it."

"Why don't we combat loss it, sir?"

"Because I want you to sign for it, Lieutenant, that's why."

Yeah, thought Eddie, *writing off that much shit wouldn't look good on your fuckin' record.* "Not going to do that, sir."

That lit Non-Charger's fuse.

"You'll sign for it, Lieutenant, or I'll put you up for a General Court Martial!"

A General Court Martial? That's where they send people to Leavenworth.

"Go ahead."

All of this in front of the grunts in the CP group. They ate it up, not even bothering to hide their grins. Without asking permission, Eddie got up and left. It was one of the proudest moments of his military service. Well, he thought, now it's out in the open.

A few weeks later, Charles completed his command tour in the field. That ticket successfully punched, he moved to the rear to take charge of the brigade Jungle School. Eddie never heard another word about the missing shit.

June-July, 1969

Captain Charles was replaced by Captain Hughes, Eddie's third CO in six months. Hughes seemed to take leadership seriously. He actually met with Eddie to see if his career goals were being met. Eddie requested to go back to the field. Two days later, he was leading a platoon again.

Eddie got lucky this time. Platoon Sergeant Ambrose Balunchkin was a career soldier, and a great one. A big, tough, competent Hawaiian with twenty years in, he was airborne to the core. He had pulled a combat tour with the 101st Airborne Division in '66, then a stint with the Golden Knights Army Parachute Team, then back to Vietnam with the 173rd. Balunchkin never complained. The Army sent him these untrained kids and his job was to make soldiers out of them. Airborne!

The mission had changed since Eddie's previous time in the bush. Then it was "search and destroy." Now it was "pacification." Pacification, they were told, meant "winning the hearts and minds of the people." He couldn't think of a worse way to do that than with a rifle platoon.

They moved north to Bong Son, a farming area along the South China Sea. Farming in Vietnam meant rice paddies, and the place was lousy with them. Dykes separated the paddies. When the paddies were dry, the platoons could walk on line. When they were wet, platoon in column. Platoon in column, the gooks knew where the GIs had to walk, the dykes. Walking the dykes meant booby traps. Booby traps were a minor problem in search and destroy. The paddies were wet when Eddie got there.

Initially, the platoons set up fixed positions. It was a mini World War I. The positions were dug into the ground with logs and sand bags for overhead cover and concertina and claymores for 360-degree security. During the day they ran patrols. At night, they sent out ambushes. There's no natural vegetation in a rice paddy, so all the villagers could see everything the platoons did. That meant, with some exceptions, contact was usually initiated by the gooks.

That meant boocoo snipers and booby traps. It was a really shitty way to fight a war.

Because of the "hearts and minds" directive, coupled with the static positions of the infantry, Eddie and his platoon had an unusual experience, battalion staff pukes in the field. It wasn't an everyday thing, but even seeing guys in starched fatigues every now and then was something new. The flatpeters figured that by providing occasional visits from medics and periodic distributions of food, the villagers would gratefully respond by giving intel on the local VC. As any grunt could have told them, when you walked through a village it was all women, children, and old men. The young men were carrying AK-47s in the surrounding hills. They were the husbands, brothers, and fathers of the mamasans and babysans targeted by the program. Getting a candy bar or a sore tooth pulled did not and could not change that. Blood was a lot thicker that policy. As a result, Eddie never received a single piece of program-generated intel that he found to be of use.

There were as many different wars as there were participants. Everything depended. It depended on when you were there, who you were with, where were you operating, who you were fighting, etc., etc. There was, however, one constant that transcended all of that, grunts hated flatpeters. Grunts hated flatpeters even more than they hated the gooks, the war, or the Army. Grunts hated flatpeters because more than anything else, flatpeters embodied the stunning unfairness of being a grunt. And, most of all, grunts wanted desperately to become flatpeters, and hated them because that just wasn't fuckin' going to happen. Fourth batt had relocated its rear area from An Khe to LZ North English. Every day at around 1700 hours, a group of staff pukes would play volleyball. Every day, 1700. Like clockwork, 1700. Then, one day, a single mortar round came in, hit the game dead center, killed some, wounded others. When this news reached the grunts in the field, the cheering was universal. Yep, grunts hated flatpeters.

Eddie was told to secure this village. They moved in and set up a perimeter. Then they herded the villagers together. A chopper landed; the battalion S-3 and some flunkies got off. The 3, speaking through an interpreter, called out one of the mamasans. Nervously, she came forward. For her great assistance in providing information, said the 3, the grateful Americans were rewarding her with xxx piastres, and handed her a wad of money. She looked like he had just given her a bamboo viper. And, in effect, he had. Two days later, she was found shot dead in a rice paddy. The story went that, somehow, she had pissed off someone of the staff pukes, so the staff pukes set her up. Cooperating with the Americans was a death sentence. The VC shot her, but the staff pukes pulled the trigger. You gotta love hearts and minds.

Eddie was running a patrol with one of the squads. They were going through a village when he heard, "All right, now! All right now!" and "*bam!*" A single shot. He ran to the front. Mather, the point man, was crouched next to a hooch.

"What happened?"

"Three gooks, sir, sittin' there bullshittin'."

Eddie saw rice bowls lying in the dirt. The gooks were gone. He took a deep breath. "Mather, when you walk point, you're on full auto, right?"

Mather blinked. "Yes, sir."

Not for the first time, Eddie reflected on the general lack of combat skills in the platoon. He and Sergeant Balunchkin had work to do.

SP4 Carter had been a first-class infantryman, having displayed both savvy and initiative on numerous contacts. In recognition of his outstanding performance, he was made sergeant E-5 right before his DEROS. He went back to the world and got out of the Army. Two months later, he was back. Completely lost in civilian life, he returned to what he knew, the Army. He re-enlisted on condition that he be sent back to Charlie Company. And so he was. Eddie eagerly made him a squad leader. It was soon clear to all that Carter was no leader. Under fire, he did what he had always done, try to kill gooks. His squad watched while Carter fought his private war. Sergeant Balunchkin counselled him that his days as a rifleman were over, that he now had the responsibility of leading a squad. A reluctant Carter shook his head in silent agreement. Not too long after that, he was leading a patrol.

Like so many patrols, there was no contact. They stopped to eat lunch, then saddled up, then moved out. They had gone about half a click when several long bursts of fire broke out to their rear. Carter swung the squad around, got them on line, and cautiously moved back. They got to where they had taken their break. They found a Pvt. Gaffney, dead as hell. He had apparently fallen asleep behind a tree. Carter, failing to take a head count, moved the squad without him. The gooks were not so oblivious. They waited until the squad was gone, and then shot Gaffney into pieces. They also took his rifle and his gear. Carter was busted back down to PFC and to the job he really wanted, rifleman.

Eddie sent one of the squads out on a daylight patrol. They had just left a village and were walking along one of the dykes when there was an explosion. No small arms fire, just an explosion. Strafucci and Gant were dead. Gant was torn up, Strafucci was blown in half. A certain percentage of American artillery was duds; the shells were fired, hit the ground, and didn't explode. That didn't mean they couldn't, it just meant that time they didn't. Duds were an important supply channel for the gooks. They took the duds, wired them up, buried them along likely avenues of American approach, and when the GIs came, *boom*. The squad figured it was command detonated because several members of the patrol had passed ahead of Strafucci and Gant. Why the gook chose to kill them, who knows. Gooks usually targeted a leader, an RTO, or a gunner. Strafucci was a grenadier, Gant a rifleman, nothing special about either. Both were nineteen years old.

The decisionmakers at battalion, realizing that operating from fixed positions was unproductive, directed the companies to saddle up and move out. Eddie, by now the senior platoon leader, was sent out on his own. There was a valley that wound up into the hills. Eddie's mission was to take his platoon and find out what was there. From the start, it was bad news. As soon as they entered the valley, they made contact. It was a short little firefight with one casualty, Sergeant Jackson. He was shot in the thigh. Laughing through the pain, he knew he was going home. They called in a MEDEVAC chopper and loaded him on. He waved; the platoon waved. Jackson was a good shit, he deserved this. A few minutes later, Eddie got a call. Jackson was dead. Now he was going home in a box.

The next day, the platoon moved deeper into the valley. They were walking a dyke when they took sniper fire. They got down behind the dyke and returned fire, semi-automatic, one magazine, then cease fire. No casualties. Sergeant Balunchkin's leadership was showing results. Eddie had an unusual experience. Like the rest of the platoon, he got down behind the dyke to return fire. He saw a papasan behind a water buffalo in the middle of the paddy. Automatically, he drew a bead on him. Then he stopped. He didn't know why, he just stopped. Later, he thought about it. Yeah, it was just a papasan, too old to go into the hills with the local VC. But Eddie knew the old bastard almost certainly was a sympathizer, and almost certainly had played some part, however small, in killing GIs. And yet, he didn't shoot him. It didn't really bother Eddie, he just wondered why.

They moved farther up the valley. The villages were closer together. The paddies smaller. The hills closer. It was spooky. Late in the afternoon they would stop, set out broad security, and wait. At dusk they pulled in the security to a single location. The gooks knew they were there. They just didn't know exactly where. That was good enough. Eddie and Sergeant Balunchkin enforced strict fire discipline. No wild firing at strange noises. That's what the gooks wanted to pinpoint the platoon's location. If the noises were really close, toss a grenade. They couldn't pinpoint off that. Then a few nights later, around midnight, there was something new:

"Bok! Bok! Bok!" "Bok! Bok! Bok!" "Bok! Bok! Bok!"

It sounded like thick bamboo stakes being hit together.

"Bok! Bok! Bok!" "Bok! Bok! Bok!" "Bok! Bok! Bok!"

Eddie put the platoon on 100% alert. He and Sergeant Balunchkin went to every position.

"They're just trying to spook us. No firing."

"Bok! Bok! Bok!" "Bok! Bok! Bok!" "Bok! Bok! Bok!"

All night long.

"Bok! Bok! Bok!" "Bok! Bok! Bok!" "Bok! Bok! Bok!"

The next morning, they saddled up and swept into the village. Eddie sent out security and heated up some chow. Eddie had a spaghetti LRRP. They questioned the villagers. Nothing. They even found some thick bamboo stakes. They beat them together in front of the villagers. Nothing. Then one of the security elements came in on the run.

"Gooks, sir! Over there!" He pointed at one of the paddies.

They saddled up and took off, Eddie in the lead, running. Then everything went weird. At that moment, he passed from his old familiar world into a new strange one. His old familiar body changed. He felt a burning sensation deep in his chest, like a red-hot wire threaded through him, and someone was strumming it, making it vibrate as well as burn. His sense of time changed. It stopped and then everything went to slow motion. He felt himself falling backwards, slowly, slowly. He hit the ground, bounced once, and then lay still. A cloud of dust rose, swirled lazily around like cigarette smoke, and covered him. He let out a deep breath. Then he noticed big red bubbles coming out of a hole in his chest, expanding and popping, expanding and popping. Blood bubbles.

Jesus, he thought, *I'm hit.* He went to wipe his face with his left hand. He saw his ring finger hanging down, barely attached by a thin strand of skin. He pinched it. No feeling. *Shit, what else?* He felt home plate. That's okay. He wiggled his toes. Legs okay. Then the medic was there.

"You'll be okay, sir!"

Of course I'll be okay, he thought. *The world can't function without Eddie Brandt.* The medic was doing something, but Eddie wasn't particularly interested. He was in pain, but it wasn't so bad. Time went by, but he couldn't say how much. They loaded him on a chopper. He noticed that Gibbs, his RTO, was there too. His arm was bandaged. Guess they got him too. Gibbs was yelling at him,

"You're goin' to be okay! You're goin' to be okay!"

No shit, Gibbs. Eddie was still discovering. The pain eased up. *This isn't so bad*, he thought, *but I am a little tired. Think I'll take a quick nap.* And he drifted off, slowly, quietly, painlessly. It was so nice. Yup, not bad at all. He was shaking hands with Death.

"Come with me, Lieutenant."

Then a stabbing pain in Eddie's chest jolted him awake. He opened his eyes. All he could see was Gibbs, close, face-to-face. Eddie's chest moved up and down, working on its own, apart from his control. Gibbs was blowing air into his lungs. He did that for a few seconds, then Eddie took over his own breathing. Then he puked, face up. *Nice going*, he thought, warm puke dripping off his chin. A small part of his brain noted: *hmm, this morning's spaghetti LRRP.* From that moment on, the pain never stopped.

Eddie was conscious of being carried off the chopper. He saw a ceiling going by. Then there were people all around him.

"What's your name, soldier?"

He told him. He went to look down at his chest. They asked him another question. He looked at them and answered. Every time he tried to look at his wound, they asked him another question. Then they pulled the dressing off and blood squirted into the air. Someone stuck his finger in the bullet hole. He had a clear plastic tube, pulled out his finger, and quickly inserted the tube.

It immediately filled with blood. Again, Eddie saw a ceiling go by. Then they were in the operating room.

"Can you scoot over to the table?"

He needed a little help, be he scooted. They did some more stuff and then the lights went out. When he woke up, he was in the recovery room. He was also in a lot of pain. It was a busy place. Just when he thought they had forgotten him, a nurse came over. Name, rank, serial number, unit. Then out to the ward.

The ward was even busier. This was a military hospital, so there were none of the civilian niceties, like privacy. There was a row of beds side-by-side along one wall, the same along the other. All told, there were about fifty beds. Most of them were occupied. They transferred Eddie to one in the middle. He took stock of his situation. He had three clear plastic tubes coming out of his right chest, a tube up his nose, another in his left ankle, and a catheter. The chest tubes emptied out into clear plastic bottles. Periodically, blood and crud worked their way from his lung to the tubes to the bottles. He had no control over the process. The bottles were about a quarter full of stuff that looked to Eddie like goulash.

"Jesus, is that shit coming out of me?" His left hand was heavily bandaged and the arm was suspended by a steel stand. He realized he was really thirsty. A nurse was going by and he tried to call out to her.

"Irk."

What the hell? He couldn't talk. Another went by.

"Irk."

Goddammit. Another went by. He tried to wave her down. Couldn't use his left arm, that was tied up. No problem, just use the right. Couldn't use that either. For some reason, it wasn't working. *Shit, shit, shit, I'm really fuckin' thirsty. Maybe I can wiggle my toes at 'em.* And so it went, irk, irk, irk; wiggle, wiggle, wiggle. Finally, a nurse happened to look over at him. She stopped, read his chart, and came over.

"Something wrong, Lieutenant?"

"Irk."

"What's that?"

"Irk!"

"Say again?" She got closer.

He whispered, "Water."

"Water? Oh, you can't have any water. You just came out of surgery."

"IRK! IRK! IRK!"

"Okay, I'll see what I can do." She left. A few minutes later, she was back with a bandage soaked in water. "Here you go. Chew on this."

It was the sweetest drink he had ever had. Of course, he wanted another one. That didn't happen.

As he began to tune back in, Eddie was told he was in the Intensive Care Ward of the 67th Evacuation Hospital in Qhi Nhon. The next morning, a technician came around and took an X-ray of his chest. Later, the doctors made their rounds. When they got to Eddie, they looked at his chart, looked at his X-rays, and got into a huddle. Then one of them came over.

"The X-rays aren't looking good, Lieutenant. You need to do deep breathing exercises to help the lung seal. Let's try. Breathe in, deeply as you can."

Eddie gave it a shot. Deeply as he could meant inhaling for about two seconds. It felt like a fat guy was sitting on his chest. And it hurt like hell.

"Not good enough, Lieutenant. Try again." The 67th wasn't big on bedside manner. Didn't have the time.

Eddie tried again, same story.

"Lieutenant, you'll have to do better than that. Do your deep breathing throughout the day."

Eddie did try, but goddammit, between the fat guy and the pain he just couldn't do a whole lot of deep breathing."

That was the routine; X-ray in the morning, ass chewing from the doctors in the afternoon, and a shitload of shots in between. On top of all that, Eddie was getting really hungry. He was on an IV, but that wasn't enough to feed a mouse. The worst part of it was he could smell the real food. The food cart came right down the middle of the ward, dishing the real chow out to the others. It rolled right by Eddie.

"IRK! IRK! IRK!"

About the third day, Eddie got his voice back. Now at least he could talk to people. He also began to take in this strange new world, the world of the wounded. It was the Intensive Care Ward, so it was the world of the badly wounded. He looked around. No partitions, no privacy screens, he saw everything. There were the amputees, booby trap victims, mostly legs, one gone, two, every now and then both legs and an arm. One poor fucker had his face blown off. Jesus!

Then there were the gunshot wounded, GSW in hospital jargon. Most of those were like Eddie, hit somewhere in the torso. Gut shot was the worst, but GSWs were democratic; you could get shot anywhere. Then there were the mystery wounds. One guy had a dent in his head that ran from his left eye straight to the back of his skull. *What in the hell did that?* Eddie wondered.

One day, as a morale booster, a starlet from some TV show visited the ward. She was a pretty girl in a frilly summer dress. She came in with her TV show smile, took about three steps, and then her eyes focused. The smile froze, she turned around and left as fast as her pretty, little TV star legs would carry her. Now someone would have to boost her morale.

Eddie was getting pissed. Not only was he hungry, but the IV in his leg was starting to hurt; phlebitis, they told him. Whatever it was, it was getting worse. It got to the point if someone as much as nudged the bed, a line of fire flashed up his leg. He asked one of the nurses, "When do all these tubes come out?"

"When we see your organs are starting to function."

"How do you know when that happens?"

"When you make wind."

Pause, then tentatively, "You mean, when I fart?"

"Well, uh…yes."

Eddie, always goal oriented, now had something to shoot for. A short time later: "Peerruutt!"

And out came the IV, the nose tube, and the catheter. The three in the unresponsive lung stayed.

"So, I can eat now?"

"Yes, indeedy."

He couldn't wait. The food cart came for the lunch meal. With agonizing slowness, it made its way down the ward. It got to Eddie. He could smell it, fried chicken. Yummy! They looked at Eddie's chart, and reached down into the cart. Jell-o, Kool Aid, and soup!

"Where's the fried chicken?"

"Oh, you can't handle that. We have to build your stomach back up." And then, with a knowing smile, "Besides, you won't be able to finish this."

Goddamn flatpeters, didn't know they were dealing with Big Bad Airborne Eddie. He couldn't even make it halfway through. Sin Loi, Malloy.

Meagre as it may have been, the low-end chow had its effect. Eddie soon had to take a dump, a huge dump. He called over one of the nurses. She came back with a bed pan and a roll of toilet paper.

"What about the latrine?"

"Too soon for that. You're still hooked up to the drainage tubes."

She slid the bed pan under him and cranked up the bed. No privacy, just fire when ready, Gridley. And fire he did with great, loud, blasting farts and gooey, drippy, foul-smelling turds. It sounded like a Pacific Rim volcano, and he half expected to see terrified villagers running for their lives. But this was the Intensive Care Ward and they had seen and heard it all before. His Homeric dump concluded, Eddie reeled off a section of toilet paper and went to wipe off. He forgot that the bed pan was only four inches deep. Gazook! His hand went wrist deep into the disgusting mess. With a sigh of weary resignation, he thought, *Of course, what else?* He spent the next ten minutes cleaning his hand, his butt, and the impact area around the bed pan. When he pulled it out, the mound of used toilet paper towered up like a monument to the Turd Gods.

"My, you really did have to go."

Intensive Care Ward, a major part of the Sin Loi Program: leave your self-esteem at the door.

"Your X-rays look terrible! You're not doing your breathing exercises!"

The friggin' doctors again.

"And, your lung is full of matter. You have to hock it up."

Why don't you hock up my butt?

"Let's try. Cough."

"A-hem."

"Not enough. Try it again."

"A-HEM."

"Still not enough. If you don't give me a proper cough, I'm going to make you cough."

Oh, yeah? How's this, ya flatpeter?

"a-hem."

The doctor whispered something to the nurse. She went off, came back a little later, and handed him something. He put it behind his back.

"Look up at the ceiling, Lieutenant."

Eddie looked up at the ceiling. The doctor whipped his hand around and fired a syringe of salt water right into Eddie's windpipe.

"AAAA-HEEEMMM!"

He held out a Kleenex. Eddie hocked a disgusting blob of red shit into it.

"See that? That's what's in your lung. That's what you have to cough up."

Fuck me to tears.

Next day, bad X-rays again.

"Lieutenant, if this doesn't improve, you're going to get the bronchoscope!"

Oooh, the bronchoscope. Big fuckin' deal. Next day, more bad X-rays.

"That's it, Lieutenant, you're getting the bronchoscope. Nurse, get him ready."

"We're going to give you a little something for the pain."

That "little something," he found out later, was morphine. She fired him up, and for the first time since he got shot, Eddie was pain free. He wasn't just pain free, he felt as good as he had ever felt in his whole life. The world turned, the birds were singing, and there weren't any goddamn birds. The bronchoscope was a tube they inserted into his mouth and guided down further into his bad lung. It had a light on the lung end and an eyepiece on the other.

"Look at this, Barney."

The doctors were lining up to check out Eddie's lung. That sparked a big humma humma. Eddie didn't give a shit if they sold tickets. Jeez, listen to those birds.

There was some kind of pump attached to the bronchoscope. When the peep show was over, they pumped the goulash out of his lung.

"See what's in there, Lieutenant? That has to come out. So, if you don't do your breathing and coughing exercises, you're getting the bronchoscope again."

Eddie immediately formulated a course of action. Not only did he not do any of the exercises, he tried not to breathe at all. All he wanted was another one of those shots. Tee hee hee, he was a sly fucker, alright.

The next day, X-rays in the morning.

"Wait 'til they see these babies," chuckled Eddie. They came around, looked at his X-rays, and went into the usual huddle.

One walked over. "X-rays look really good, Lieutenant. Good work."

"Good X-rays?"

"Yes, indeed."

"So, no more bronchoscope?"

"Oh, you won't need that anymore," and walked off.

Jesus, did the Sin Loi Program ever stop?

In addition to the doctors, nurses, and patients, there were others in the ward. Once, there was a gook. VC? NVA? Who knew? One thing was clear, he was a salty little fucker.

"GI numba ten! GI numba ten!"

There was an MP guarding him. Eddie wasn't sure if it was to keep the gook from escaping, or to keep the GIs from killing him. Yep, tough little fucker.

Orderlies were there too. They wore starched and pressed fatigues. Their boots were polished. They had neat haircuts. Jesus, they were clean. One in particular came by regularly to chat. Sure, he was a flatpeter, but Eddie liked him anyway. He was so clean.

"What's that you're wearing, pal?"

"Say what?"

"Your aftershave. What is it?"

"Old Spice."

Eddie used Old Spice aftershave for the rest of his life.

Recovering from a serious wound was as much emotional as physical. Eddie's body was beginning to heal. His mind was another matter. The medical part of the Army's care for the wounded was first rate. The bedside manner part was marginal. Given the number and severity of cases, this was understandable. As a patient, it could be rough. They took the bandages off his left hand. The ring finger was gone and the rest of the hand was atrophied up into a bird-like claw. It didn't even look like a hand anymore. *Oh, well,* he thought, *a glove could hide that.* The lung was harder to take. The bullet had gone straight through, but erratically, tumbling and zigzagging along the way. It churned up the one lobe and damaged the other two. The surgeons sliced into his chest, cutting from his sternum under his right arm, around to his backbone. They removed the destroyed lobe, cleaned up the rest, and sewed him up. That engendered the daily bedside debate: could they save the remaining lobes, or did they have to come out as well? The worst-case scenario, the one they gave him most often, was the likelihood of a future a life with one lung, and its attendant physical limitations. Eddie knew they were trying to scare him into doing his exercises, but goddammit, it was scary nonetheless. In addition, the massive incision to his right side had destroyed most of the muscles on his right torso, so erect posture was going to be a challenge. *Great,* he thought, *life as a hunched over, chicken handed, semi cripple.* It was depressing. Then they wheeled in a young kid next to him. He was missing both legs above the knee and part of his right hand. In the odd moments when he talked, he told Eddie his story. He had come in with the latest batch of replacements. It was his first night in the field and he had to take a shit. He didn't want to stink up the position, so he crept outside the perimeter. He didn't want to disturb the rest of the platoon, so he didn't tell anyone. He went out and crouched down; it was right in front of a claymore mine. When he went to wipe his ass, they blew the claymore. It sent a couple of hundred steel balls in a fan-shaped killing zone. If he had been a few feet farther out, it would have killed him, but he was so close it just took off his legs and the hand he was using to wipe.

They put a tent over his lower half so you couldn't see his legs were gone. Every so often, he would lift the sheet, take a look, and start crying. Usually, when someone was having a bad time of it, those around him would tell him it was going to be okay. No one even tried with this kid. He was fucked. He knew it and they knew it. Even the nurses didn't try. It had an odd effect on Eddie. Looking at this kid, he didn't feel so bad.

"Yeah," he said to himself, "I'm banged up, but not as badly as he is."

The Intensive Care Ward; sin loi, Malloy.

Some members of the platoon came to see him. They filled in the blanks. He had apparently taken a burst of automatic fire right up the front. His equipment saved his life. His rifle absorbed most of the hits and was shattered into pieces. The two ammo pouches, left and right on his pistol belt, both took several rounds. Two bullets got through, one clipping off his left ring finger, the other passing through a purple smoke grenade hanging from his web gear, then passing through his right lung.

"You were lucky, LT."

He didn't feel lucky.

The doctors filled in another part. The peaceful little nap he took on the chopper was death; he had stopped breathing. Gibbs, his RTO, a black kid from Shithole, Texas, gave him mouth-to-mouth, saving his life. The only people who were trained in that were the medics. Gibbs was an infantryman. Where in hell did he learn that? Eddie never saw him again. It was a question he never got answered. The impersonal force of chance and happenstance; how many times had it profoundly affected Eddie's life? Was it luck? He didn't buy that at all. A later generation summed it up exactly: shit happens.

The physical therapist was a female captain. She scared everyone in the ward. She was a pain maker and they all had had their share of that. Eddie watched her go by. She watched Eddie. One day she stopped, read his chart, looked at him and said,

"I'm Captain Pain Maker (Eddie couldn't remember her name). I'm the physical therapist."

Eddie looked at her like a small rodent looks at the descending hawk that will rip his guts out in the next second. "Mumble, mumble," or something to that effect.

"Let's see. Here we are," and she pulled a dumbbell out of her bag. She placed it in his right hand. "Why don't you press this over your head."

It wasn't a question. He got it to his ribcage. The incision had atrophied most of the lifting muscles on his right side. He got it to his shoulder. Sweat popped out on his forehead.

"Aarrgghh!"

He got it an inch over his head and dropped it back down to the bed. He was in a full-blown sweat. The goddamn thing weighed all of two pounds.

"Very good. Now let's see four more."

Now this shit was part of his daily routine.

Eddie's lung sealed. The crud stopped inching its way along his drainage tubes. The goulash stopped collecting in the bottles. He was getting better. It was about time, he thought. Most patients were in and out of intensive care in two or three days. Eddie was there nineteen. They pulled out the tubes and sewed up the holes.

"You can get up now, Lieutenant."

"What?"

"You can get out of bed. Walk around. Take a shower."

A shower! Jesus. Eddie swung his legs over the side, grabbed on to the head rail, and pulled himself upright for the first time in nineteen days. He was stooped over forward and canted to the right, but he was up and moving.

"Wait just a minute, Lieutenant!"

They swooped in on him. One straightened his back, the other straightened his shoulders. His battered body popped and snapped in rebellion.

"That's more like it."

Eddie frog marched himself out of the ward. Once outside, he looked around, saw no nurses, and eased back into his B-movie monster stance.

"Aaahhh!"

Eddie hobbled along. He was the Hunchback of Notre Dame and loved every minute of it. He found the men's shower, looked in the mirror, and, if he'd had his old body, would have jumped back in revulsion. He looked like pure shit. The hair on the right side of his head was flaked with purple crud. That must have come from the smoke grenade. There was a light sprinkling of some red shit. That must have come from the spaghetti he puked up. The OR had just cleaned the wound. He would have to clean the rest. Also, always muscular, he was now gaunt, almost emaciated. He was amazed at how little time it took for the body to degenerate.

"Ah, who cares? I'm taking a fuckin' shower!"

It was heaven. He turned up the hot water until he could hardly stand it and then washed himself, and washed himself again, and then just stood luxuriating in the hot, healing, cleansing water. Everything hurt, but it was the best shower of his life. The next day, they shipped him to Japan.

Eddie thought it would be Camp Zama, but it was Kishine Barracks outside of Yokohama. They assigned him a bed, but he was ambulatory, so he spent most of the day walking around or just sitting in the sun. It was so nice to sit there and not worry about anything. He had bad dreams at night. The details varied, the situation was always the same, they were in contact and he couldn't function. Sometimes he was trying to shoot, but no matter how hard he squeezed, the trigger was frozen. Most often and most frightening, he was on the radio and couldn't remember the call signs. No matter where or what, he had no control. Sitting in the sun, control didn't matter. It was so nice not to be in charge anymore.

On one of his walks, Eddie just missed getting hit by an Army bus.

The driver yelled out the window, "Just because ya didn't get killed in Vietnam, don't mean ya can't get killed here!"

Eddie wondered if any jury would convict him for killing the worthless prick.

He received a partial payment and was told he could go into Yokohama. He went to the PX, bought some civilian clothes, and went back to the ward. He put his new clothes on the bed, his money in a pocket, and went to take a shower. When he got back, the clothes were there, the money was gone. No Yokohama. The Sin Loi Program wasn't just in Vietnam.

A doctor interviewed him, asking the usual questions. Then, conversationally, he asked him who performed the surgery. Eddie didn't know. Who were the other doctors? Didn't know. Therapist? No clue. Nurses? Ditto. It then occurred to Eddie that every player in this, one of the most important events in his life, was and always would be, a stranger. So, it seemed in wartime even lifesaving was anonymous and impersonal. Then the doctor posed the infamous Roger Parker question: Did he want to go home or go back to Vietnam?

Eddie couldn't help but laugh.

"I have to ask, you know."

"Home."

The doctor checked his home of record to determine which hospital. "Walter Reed or Valley Forge?"

"Reed."

And that's where they sent him.

They flew from Japan to Alaska, then Scot Field, Illinois, then Baltimore-Washington International Airport. The last leg was an Army bus. It was late afternoon and they hit the parkway during rush hour. Eddie looked out the window; pissed off commuters dragging their tired asses home after a shitty day at the office. No one looked at him. No one realized in that nondescript Army bus rode young men returning from the most extraordinary experience of their lives. It was just another vehicle slowing them down, keeping them from getting home on time.

When the bus pulled into Walter Reed, a guy with a clipboard told them where to go. Eddie filed off with the rest. He was still wearing his hospital robe and carrying a plastic bag with his few personal belongings.

As he was walking through the main entrance, a pleasant looking middle-aged man in a suit and tie quietly asked him, "Just back from Vietnam?"

"Yes, sir."

"Welcome home, son."

The trip over had been impersonal. So had the trip back. That hadn't bothered Eddie. For some reason, this small human touch did. He started to tear up. That set the pattern for the rest of his life. Books, movies, news reports, any mention of soldiers coming home, it made him emotional. It always would.

They put him in another ward, gave him another bed. This time the officers and enlisted were separated. His roommate was Captain Rocky Riviera. Rocky had been assigned to Special Forces in the Mekong Delta. Riding in a fast boat one day, he saw movement along the shore and ordered the boat to land. When he jumped off, he took a round to the chest and went down. A gook ran over and shot him six more times. They got him to a hospital where, to everyone's surprise, he lived. When Eddie met him Rocky was still a little shaky, but the son of a bitch was alive. He was just back from Puerto Rico where they held a parade in his honor.

"How was that, Rocky?"

"Great, I got laid three times."

They gave Eddie a thirty-day leave. He phoned his father, who drove down the next day and picked him up. They went to the small town in Pennsylvania where the old man had retired. Eddie was home.

Rural Pennsylvania was great. His father had bought a few acres from a farmer and built his house there. It was surrounded by farmland. Eddie spent hours sitting there looking at it. The jungle in Vietnam was hard. Pennsylvania was soft. The fields were light green, the hills rolled gently, the air was sweet. Not a trace of burning shit. It was Mennonite country; the farmers were hard-working and soft-spoken. A few came around to be neighborly. They chatted with his father. Eddie just listened. There was no profanity, no anger, no sin loi. It was just nice. Everything was nice. He took enormous pleasure in the small things. He loved making coffee in the morning, and then sitting at the breakfast table holding the cup, letting its warmth soak into his hands. He walked around the garden, his father pointing out the different flowers. Before Vietnam, Eddie had no interest in gardening. Now he loved it. Plant life in Vietnam was ominous. What was hidden behind all that malignant vegetation?

Here, it was simply pretty, sweet smelling, pleasant stuff. He even loved watching television with its mindless sitcoms and trivial commercials. It was all so unimportant, so non-threatening, so…normal.

One day, his father happened to mention a groundhog was digging up the garden.

"I'll take care of it, Pop."

Eddie took the old .22 rifle and hunkered down, looking at the wood line. After a while, the groundhog shuffled out. Eddie fired. He walked over and looked down. It was still alive, eyes blinking, paws shaking. Eddie finished it off. For the rest of his life, he never shot another living thing.

At Reed, they asked him where he would like to go when he returned to duty. He said Ft. Benning. When his leave was up, that's where he went.

Eddie was assigned to the Infantry School. An infantry officer with a CIB, he was naturally slotted as an instructor. It had a nice symmetry. A year earlier, he was the raw material being squeezed through the Vietnam pipeline. Now, a year later, he was part of the machinery doing the squeezing. The CIB worked its magic; he had instant credibility. His 173rd combat patch just added gravitas. Additionally, there was the comparative oddity of his being a first lieutenant. Normally, given that he survived, an infantry officer returned from his year-long tour in Vietnam as a captain. The received wisdom was that coming back as a first lieutenant usually meant having been wounded in action. As Eddie quickly discovered, having a CIB was cool; having a CIB with a purple heart was even cooler. Coolest of all was a CIB, a purple heart, and a salty looking wound. Salty meant highly visible, maybe even slightly disfiguring, but not disabling or repulsive. Check, check, check; Eddie had all three. For the first time in his military career, he was afforded immediate respect. It was seductive.

After completing a two-week instructor preparation course, Eddie was made the Principal Instructor for Combat Formations and Battle Drill, or, simply stated, what you should do when you come under fire. The students were OCS and NCOC candidates, and as far as Eddie was concerned, it was the most important class they would receive. After some initial stage fright, he settled in and made an interesting discovery: he was a good instructor, not just competent, but great. He found he was able to capture the attention of the class, and then, with a mix of information, personal experience, and a bit of humor, lead them through the lesson plan. His acknowledged stature as a recently returned combat veteran made his words ring with truth. It was the most satisfying assignment he'd had in the army. He enjoyed it immensely.

Eddie instructed twice a week. When he wasn't on the platform, he was a lane grader for other tactical training classes. Lane graders supervised the practical exercises in which the candidates implemented in the field what they had been taught in the class. They were closely observed and formally evaluated. Eddie enjoyed that too. He particularly enjoyed it as it gave him the opportunity to cut the punitive horse shit that practical exercises were when he was a candidate. When the class had formed up into platoons, their Tac officer would approach him, salute smartly, and hand him a list of names to fill each one of the exercise leadership slots. It was a hit list, as he remembered all too well. These were the candidates they were trying to bust out of the program, and Eddie wanted no part of that nonsense. The platoon watched in dread as the paper changed hands. The Tac saluted smartly again, did an about face, and moved off to the side. Eddie read out the op order. Everyone wrote up the patrol order. Now, let the bloodletting begin.

Eddie looked at the paper given to him by the Tac, and then at the platoon. No one met his gaze. He walked leisurely from one side of the formation to the other, paper in hand.

"Your Tac officer has given me a list of names to fill the leadership positions."

Silence. Staring at the ground.

"I'm not going to use it."

Immediate attention, all eyes now on him.

"I want volunteers."

Pause.

"Who wants to lead this patrol?"

Silence.

"A platoon of officer candidates, and no volunteers?"

A ripple in the ranks.

"Gentlemen, the mistakes you make here are free. The ones you make a year from now are not."

Pause.

"I will not let you make mistakes. I will work with you to make sure the leaders do it right and the rest of you see it done right."

Pause. Looks left and right.

"I say again, who wants to lead this patrol"

Two, three, four hands. He picked one and motioned him forward.

"I want you to pick your platoon sergeant. Don't pick your best friend. Pick the best man."

He selected a candidate. Eddie motioned him forward.

"I want you two to select the squad leaders. Select the best."

They choose their squad leaders.

"Platoon Sergeant, organize the platoon. Platoon Leader, come with me."

Eddie took the platoon leader aside. Together, they went over his patrol order. Eddie never told him what to do. He just asked questions. The platoon leader figured it out on his own. When the patrol order was in decent shape, the platoon leader assembled the patrol and read it to them. And so it went. Eddie moved from leader to leader as they prepared, practiced, and executed, always asking questions, never giving direction. He could feel the enthusiasm: goddamn, things done right! This was the way Eddie had hoped his training would be like.

He made full use of the Infantry School Library, both to supplement his lesson plan, and just to explore what was there. There were the standard histories, biographies, and memoirs of all the wars in history. To be expected, the war in Vietnam was heavily covered, not only published material, but the internal after-action reports, analyses, and reports. One day, Eddie found a report on his battalion for the first quarter of 1969, his time. It was fascinating. The report stated that for the first three months of that year, the battalion had incurred thirty KIA and ninety WIA. That's 120 casualties in a quarter of a year. He did the math: 120 times four to estimate the full year…480 casualties. Eddie did a rough battalion headcount for the units in the field. The rifle companies were running around a hundred men, Recon Platoon about fifty. So, 450 men would take about 480 casualties. The battalion wasn't in any major battles, just firefights, ambushes, snipers, and booby traps. Eddie realized it was just a rough estimate. He never saw the actual numbers. He didn't have to. It was infantry math. It lined up exactly with his own worm's eye view of the war. The platoon leader ahead of him was wounded, he was wounded, the one after him was wounded. Of the three lieutenants who went in together, Parker, Crane, and himself, he was wounded, Crane got sick and sent home, and Parker was killed. He heard Sergeant Balunchkin got hit with a booby trap and sent home. The conclusion was grim: if you were a grunt in Vietnam, chances are you were going to get hit. Infantry math.

The My Lai Massacre story broke. In the spring of '68, a lieutenant in the American Division had run amuck, leading his platoon in the killing of some 200 villagers, mostly women and children. Charges were brought against him and he was under house arrest in Benning. His name was William Calley. It was the talk of the post.

Eddie's boss, Captain Mann, said half-jokingly, "Jesus, I hope they never investigate the 9th Division." Nervous laugh.

There were lots of dirty little secrets. Eddie certainly had his. He went over his time in the bush. Was he a war criminal? Let's see. He ordered that wounded gook shot. True, but he wouldn't have made it anyhow, too badly torn up. Mercy killing? Not really, Eddie had a gallon of testosterone raging through his veins and he wanted blood. Besides, hadn't the gooks outright executed Gaffney? What about burning those Montagnard villages? Just following the guidelines. And the Yards probably really were helping the VC. Then there was writing up that phony After Action Report to protect Sergeant Rojas. Well, Rojas didn't mean to kill that ARVN. Captain Charles beating the shit out of that mamasan? Shouldn't Eddie have reported that? Nah, loyalty to the commanding officer, even if he was a dickhead. But here was the real test: how did he feel? Any guilt? Any remorse? Any bad dreams? None at all. Not then, not fifty years later. He had to hand it to the Army. The tactical training may have been half-assed, but the emotional preparation was first rate. Eddie went to Vietnam ready to do some serious damage, and he did just that. So, what about Calley? Killing 200 women and children is, by anyone's accounting, some really serious damage.

Eddie remembered a quote: "The essence of war is violence. Moderation in war is imbecility." That didn't come from Hitler or Stalin or Atilla the Hun. It came from John Fisher, an admiral in the British Royal Navy in World War I. Eddie looked him up in the Infantry School Library. He found something else Fisher said:

"If you rub it in both at home and abroad that you are ready for instant war...and intend to be first in and hit your enemy in the belly and kick him when he is down and boil your prisoners in oil (if you take any), and torture his women and children, then people will keep clear of you."

Jesus, Admiral! He sounded just like the old NCOs around the fire barrels: "Kill 'em all and let God sort 'em out."

Eddie was beginning to realize there were two faces to war. There was the public face; neat, clean, and honorable. This was the face the Army showed to outsiders...the press, the movies, the recruiting posters. Then there was the private face. It wasn't shown, it was experienced, lived, and felt by the grunts in every war, from Vietnam down to the ancient Greeks. It was sensory overload. Eddie had smelled it, seen it, felt it, tasted it, and heard it. It was like fucking a disgusting old hag: she smelled bad, looked bad, felt bad, tasted bad, and sounded bad. She took his combat cherry and that repulsive old cunt left him with an incurable dose of reality. He would spend the rest of his life learning to live with it.

This discrepancy between appearance and reality was, Eddie saw, a serious problem for the army of a democracy. How does it prepare its soldiers for hard war while maintaining the fiction of "playing nice?" He examined his own journey. From the outset of his training, he had noted a discrepancy in messages. There was the one sent in the classroom, and then there was the one told by the old NCOs around the fire barrel. The classroom was the appearance message; the fire barrel was the reality. Not for the first time Eddie wondered if deep within the bowels of the pentagon, the trolls who pulled the Army's levers knew this. Was there some dark-hearted son of a bitch who thoroughly understood the effect infantry combat had on soldiers? And did this evil genius know combat veterans always had and always would talk about what they had seen and done? And had this manipulating prick arranged matters so the veterans and the novices would mingle around the fire barrel, with the veterans inevitably passing on the realities of combat?

Once again, Eddie sorted through his own experience. His classroom instruction was like a pleasant little ditty, a nice tune to hum when you took a stroll on a sunny day. The fire barrel talks were the bass to that pretty melody, the drum beat that resonated, the pulsating rhythm that gave him the hypnotic marching tempo so easy to follow. This arrangement was, he reasoned, fiendishly effective. The classroom lesson plans were open for inspection. It was all tight and tidy. Everything according to "playing nice." The fire barrel talks were invisible, just hearsay, no audit trail. The cynicism was stunning. For the rest of his life, Eddie never trusted any organization.

When Eddie looked at LT Calley, he realized there was a weak link in this chain: it required a smidge of common sense to be effective. Infantry officers had to supply that smidge. They had to understand that "kill 'em all and let God sort 'em out," was hyperbole. In hard war, you could kill lots of 'em, but you couldn't really kill 'em all. It was the unwritten rule of the infantry the officer in charge had to tightly control the murderous urges of young Americans with deadly weapons.

Eddie knew this firsthand. When he ordered one of his men to shoot the wounded gook, the soldier did so without hesitation. Same when burning down the Montagnard villages. There was a fine line between hard war and atrocity, and it was the job of the officer to make sure that line was not crossed.

Unfortunately for Calley, he just wasn't very smart. A captain on the Platoon Tactical Committee went through OCS with him.

"He was always a marginal candidate."

That was code for "under peace time conditions, he wouldn't have graduated." So, Calley marched to the dark drum beat that had been given to him. Now he was facing life in prison.

Life was good for a single officer at Benning during the war. Every Thursday night at the club annex at Custer Terrace, things were jumping. It was a serious meat market. Eddie followed the herd. It was standard practice for the married officers on orders to Vietnam to stash the old lady at Benning. When the back channels started leaking stories about all the boom boom going on over there, the result was predictable. Most of the girls had an itch. A good number of them decided to get it scratched. Tit for tat. Lots of scratching at Custer Terrace.

One night, Eddie was chatting up one of the stashed wives. He was all set to get his own itch scratched that night, no sweaty da. Then during the preliminaries, he let slip he had been in the Herd.

"Ooh, that's where my Jimmy is! Maybe you know him?"

When she told Eddie her last name, sure enough, he knew the prick. Laying pipe with a stranger's wife was not a problem. With the old lady of an acquaintance, bad form. So, no boom boom for the Ed-man that night. A man has his principles.

One day, Eddie was called into the CO's office. The boss was on the phone.

"…And I'll send over one of my tactics experts."

He hung up.

"Eddie, I want you to go over to…"

To his astonishment, Eddie realized he was "the tactics expert." Well, shit in my hat.

Another day, Eddie was called into the CO's office.

"Why don't you make the Army a career?"

That was the re-enlistment speech. Eddie signed the paperwork to get out. The next day, he was instructing. His assistant came to him during the break. The Commandant of the Infantry School was flying out for an unscheduled visit. A short time later, two birds came in, the general and his staff. He sat in the bleachers observing Eddie's class. At the break, he and Eddie had a pleasant chat. His staff hovered behind him. Then he walked over to the woodline. His staff followed. Then he unbuttoned his fatigue pants and took a piss. The staff unbuttoned and pissed too.

Yup, thought Eddie, *I'm not going to miss this shit.*

One of the regular ads in *The Army Times* was a recruiting firm that specialized in finding jobs for people getting out of the service. It showed guys smiling. *Why not?* thought Eddie. He gave them a call, sent in a form, and they set up an appointment. He drove to Atlanta and went into the office. The waiting room was full, lots of guys wearing suits and ties. Eddie had on a sports jacket and no tie. Lots of briefcases. Eddie had the ad he'd cut out of the paper. Lots of guys with glasses. Eddie saw like a friggin' eagle. All the "Briefcases" were reading folders. Eddie read a magazine. Three magazines later, a lardass came out and called his name. Eddie followed him into a small office. Lardass introduced himself, they shook hands, and sat down. Unconsciously, Eddie wiped his hand on his pants.

"Well, Mr. Brandt, or can I call you Eddie? You're the kind of guy we used to sing about in Basic Training. Ho, ho, ho."

Basic Training for what, the Girl Scouts?

"Now then, what would you like to do with the rest of your life?" Big fuckin' smile.

"I don't know."

"Well, where would you like to live?" Smaller fuckin' smile.

"I don't care."

"How much do you want to make?" No fuckin' smile.

"It doesn't matter."

"You know, Eddie, you're not making this very easy."

"If I knew the answer to those questions, I wouldn't be here."

"Have I offended you? Would you like to see another agent?"

"Relax, you're fine."

Lardass looked through some papers.

"Tell you what, Eddie. Why don't you go get some lunch and, when you get back, I'll have some options for you. How's that sound?"

"Sounds fine."

"Oh, and see if you can find a tie. See you at one."

Eddie ate a hot dog from a street vendor, walked around for a bit, bought a tie from another street vendor, and went back to the office at one. He was reading another magazine when Lardass breezed in.

"That's much better," he said, looking at Eddie's two-dollar tie. "Why don't you read through this and, when I get back, then we'll talk." He handed Eddie a brochure and left.

Eddie took a look. Insurance. The job was selling fucking insurance. Ten minutes later, he was on the highway heading back to Benning. Jesus, he hated flatpeters.

Eddie's last day in the Army was coming up. He reported to the hospital for his end of service physical. The doctor examined his wounds to determine if he rated any disability.

"Let's see. Missing left ring finger. You right or left-handed?"

"Right."

He checked a chart in a manual. "Nope, no disability."

"I could be wrong here, Doc, but I don't think it's going to grow back."

"Just following the regs, Lieutenant. Nothing personal. What's this?" he said, pointing at the scar on Eddie's chest.

"Gunshot wound, right lung. They took out one of the lobes."

"Mmmm," checking another chart in the manual, "nope, no disability."

"Aren't you going to ask me if I'm right or left lunged?"

"Ha, ha, good one. Like I said, Lieutenant, nothing personal, it's the regs. Good luck in civilian life."

Last day. Eddie reported to one of the classrooms. It was filled with other guys getting out. No one spoke. A staff officer handed out some forms, then told them what to read and where to sign. Eddie signed, and just like that, he was a civilian.

1970-1974

Eddie drove to Pennsylvania to see his father. It was strange. His father had always been the tough guy. He was the street fighter, the kid from the wrong side of the tracks, the veteran of two wars, etc., etc. But he'd never been in combat and Eddie had. Eddie had led an airborne rifle platoon; the old man had ridden a desk. Eddie had been a grunt; the old man had been, let's face it, a flatpeter. Their relationship had changed forever. He couldn't talk about it, even when his father asked. He just couldn't. It just didn't feel right. After a few days, he hit the road to California to see his sister.

She was thrilled to see him. She lived in a condo with all the California condo stuff…pool, hot tub, sauna, outdoor bar. When she went to work the next day, Eddie hit the pool. He was a piece of work in a bathing suit. It would take years for the scars to fade. In California, they were still bright red and nasty. He didn't know or care if people looked. He spent most of the time asleep in a lounge chair. At night, he went out. There were lots of bars filled with lots of California babes. In any given ten, five were okay looking, three were pretty, and two were knockouts. He even talked to a few of them, but that seemed to be too much work. Sleeping around the pool was easier.

After a week, his sister asked, "So, what are you going to do?"

"Thought I'd hit the pool."

"No, sweetie, I mean with the rest of your life."

"Oh, that. I really don't know."

"Listen, I was talking to a friend, and he knows a company that's looking to hire veterans."

"Uh-huh."

"Why don't I have him set something up for you?"

"Sure, why not."

This time, Eddie wore a tie. It was an asphalt company and the boss was a big, friendly guy. They went through the usual chit chat. Then he told Eddie about the asphalt business and the great future for it in booming California.

Eddie nodded.

"So, Eddie, know anything about asphalt?"

"Not a thing."

"Uh-huh. They tell me you're a veteran. What branch were you in?"

"The Army."

"Army, that's great. We have a lot of Army guys here. What did you do, engineers?"

"Infantry."

"Uh-huh. Gee, we don't get a lot of infantry."

"In the infantry, we didn't get a lot of engineers."

"Uh-huh. Well, can you tell me how an infantryman could work in the asphalt business?

"I guess I'd just have to learn it."

Driving back to his sister's place, Eddie was pretty sure there wasn't going to be any asphalt in his future. A week later, he hit the road again.

Eddie drove around to places he'd never been, the North, the Midwest, the mountains, the plains. He was driving up the Mid-Atlantic when he remembered a pal from Benning saying he was going to go to school at one of the state universities nearby. Eddie went there and checked with the registrar; no record of the pal. Conversationally, he asked about what it took to enroll. And, just like that, Eddie was scheduled to start classes in the fall.

Eddie had a few months to kill before the semester started. He happened to be in Harrisburg, Pennsylvania. He bought a local paper, checked the want ads, saw one for a security guard, and drove to the main office.

"Just got out of the Army?"

"Yes, sir." Goddammit, he'd have to break that habit.

"What branch?"

"Infantry"

"Vietnam?"

"Yeah."

"That's what we're looking for. You're hired. Go next store and get a uniform. Got a gun?"

"No."

"Here, use this until you get one of your own." He handed Eddie a revolver.

Eddie got the uniform and went to the YMCA and got a room. He put on the uniform and the pistol and looked in the mirror. Goddammit, a fucking security guard. So much for that great leadership experience.

Eddie's job was to check a bunch of locations at night. To make sure he actually went there, they gave him a time clock to punch in at each location. It was mostly factories, dimly lit, in the shitty section of town. The second night, he was punching in somewhere when he thought he heard a noise. Automatically, he put his hand on the pistol. He thought he heard another noise; he drew the pistol. He spent the rest of the night punching in, pistol drawn. The next day he quit. He didn't come through Vietnam just to shoot some asshole in Harrisburg, Pennsylvania.

Eddie got a job as a security guard in a hospital, no uniform, no pistol, just checking the hospital four times a night. He had lots of time to read.

The fall came and Eddie started going to class. His attention span was about zero. He was interested in a lot of things, just not the stuff they taught in class. He loved wandering through the stacks in the library, pulling out books that caught his fancy. Hours later, he realized he hadn't done any homework. He loved going to the music room and listening to records. No homework done there either. Every year he switched majors. The GI Bill was paying, and they didn't seem concerned over his aimless pissing away of government money. Eddie didn't care either.

The university had the usual assortment of student clubs. One of them was the Veterans' Club. Just for laughs, Eddie checked it out. He actually attended a meeting. He wasn't sure what he expected to find there, but there was one surprise: there weren't any grunts. Everybody had been in the Navy, the Air Force, or stacking toilet paper in the Army. There was no one like him. Jesus, were all the infantrymen dead? The topper was the club display window in the Student Union. Front and center was a Dishonorable Discharge. So much for the Veterans' Club.

A local widow was renting rooms to college students and Eddie found a place there. There were three other boarders. Two were kids, the third was Thaxter, a former Marine. The kids were all right; Thaxter was a searing pain in the ass. Eddie had almost no experience with Marines. To him, Vietnam was Army, with a bit of Air Force thrown in. Thaxter was his introduction to

Marine Corps horseshit. Goddammit, he talked a good fight. Just when Eddie was wondering who was going to play him in the movie, he discovered Thaxter had been a support puke, a fuckin' flatpeter. There was no getting around it, he hated fuckin' flatpeters, Marine or otherwise.

There was a sprinkling of vets in his classes, and every now and then Eddie spoke with a some of them. One of the least annoying told him he was drawing a disability from the Veterans Administration.

"Wounded in action?"

"Nah, dicked up my back lifting stuff. I get 30%. Puts me in the Vocational Rehabilitation Program. The VA picks up my tuition and gives me a monthly payment. Good deal, huh?"

He asked Eddie if he'd been hurt. Eddie gave him the details.

"How much are you getting from the VA?"

"Zero."

"Zero? Listen here, pal," and he told Eddie about the Disabled American Veterans.

"Give them power of attorney and they do the rest."

"How much does that cost?"

"Not a thing, partner, not a thin dime."

Eddie reached out to the DAV, gave them power of attorney, and six months later was officially a disabled veteran, rated at 40%, and admitted to the Voc Rehab program. So, just like that, he began sucking the government tit. He did it for the rest of his life.

Even with the disability payments, Eddie was running low on cash. He tried a few part-time jobs, but they bored the shit out of him. So, reluctantly, he went back to what he knew, the Army. There was a reserve unit not too far away, and he went to see them. A fat NCO (there's a fuckin' surprise) was sitting behind a desk. Eddie showed him his DD 214. Fat City read through it.

"You know, there's a Nation Guard Special Forces battalion north of town. That might be a better fit with your background."

"Nation Guard Special Forces?"

"Yep. Here's the number."

National Guard Special Forces. Who'd a thunk it? So, he made the call, set up an appointment, and drove on up. Another desk, another fat NCO, and Eddie was in.

He took his fatigues to the local Army base to get a military starch. He spit shined his jump boots. He even got a haircut. 0800 Saturday, drill weekend, he was standing tall in front of the battalion commander, Lieutenant Colonel Fife. Fife, as Eddie found out later, in his civilian life, was a meter reader for the power company. Oh, well, at least he 'wasn't fat.

One of the company first sergeants came in, greeted Eddie, and led him out of the CO's office. They went to a nearby building. It was being painted. He handed Eddie a paint brush.

"What's this?"

"Paintbrush, sir. We're painting the building."

"Officers don't pull detail."

"This is Special Forces, sir."

The first sergeant left. Eddie looked at the paint brush, looked at the walls, and started for the door to get the fuck out of National Guard Special Forces.

A captain looked in. "You new here?"

"Yeah."

"Got you painting, huh?

"Yeah, I'm going home."

"Ah, come with me."

They went to the captain's car, got in, and drove to Dunkin Donuts. The first sergeant never said a word.

During the late sixties' and early 'seventies, everyone knew what service in the guard and reserve meant: it meant you weren't going to Vietnam. You did your one weekend a month and two weeks in the summer and that was it. The government figured that calling up the reserve components would sound too much like a national emergency, and that was not the message they wanted to send to the American people. So, the Guard and Reserves sat this one out. The twist with NG Special Forces was the green beret. You could wear the beret and strut your shit, secure in the knowledge you weren't going any farther east than the Potomac River. It was flatpeter heaven. It was flatpeter heaven, that is, until the veterans started to come in. They razzed the guardsmen unmercifully, lifting their giant fig leaf to reveal the tiny pecker underneath. The guardsmen hated them for it.

Eddie took particular pleasure in twisting National Guard tits. When the Army went into Cambodia, riots broke out in protest across the country. The students at Eddie's school followed suit, and his Guard unit was activated. Eddie's team was given the mission of guarding the administration building. To his astonishment, they were issued live ammunition. Once inside, he briefed them.

"First, no one loads their weapon. Keep the ammo in the box. Second, if they come in the front door, we're going out the back. Nobody is going to get hurt fighting over some fuckin' administration building."

When no one was looking, Eddie loaded a magazine. Just in case. He was going to make damn sure no one on his team would get hurt in this stupid shit.

Nothing happened, and a few days later the battalion stood down. When they went to hand in their ammunition, everyone on the team turned over the unopened ammo boxes. Eddie dumped twenty rounds on the table.

The warrant officer in charge looked at the ammo and then hard-eyed Eddie. "You were endangering people's lives, sir."

That was the wrong thing for a guardsman to say.

"Endangering people's lives? What the fuck do you know about endangering lives? All you've ever done is stack toilet paper in the supply room."

So, Eddie short-dicked a guardsman. Needless to say, he made an enemy that day. He loved it.

Once a year, there was a statewide field exercise involving all the National Guard units. The SF unit played the aggressors. Eddie and his team moved out to their area. Eddie's team sergeant was an E-6 named Ronnie. Ronnie was a good guy and everybody liked him. Unlike most of the career guardsmen, Ronnie had actually been in Southeast Asia. He'd spent time as a civilian working for Air America, kicking door bundles out of airplanes. Ronnie was a good guy, but his Air America stories started to wear a little thin with Eddie. Then Ronnie started to set up for the night, five two-man positions spread out all over hell. In front of the whole team, Eddie carved out his asshole.

"Sergeant, I am the team leader and I will decide how and where to set up. You are the team sergeant, and you will see that my orders are carried out. Is that clear?"

"Yes, sir."

So, Eddie short-dicked another guardsman. There really wasn't any call for reaming out Ronnie, particularly in front of the team. Eddie made another enemy that night. Nice guy be damned, he hated flatpeters.

Eddie was put in charge of mortar training. Three drills in advance, he called a meeting of all the 11C senior NCOs. He designated the NCO in Charge (NCOIC), made the training assignments, and asked if there were any questions. There were none. Two drills in advance, he called another meeting of the NCOs. He asked if there were any issues with their preparation for training. There were none. One drill in advance, same, same. On the drill for the mortar training, they loaded the weapons and equipment on the trucks, loaded all the troops to be trained, and convoyed to the training area. They went to the ammunition supply point, drew a hundred rounds of 81mm ammo, then went to the range. Eddie directed the NCOIC to set up the mortars and begin training. He then drove to the Officers' Club for coffee. An hour later, he went back to the range. The troops were milling about. The mortars had been set up, but the aiming circles were laying on the ground. Pissed, Eddie called the NCOIC aside.

"Sergeant, what the hell is going on?"

"Well, sir, uh…"

"Well, what?"

"You see, sir, uh…"

"Goddammit, Sergeant, what's the fuckin' problem?"

"Well, sir, uh…we, uh…don't know how to set up the aiming circles."

"What? You're school trained 11Cs! What do you mean you don't know how to set up the aiming circles?"

"Geez, sir. That was a long time ago…"

"Why the fuck didn't you say something before this?"

Silence.

Eddie was so pissed he was getting dangerously close to choking the shit out of this worthless turd.

"You are aware we can't turn in this ammunition, right?"

"Yes, sir."

"That we will have to fire it all up, right?"

"Yes, sir."

"Okay, no aiming circles. Just drop the rounds in the tubes and fire them up. Can you do that, Sergeant?"

"Yes, sir."

The three crews went to their weapons, picked up a mortar round, and looked at each other.

"Now what's the matter?"

"Well, sir, uh…"

"What?"

"It's the charges, sir. How many do we use?"

"Jesus fuckin' Christ, Sergeant! Does anyone here know anything about this fuckin' weapon?"

"Uh..."

"Goddammit, tear off a couple of fuckin' charges and fire the fuckin' weapons."

They tore off two charges and dropped them down the tubes. They looked down range to see where the rounds landed. Way off in the distance they heard them hit, way out of sight. Eddie had a nightmare vision of shoppers in the commissary getting blown to bits.

"For fuck's sake, tear off all but two!"

Well, at least they saw where these landed. As quick as they could, they fired the one hundred rounds, packed up, and got the fuck out of Dodge. For the next week, Eddie was afraid to answer the phone or open the door.

The following drill, Eddie was summoned in to the battalion commander.

"You fucked up mortar training, Lieutenant. I want your resignation."

That really punched Eddie's buttons. Evil Eddie came roaring out of his cave spitting fire. Colonel Meter Reader wasn't used to dealing with raging assholes.

"…And another thing, this unit discriminates against veterans!"

Meter Reader scraped together what was left of his scorched self-importance. "That's not true, Lieutenant."

"Yes, sir, it is, and don't just take my word for it." Eddie went out into the hall. Two of the vets happened to be passing by. He corralled them into Meter Reader's office. "Here you go, sir, ask them."

Half an hour later, the two vets left. A small voice came out of the smoking hole that had been Meter Reader's desk. "Well, Lieutenant, let's talk about this later."

Eddie never heard another word about mortar training. But the gauntlet had been thrown down. He was going to short-dick every one of these flatpeters.

On paper, the battalion was impressive. Everybody passed the annual PT test with a high score and almost everybody fired expert on the annual rifle qualification. After the mortar fiasco, Eddie began to question these paper credentials. Sure enough, when the qualification drills rolled around, he saw massive fudging. They even joked about it:

"Yep, fired expert with the M-16 pencil."

The most outrageous fudging was on the Special Forces correspondence course. In the first place, Eddie was astonished to learn it was possible to get qualified through the mail. You had to be in an SF unit, sign up for the correspondence course, and then pass the written tests. That plus attendance at one two-week annual training and, bingo-bango, you were Special Forces qualified. There was no note in your records you were a correspondence course commando; you were SF just like the guys who went through the real course. Eddie signed up. Six months later, he was a bona fide John Wayne snake-eater. He thought it was hilarious and told the story for years. The enlisted had their own course. One drill, Eddie happened to be walking by one of the classrooms. He looked in and saw a group of EM taking the test. He also saw a captain in front of the class reading off the answers. Like a pilgrim discovering the promised land, Eddie rejoiced.

"Gotcha now, fuckers."

He huddled with two other vets to plan their attack. They decided on taking it to the local congressman. Once they figured out who he was, they called up, got through to an aide, and outlined the situation. The aide made an appointment. They were locked and loaded. On the appointed day, they drove to the capitol and went to his office. Of course, the meeting was with the aide, not the congressman. No big deal, it was still democracy in action, power to the people. After dropping a dime on the battalion, they stopped off at a bar to celebrate victory. Two drills later, a team from the congressman's office showed up. They interviewed a few people and left. And that was the last they ever heard about test fudging. Within a year, Eddie and the other two whistleblowers were out of the unit.

A slot opened for Ranger School.

"Go on, take it," said dumb Eddie.

"Run for the woodline," said smart Eddie.

Dumb Eddie won.

He reported in that November. He was going to be a winter ranger. That meant, on top of all the ranger horseshit, he was going to be cold—really, really cold.

They started with Benning Week; seven days designed to "get you in shape." First, there was the run, "progressive PT." Rangers had their own unique idea of progressive: one mile the first day, then three, then five, then nine, all with equipment bouncing up and down. The laws of human physiology begged to differ with the Ranger Department. Running like this didn't build you up, it just beat the shit out of everyone. Then there was a mix of other so-called preparatory stuff: obstacle courses, the slide for life, and hand-to-hand. The culmination was "the Pit." They put the whole class in a big pit, paired everyone up, and ordered them to fight their way out. Supposedly, this was not only practical work in applying the hand-to-hand techniques recently acquired, but also competition to identify the toughest ranger. Old timers like Eddie got themselves eliminated in the first round. The younger and dumber one battled it out. Finally, there were two left, a Marine and a guy from the Greek Army. Naturally, Eddie and the others rooted for the Greek.

"In the balls!" they shouted. "Kick him in the balls!"

The Greek, handicapped by 2,500 years of culture, paid no heed to this guidance, and the Marine's testicles emerged from the contest not kicked. In the interests of international harmony, the committee called it a draw.

The next stop was Mountain Phase in northern Georgia. There was perfunctory training in how to operate in the mountains, specifically, rock climbing.

"Rangers, do not do this in the rain," proclaimed the instructor, wearing a slicker to keep dry in the downpour. They practiced a few time on a rock cliff, and then were run out to the woods. Once tactical, they were reduced to one box of C-rations per day. Immediately, everyone was hungry. Every day they got wet, so everyone was cold. Morale sank with the temperature, so everyone was pissed off.

"Rangers, you all have a bad attitude. If this was unit training, you would not get the tab."

That pissed off everyone even more.

Eddie was the patrol leader for a night movement to the objective. They came to a stream. Eddie went forward to check it out. Off to the left was a bridge. Eddie looked at the bridge and then at the stream and then at the bridge again.

The Ranger Advisor whispered in his ear, "I know what you're thinking, Ranger, and I am advising you not to take the bridge. It's a danger area."

They were wearing their last pair of dry fatigues. The temperature was below freezing. Eddie went back to brief the patrol.

"We're taking the bridge."

"Ranger, I am advising you in the strongest possible terms, do NOT take the bridge. It is a danger area."

"As I said, we're taking the bridge."

Eddie failed the patrol.

By the time they got out of the mountains, they were half starving. It was that rarest of moments in military life when no one talked about pussy. It was all about food. The end of Mountain Phase was right before Christmas, and they were due ten days leave. When they got back to Benning, they were released prior to going home the next day. Eddie and a group got a motel and then went out to eat. There was a restaurant right outside the main gate. Knowing their clientele, they seated the boys at a table and gave them a menu and a large pizza. The pizza was gone in seconds. Another one appeared. The first item on the menu was the "Ranger Special." It was all you could eat. They read no further.

"Five Ranger Specials and another pizza."

The food came and came and came. There were huge platters of beef, chicken, Italian, and bread. Eddie had never eaten so much so fast. After a while, it actually hurt. They staggered out of the restaurant. Eddie leaned up against the car. Pain was shooting up and down his stomach. He tried to puke, but his body refused to surrender the precious food. Groaning, they stumbled into the car and drove to the motel.

Halfway there, someone said, "Man, I sure could eat some ice cream."

In a flash, they were at a convenience store. Clutching a gallon of ice cream and a cherry pie, they raced to the motel. Someone with masterful planning potential had bought spoons, paper plates, and Pepto Bismol. As if there had been no Ranger Specials, they dug in. Eddie was beginning to feel as if he had incurred serious damage.

"Pepto Bismol?" he moaned. Someone pointed to the kitchen. Lurching like a walking wounded, he went over. Just as he was about to chug a big slug of the pink shit, he saw a lone piece of pie on the counter. Boomo, the Pepto Bismol hit the floor. Gaslorp, no spoon, no plate, the pie disappeared. Eddie slid down and passed out.

His landlady welcomed him back. He nodded and went to the fridge. He ate for ten days straight. He didn't really have meals, just a continual intake of food. There were hamburgers, cheeseburgers, hot dogs, chili dogs, pizza, chicken wings, Chinese, Italian, Mexican, Thai, and cookies, potato chips, pretzels, and, let's not forget, the sacred ice cream.

"What are you doing, Eddie?" His landlady was concerned.

"Mmmrf, grumpf, gezork," said Eddie through a mouthful of food. And, just like that, the ten days were up.

The final segment was Swamp Phase in Eglin Air Base, Florida.

Florida, Eddie thought, *gotta be warm.*

It was the panhandle and it wasn't warm. Some more preliminary horseshit and then into the swamps. It snowed. It didn't stick, but goddammit, it snowed in Florida. They got wet every day, and that combined with not enough food and too little sleep, everyone was sick. It was not uncommon when a patrol order was being read out, the patrol leader would have to stop and wait for the coughing to subside in order to be heard.

There was a contingent from Laos, and they suffered the worst. They were short, so when the Americans were waist deep in water, the Laotians would be up to their necks. One time a patrol was wading through the swamp when one of the Laotians peeled off the column, hopped up on a little island, lit a fire, and refused to go any further. They had to send a boat in to get him. Another time they were loaded aboard a Coast Guard cutter, taken out to the bay, and loaded on to rubber rafts to infiltrate the beach. The plan was to have all the rafts rendezvous in the gulf, and then conduct a coordinated movement to the beach. Eddie was in charge of one of the rafts. They rolled around in the water, waiting for the other rafts to load. They were wet and it was cold.

"Fuck this," said Eddie, and ordered his raft to row for the shore. The other rafts saw this and followed suit.

The Ranger advisors were pissed.' "If you fuckers were going through as a unit, you wouldn't get the tab."

Eddie mused they could stick the tab up their ass.

One day, they were taking a break prior to crossing a river.

One of the Ranger advisors walked up and looked over them. "You're cold, right?

They all nodded.

"And you'd do anything to be warm, even just for a few minutes, right?"

They all nodded again.

"So, piss your pants."

"Wha?"

"Piss your pants. You're going to get wet anyway. Piss your pants."

Everyone turned it over in their minds. The logic was irrefutable. Soon all up and down the column you could hear the contented sighs of relief. Ahh, warmth. There were times when even the Rangers got it right.

On another exercise, they were making a night jump to infiltrate the area of operations. They chuted up and waited. Eddie was famished. He went to the medics and complained of a sore throat. They gave him a bottle of cough syrup. He slugged it down. Five minutes later, he was asleep.

"Let's go, we're loading."

He schlumped into the plane, sat down, and went to sleep again.

"STAND UP!"

He followed the jump commands. They were on jump run. He fell out the door, oscillated a few times, and hit the ground. Best military jump he ever made.

They finally finished up Swamp Phase and motored back to Benning. By now, everyone was really sick, coughing continuously and hocking up disgusting lungers. No one admitted it, but the reality was that they were in the initial stages of death by exposure. Another thirty days of this shit and people would have begun dying.

Graduation was the next day and after a good night's sleep and a big breakfast, they fell out to the parade ground to practice for the ceremony. After the address from some VIP, they were to pass in review. Rangers don't just march in review, rangers run in review and chant while doing so.

"Rangers, run in review."

"Rah, rah, rah!" left turn, "rah, rah, rah!" left turn, run in front of the reviewing stand. "Rah, rah, rah!" left turn, "rah, rah, rah!" left turn, "rah, rah, rah!" Back in place. The coughing started.

"Not good enough! Do it again! Rangers, run in review!"

"Rah, rah, rah!" etc., etc. Now everyone was coughing and hocking.

"Not good enough! Do it again! Rangers, run in review!"

To a man, the whole class sat down.

"Get up! Get up, you sorry fuckers! Get up!"

No one moved. A jeep with the VIP pulled onto the field. Everyone got to their feet. Forgettable words were spoken. Ranger tabs were passed out and pinned on. They were rangers.

As they were packing up to go home, Sergeant Keel, the NCOIC, stormed into the barracks.

"If you sorry fuckers had went through as a unit, ya wouldn't a got the fuckin' tab!"

Just then, one of the guys from the class stuck his head in the door. "Sergeant Keel, there's a Ranger squad outside waiting for you to lead them."

With a puzzled look, Keel went outside. Everyone rushed out behind him. There in a neat row were ten black ranger berets. In each one was a nice, fresh turd.

You know, thought Eddie, *someone's wasting his talent in the Army.*

At his last summer camp in the Guard, there were some Brits from one of their SAS units. The regimental sergeant major was a cocky fucker named Rover. He was a Sean Connery look-alike, complete with moustache, accent, and kiss-my-ass demeanor. No doubt about it, RSM Rover had all his shit in one pile. Eddie took an immediate dislike to the prick.

One night, they were all in the club. An American female lieutenant was there, and Rover had his heat seeking missile locked in on her. His bullshit was reaching tsunami levels and then he fucked up.

"Gotta hit the loo, luv. Back in half a sec."

Big mistake, Rover.

Eddie leaned over the table. "Whaddya say, toots?"

And Eddie and the babe were out the door. He enjoyed hosing the babe. He really enjoyed hosing the regimental sergeant major. Suck on that, Rover, you limey fuckwad.

Three of the oddest ducks Eddie ever met, he met there in the National Guard: Fritzie, Beast, and Wacky Willy.

Fritzie: The only thing wrong with Fritzie was a serious case of SPS – Short Pecker Syndrome. Eddie got that insight from wife one, who observed it was really men who had penis envy, not women. All in all, Fritzie got dealt a pretty good hand: He was relatively tall, relatively handsome, relatively intelligent, and generally a pretty good shit. What outweighed all that was he wanted to be a tough guy and Fritzie wasn't tough. He wasn't even semi-tough.

Truth be told, he was uncoordinated, unathletic, four-eyed, a little bookish, and, let's face it, in his heart of hearts, a little wimpy. In other words, perfect material for the Marine Corps.

To be sure, the Marines draw from a variety of recruitment pools, but the dirty little secret is, historically, their best source is and always has been the short pecker syndrome mooks. "The Marine Corps builds men." That's the public message. The subliminal one is a lot more compelling: "Hey, brother, got a little dick? Become a Marine and we'll give you that extra yardage nature forgot." It's worked for generations. It sure worked on Fritzie.

Eddie met Fritzie in the National Guard which he joined after getting off active duty. They both needed the money. At that time, the bug was only a little ways up Fritzie's butt. His stories were at first of a low-grade order, taking what really happened and jazzing it up a little. But that's the thing about SPS; that little wienie casts a big shadow and Fritzie never felt like he'd walked out of it. So, his jazzing up moved from tiny turdlets to massive, steamy, smelly, full-blown bullshit. His honorable but modest war soon metastasized into Hollywood style bayonet charges (there weren't any), a battlefield commission (there weren't any), and that perennial Marine Corps favorite, hand-to-hand combat (so rare that for all practical purposes there wasn't any of that either).

Here's the problem: bullshit is some pretty thin ice, putting the serious bullshitter in constant danger of falling through. Fritzie's bullshit was so outrageous that just about everyone took it as such. And yet they cut him some slack. He was, after all, basically a good egg. Then he made the stupendous mistake of bringing out one of his wartime buddies, Shorty. Shorty was the feather that broke Fritzie through the ice. In a night of drinking with the gang, inevitably the talk turned to the war.

That's when Honest Injun Shorty dropped his innocent bomb: "Yeah, we really didn't see much action."

With an expression like he had just caught his jimmy in a zipper, Fritzie squeaked "Whaddya mean? Sure, we did."

For the rest of the night, Shorty's money was no good.

Skydiving was another pecker extender and, therefore, predictably, another siren call for the Fritzer. Again, predictably, he strutted his stuff, but in fact it scared the shit out of him, literally in this case. Another seemingly innocent bomb was dropped, his wife woofing about having to clean the skid marks out of his skivvies. Poor old Fritzie.

His divorce opened virgin bullshit territory for him…nookie. He went from happily married Faithful Fritzie to swordsman extraordinaire, or so his story went. At least once a week he'd call Eddie and forklift it on. "Yessiree, buddy," he expounded, "I'm layin' some heavy pipe."

Sure, Eddie knew it was just more Fritzie crapunza, but it was entertaining crapunza. And where was the harm in it? Meeting no resistance, Fritzie expanded the act to include whipping ass. So, it was a small step from Fucking Fritzie to Fighting Fritzie:

"Ya shoulda been there, Eddie. These two big guys come at me and zip, zippo, zippy, they're on the floor bleeding." Given Fritzie's unimpressive physical equipment, this one was a little harder to take, but again where was the harm.

Then came the fight in the diner. Coming home late from a party one night, he and his buddy Willie Boy stopped off at the diner to get some coffee. The local rugby team was there celebrating a victory. Words passed and Willie punched one of the rugby dicks in the throat. His pals came at the two of them like the opening scrum of a match. Willie went down swinging. Fritzie, on the other hand, claiming he was wearing a back brace, stepped into a neutral corner, and watched Willie get the fondue beat out of him. No more Fighting Fritzie stories after that.

War, fucking, fighting, the final pecker yardstick was money. This one was harder for Fritzie to fake. And then he married Angie. Angie had put her head through a windshield in a car accident, sued the other guy, and walked away with a serious shitload of money. For the first time in his life Fritzie, who was coming off a string of nowhere jobs, was in the chips and it felt good. He was soon living in a mansion on a hill and driving a Mercedes. He also discovered multilevel marketing where his in-your-face lifestyle and his superb bullshitting skills combined to make multilevel marketing magic. Fritzie found his element and took off. He was in the one percent that actually make money in that scam. In no time at all, he was living in an even bigger mansion and driving an even bigger Mercedes. He even self-published a book, the reflections of the master sharing his secrets to success. Sure, it was one whopper after another, but no one seemed to call him on it. And why would they? Who wouldn't believe a war hero, a skydiving champion, a martial arts expert, and a really rich guy? So, Fritzie had built the good ship Horseshit and by God it floated. He was living the legend. So, mused Eddie, maybe he really was a master. He certainly broke the code on success in America. “Good on ya, buddy. Your secret is safe with me.”

Beast. Beast could have come right out of central casting – good size, good shape, and, on top of that, he was a dead ringer for Burt Reynolds, an accident of nature he played up to the max. He was a National Guard legend. With a beret on his head, an athlete’s spring to his step, and the practiced cool of his look-alike, he wasn’t just the picture of your basic tough motherfucker, he was “the Beast.” That act worked when the Guard was full of Guardsmen. When the veterans started coming into the unit, suddenly Beast wasn’t so beasty. In their eyes, he was just another draft-dodging dork hiding out in the Guard while real soldiers were getting the big green dick in Vietnam.

Just about all the Guardsmen suffered the vets’ razoo with hateful but quiet resignation. It was a small price to pay for getting their immunity from the war. Not so, Beast. Their digs cut deep to that sorest of his sore spots, his small pecker. Once again, the US Marine Corps to the rescue: Beast enlisted. He caught the tail end of the war…not enough…the small pecker is a hard master. He quit the Marines, went to Rhodesia and led a platoon in their war… not enough. He quit the Rhodesians, came back to the states, and led training teams in El Salvador for Mercenary Magazine…still not enough…aw, me, Sapphire, what’s a small pecker to do? Beast made the terrible discovery: There is no cure for the Small Pecker Syndrome because it’s never enough. So Beast and his small pecker just got old together.

Wacky Willy. There was nothing in Willy’s upbringing that could in any way have foretold the strange short life he led. According to his high school pals, Willy was kind of a quiet, preppy, button-down kid, to the point of being almost but not quite dorky. He joined the Army, got commissioned, went to jump school, and got to Vietnam in time for the ferocious battle of Dak To. Back in the world, he completed Special Forces training and went for his second tour in kooky, spooky Command and Control North (CCN), the black ops dicks who sent people “north.” Then home again for the Advanced Course to prepare for battalion level assignments. On track, tight and tidy. But Vietnam was winding down and the inevitable reduction in force hit. Problem: Too many captains. Solution: Shitcan those without college. Result: Adios

Willy. Now the lug nuts on his wheels start to come loose. He became a cop… uniform, weapons, power…close enough. When he shot and killed someone, the wheels started to wobble. Questions were raised, an investigation was opened, and one night the officer in charge of the investigation was sitting in his living room when a bullet came through the front window. Charges were never brought, but not too long after that Willy quit the cops and took off for Saudi Arabia to train the Royal Saudi National Guard. A year later he was back. Why, Eddie never found out.

Then the lug nuts popped off: Willy went to Rhodesia and got commissioned in the Rhodesian Army. He brought Beast over and he too got a commission. Beast, whose emotional gyroscope was slightly less skewed than Willy's, actually went to the field and did some fighting. A year later, Willy was taken under armed guard to a plane and sent back to the states. According to Beast, who was himself a little fuzzy on the details, Willy finagled living quarters in an abandoned estate square in the middle of Indian country, complete with a local babe, her daughter, and D-Day levels of guns, ammo, and explosives. There was also talk of roughing up the black enlisted men and of selling weapons on the black market. Whatever, the Rhodesians had enough of Willy, and led him in handcuffs to the airport. So, he was shitcanned from his second army.

Then the first wheel came off: Willy got involved in the MIA controversy. He claimed North Vietnam had not returned all the POWs. He also claimed firsthand experience of this resulting from his classified missions "north" when he was in CCN. Eddie might have dismissed this behavior as nutty but harmless until Willy started schmoozing with the League of Families, the relatives of the unaccounted MIAs. He went with Willy to a meeting of the League and saw him pump up these vulnerable souls with false hope. More than one actually gave him a hug. Face-to-face, Eddie told him "You know these guys are all dead, right?" He just smiled. And with that, he metastasized from funny old weird Willy to out and out Wacky Willy. But all that bullshit somehow got him an intro to billionaire and former presidential candidate H. Ross Perot, who sent him to England, to do what Eddie never found out.

Then the second wheel came off: In England, the weird shit got weirder. Somehow, Wacky Willy got in a punch-up with the local cops, who, after pounding the crap out of him, uncovered several phony IDs and a pistol (Willy was always armed). He went to trial and got a six-year stretch, for what Eddie never found out. In prison, as far as Eddie could piece together, Willy went on a hunger strike, got interviewed by a babe from the US Embassy, he told her he was framed, she, of course, fell in love with him, etc., etc. The secret to the successful incarceration experience, according to Wacky Willy, is to align with a power group. "All for one, one for all," good for the three musketeers, Hell's Angels, and Her Majesty's Prison Parkhurst. So, he joined forces with the Irish Republican Army, in the process shedding the vanilla-flavored "Willy" for the more Celtic "Liam." Six years and another armed guard escort to an airport and Wacky Willy was back home.

Then the third wheel came off. Drawing on his newly self-developed Irish heritage, Willy blossomed from a bush league bullshitter to a major league crap artist. First things first. He married a nice, unsuspecting, well-employed, Catholic girl (a man has to eat). Then he glommed enough money off her to buy a nice suit (a man has to have a good image). Finally, he hung out at the local power bar (a man has to drop his line where the fat fish swim). Re-purposed as Colonel Liam (a man needs an impressive title), he began to reel in the suckers. He targeted the old money dicks, the tall, skinny, pear-shaped putzes with last names for first names whose ivy league connections got them positions in the power structure. Eddie had to give him credit, Willy was pretty good at conning these dorks. He had learned the secret to power bullshitting; less is more. Using the indirect approach, he dropped a hint here, a suggestion there, reinforced with a well-timed arched eyebrow and the occasional pregnant pause, and the absolute clincher, "Can't really talk about that." The fish dutifully filled in the blanks. In no time, Colonel Liam was Mr. Black Ops. Separately, he hit each one for money which they were eager to fork over. One even took him home to show him an expensive coin collection. Not long after the house was burgled and the coin collection disappeared. Funny about that.

One of the dorks was on the National Security Council, and Willy went for him like a heat seeking missile. The guy actually asked Willy for a proposal to train contras in South America. Willy didn't know a proposal from a loaf of bread, but Eddie did, so for laughs he whipped one together just to see how far Willy could run with it. And, goddammit, he ran the shit out of it. It went to the Pentagon and the State Department and Willy started to dust off his jungle boots. Then the Iran-Contra scandal hit and everyone disappeared like cockroaches in a kitchen light. Poor old Willy was left standing with his pecker in his hand and a bewildered look on his face…soooo close.

Another potential fish was a female fire-breather who ran an organization that supported the opposition to the Russians in their Afghanistan war. She was also a major in the Army reserves. Willy gave her the big time humma humma and so Major Brunhilda asked him if he could train Afghans. Said Willy, "Does a cat have an ass?" or words to that effect and laid the South America proposal on her. This was talking her language. Once again, Willy dusted off his jungle boots. Then Alcohol Tobacco and Firearms arrested him. Once again, soooo close.

Then the fourth wheel came off. As usual, Eddie never got the full story, but apparently the ATF found some of the stolen coin collection in Willy's car. Not good. He was a convicted felon found with a firearm. Not good. They also threw in impersonating an officer. Not good. He went to trial where some other not good stuff came out and Willy got hit with eight years. He had one thing left in his trick bag, PTSD, which he parlayed into avoiding hard time, serving instead at Butner Prison, the locus for federal prisoners with "behavioral problems." Then, a few years into his sentence, the Bureau of Prisons stepped on their government dick: They released Willy through an administrative mix up. Oops. No matter, instead of disappearing into the hinterland, Willy went back to his old haunts, the power bars around Washington. Wacky Willy indeed. With minimal effort the feds spotted him, bagged him, and re-Butnered him. He got divorced by his wife, served his time, and scammed a female pen pal. Upon release from prison, he moved in with her, maxed out her credit cards, had a brain aneurysm, and died.

His last scam was to get buried at Arlington Cemetery with full military honors – the caissons, the horse drawn carriage, the honor guard, the flags, the works. Eddie watched it all, and just when he was about to salute the fucker for pulling off a final good one, three of the horses dropped enormous turds all over the road, causing the marching guard to hoochie-coochie around to avoid messing up their boots. *Right there*, thought Eddie, *is the story of Willy's life: A good show dorked up by a few untimely turds. Soooo close.*

A couple years later, Eddie was drinking with one of the vets who had been in the Guard with him.

"You know, Eddie, the battalion was full of fags."

"What are you talking about?"

"Homos, big time, lots of 'em."

"Homos? Like who?"

He reeled off a bunch of names.

"And Sergeant Major Thorn and Captain Poser were the ringleaders."

"Are you shitting me? How do know all this?"

"I bunked with 'em one summer camp. They were open as hell about it."

"Why in hell didn't you tell me? I would have burned 'em to the ground with this."

"Ahh, who really gives a shit."

Point taken. Who really gives a shit?

1973-1981

Eddie took up skydiving. It seemed a natural next step, paratrooper to skydiver, military to civilian. Just the term "freefall" said it all, free, no jump commands. Anything with no commands was the ticket for Eddie. There were a bunch of licenses. His immediate impulse was to ignore anything involving steps and progression, but there was a chance he could instruct, and to do that you needed the goddamn stuff. So, he picked it all up, A license, then B, C, and D. Then jumpmaster, and finally, thankfully, instructor. He got the first jump course and loved it. Yeah, there was no getting around it, he was a good instructor. Skydiving also introduced him to dope, and he loved that too. There was no hard stuff, just hash and grass. Then he got turned on to acid, and he really loved that. As someone said, it was the most fun you could have in the vertical position. He even made a blast tripping. All the way to altitude he kept reminding himself to pull the ripcord.

"I don't care how pretty it is, don't forget to pull."

It was pretty and he did pull.

Eddie was having a great time. Between his disability, the GI Bill, and instructing, he was taking in all the money he needed. Yep, life was good. Then he turned thirty. An annoying little voice in his head asked him if he could hide out like this for the rest of his life. Just maybe he should get a real job. Someone told him about an opportunity with one of the big fruit companies in Pennsylvania. He called them up, got an interview, and drove up there. He met with two of the managers and they couldn't have been nicer. It was more like three guys chatting than an interview. Then they showed him around the plant. Finally, they told him that the best way to learn the business was to take an internship and get his hands dirty from the ground up. They set it up for him starting in June. They couldn't have been nicer. He drove home. Damn, they were nice guys. Fruit business, here we go. June came around, Eddie went back to Pennsylvania, drove around the town for an hour, said, "Fuck this," and went home. And, just like that, his career in the fruit business ended.

Eddie always wanted to weld and conned the GI Bill guys into paying for a twelve-week welding course. They taught him gas, stick, MIG, and TIG. He liked it. The school was a pipeline to the shipyards and that's where he went. They were building a ship, and Eddie and another new guy were assigned to weld down in the hold. It was dark, there was no ventilation, and it was all overhead welding. Overhead welding meant all the sparks and burning metal rained down all over you. Eddie did it for half an hour. Then he turned to the other new guy.

"This sucks."

"Yeah, it really does."

"I'm quittin'."

"Yeah, me too."

And, just like that, Eddie's welding career ended.

He finally actually completed a course of study at the university…industrial arts. He interviewed at one of the local high schools to be a shop teacher.

"Eddie, we like the fact you have a few years on you. We need a man who can take charge of the shop. We're growing and we want someone to grow with us."

They offered him the job on the spot. A few days later, he got a thick packet in the mail. It was all the stuff he had to fill out for the school district. He put it on the counter in the kitchen. He looked at it every morning when he was drinking his coffee. It was June, then July, then August. He was still looking at the untouched packet. Two weeks before school started, he got a phone call from the head of the Industrial Arts Department.

"Eddie, we haven't received your paperwork. You need to send it to us right away so we can get you set up."

Shit.

"Uh, I'm really sorry, but there's been a family emergency. I won't be able to take the job."

Shit.

"Oh, I'm so sorry, Eddie. I hope it works out for the best."

Shit, shit, shit.

And, just like that, his career as a shop teacher ended.

One day a woman named Connie came out to the drop zone. She and Eddie hit it off. They were true opposites, and as such fascinated each other. She had been in the Peace Corps. Eddie, of course, had not. Connie had never known anyone who had been in the war. Eddie had never known anyone who had been in the Peace Corps.

"So, you were in Vietnam?"

"That's right."

"That must have been interesting."

"Oh, yeah."

"What was it like?"

"Huh?"

"You know, the country, the people, the culture."

"I didn't really notice."

"Well, what was the architecture like."

"I don't know, huts made out of wood and stuff."

"How about art work?"

"Never saw any."

"Music?"

"Never heard any."

"History?"

"Never read any."

"You were there, right?"

"Sure."

"Did you pick up any of the language."

"As a matter of fact, I did."

"Great! Like what?"

"Well, let's see…*dung lai*."

"What's that mean?"

"Stop…*ra dey*."

"And that?"

"Come here…*chu hoi*."

?

"Give up…*di di mau*."

?

"Get out of here…*dinky dau*."

?

"Crazy...*sin loi.*"

?

"Tough shit. Then there was pigeon English. *Ti Ti* was a little, *bookoo* was a lot, *chop chop* was food, *boom boom* was, well, you know, *numba one* was good, *numba ten* was bad."

"How do you say 'hello'?"

"Don't know."

"'Please'?"

"Never used it."

"'Thank you'?"

"Didn't need it."

"So, basically it was, 'stop,' 'come here,' 'give up,' 'get out of here,' 'crazy,' and 'tough shit'?"

"Pretty much. Seemed to be all we needed."

"Good God."

A month later, Eddie moved in to her place.

Connie was a management consultant. Eddie had never heard of it. She did something involving health care. Eddie wasn't interested in it. Her condo was a mess, a bunch of half-finished projects sitting there half-finished. Eddie finished one, then another, then another. Connie thought he was a magician.

"Take 'em one at a time, toots. No magic about it."

She was still impressed. Every so often, Connie asked the inevitable question: "What are you going to do with the rest of your life?"

"Jump out of airplanes."

"Come on, be serious."

"Hell if I know."

Then Connie was offered a consulting job in Bolivia. The pay was good, so was the opportunity.

"You should come along."

"What the hell am I going to do in Bolivia?"

"Learn Spanish, build relationships; this would be a great way to get back into the real world."

"Who wants to go there?"

Well, he was getting older. And, who knows? Bolivia might not be so bad. Ah, hell, why not?

"You know we'll have to get married."

"Hah?"

"They'll only allow family members, not shack ups."

Connie arranged it all. It would be small, right there in the condo. A minister, longtime friend of the family, would perform the ceremony. Her folks, his folks, no problem.

The designated day, they were all there, all except the minister. They waited; no minister.

"You know," Eddie said to her, "I don't think this guy's coming."

"I've got an idea," she said and went into the other room. She came back with a book in her hand, opened it, read a poem, and looked at him.

"Uh, yeah, me too."

The next day, they flew to Bolivia. A week later, Connie got a letter from the minister, full of effusive apology. He had thought she was kidding and had gone fishing. Along with the letter was a marriage certificate.

So, Eddie was a dependent spouse. One day, the ambassador's wife held a thing for the spouses. It was Eddie and a room full of women. They all thought it was cute. He thought it sucked. He never went to another one.

Eddie did take Spanish lessons at the embassy. Funny thing was he was great at the written stuff, but couldn't manage to speak it. He didn't like making mistakes in front of strangers. He'd had enough of that shit in the Army. One day, he needed to buy some writing paper. He spent half an hour practicing the request: "Yo quiero papel, por favor." How hard could that be? He found a stationary store, waited until there were no other customers, and then strolled in like it was no big deal. He ambled up to the sales clerk, a woman.

"No big deal," he reassured himself.

"Buenos dias."

"Buenos dias."

"Yo quiero papel, por favor."

"Si, senor."

She went into the back room. A minute later, she came back...with drawing paper. No big deal, slightly less reassured.

"No, no, senora. Papel, por favor."

Back to the back room. She came back with wrapping paper. No big deal, completely un-reassured.

"No, papel," and he pantomimed writing, "Papel."

Graph paper, tracing paper, toilet paper. *Fuck me*, thought Eddie, getting ready to sprint for the door.

"Esto?" she asked timidly, holding up a pad of writing paper.

"Si, si, si, esto!" as if he had just won a door prize.

She wrapped it up and Eddie paid. He asked her what writing paper was in Spanish.

"Como se dice esto?"

"Papel," she said.

Eddie hated Spanish.

Eddie hated Bolivia. Then Connie came down with hepatitis and they were shipped back to the States. Sometimes shit happens for the best.

He had applied to the State Department. They sent him an appointment to take the competitive exam. He passed that and they sent him an appointment to get interviewed. It was a stress interview, three on one, rapid fire questions in no particular order. He was starting to get pissed. Then they asked him what would he do if he was on duty one night at an embassy and received a call that a group of Americans was tearing up a party at the local hotel. Eddie said he'd take the embassy guards, go to the hotel, and beat the snot out of the miserable fuckers. And, just like that, his career in the State Department ended.

Connie talked him into going back to school for a master's degree. He still had some GI Bill left, so he gave it a shot. To his surprise, his application was accepted at a place in Arizona. Off they went. It was a program for international business, and for the most part, it bored the shit out of him. Connie was his rock and kept him focused. Even so, it was tough sledding. First, there was the bureaucratic horseshit. He got called into the registrar's office one day.

"You didn't take the GMAT."

"That's right."

"You have to take the GMAT to be accepted."

"But I've already been accepted. I've been here for a month."

"No matter. You need to take the GMAT."

"Just for the sake of argument, what would happen if I dork up the GMAT?"

"That's irrelevant. We need to show in your record that you took it."

"Okey dokey."

Eddie took the worthless GMAT and was out of there in fifteen minutes. Box checked, that was the last he ever heard about it. He was learning that army or civilian, bureaucracy is bureaucracy.

One of his professors was a cutie pie. A product of academia with no real experience in the business world, he liked his little games in the classroom. Eddie quickly identified him as a business version of a flatpeter: no time in the field. For the midterm, he announced the entire test would be working through the multi-step process of determining some metric apparently of large importance to business managers. Everyone diligently studied the stuff. Professor Cutie Pie handed out the midterm, and, true to his word, it consisted of a single question: the multi-step process. The rascally funster, however, provided the answer, instructing the class to work the process in reverse. The groans were audible and growing. Eddie looked at the test for about five minutes. Then his internal Horseshit Meter started beeping:

"Danger. Major horseshit ahead."

He walked up to Cutie Pie and dropped the test book on his desk.

"You're finished?" from a surprised CP.

"Yeah, this is horseshit." And left.

Half the class followed him.

A week later, they got the results. Out of a class of twenty students, there were eleven zeros, not F's, fuckin' zeros. The class attacked Cutie Pie. Of course, he never acknowledged making a really stupid move, but he did allow a re-take. Jesus, Eddie hated flatpeters.

Eddie and Connie were coming apart. The agreement was, so he thought, that he would get his degree, get a job, and that's where they would go. He followed her to Bolivia; she would follow him to wherever. Sounded fair to him. Then she started making noise she really liked Arizona and wanted to stay there. Eddie hated the fuckin' desert and told her so. She still wanted to stay, and twisted his arm into using his GI Bill to buy a house. With herculean effort, he finished the program and got some soul-destroying job in Arizona. Just as he was about to go certifiably insane, he got a call from Reserve Affairs in St. Louis. How would he like a forty-day reserve tour in England?

"Hell, yes. What is it?"

"Well, you're Special Forces qualified, right?"

"You know it, brother." (Correspondence, hardee har har har. Goddammit, this was funny.)

"And you got a CIB, right?"

"Yes, indeedy."

"It's the annual worldwide Special Forces exercise. You'd be working in headquarters." (Flatpeter city)

"Send me in, Coach."

Three weeks later, Eddie reported in to Group Headquarters. Tally-fuckin-ho!

Eddie's job was to present the strategic intelligence update as part of the morning and evening briefing to the group commander. On a tough day, preparing and presenting might take an hour, tops. Why this required a combat experienced captain, who knew. True, Eddie hated flatpeters, but he loved being one.

There were five other reservists attached to group for the exercise. Like Eddie, all were combat experienced captains. Also, like Eddie they didn't have a lot to do. So, they fucked over the regulars. The war had now been over some five years with the result that the majority of active-duty captains had missed Vietnam. Under normal circumstances, reservists were treated as second class shit stains. But here come Eddie and the boys, reserve captains with CIBs bigger than hell. It was immediate and unquestioned short-dicking for their regular counterparts. They didn't like it, but there was nothing they could do. In Army World, CIB always trumped non-CIB, and they knew it. So did Eddie and the boys. Let the games begin.

Part of the exercise called for the insertion of a SADM team. SADM was short for Special Atomic Demolition Munition…basically, a back-pack nuke. The concept was simple: the team parachutes in to a likely area of enemy advance, places the SADM on something of strategic value, punches the timer, and runs like hell. In theory, the timer would give them enough of a margin to get beyond the blast radius.

The SADM team was a cocky bunch of dicks. Eddie knew raw meat when he saw it. One night in the club, he ambled over to their table.

"Hiya, boys. Mind if I take a seat?"

Noting his CIB, they nodded.

After some really small small talk, Eddie leaned across the table confidentially. "You're SADM, right?"

"Yeah."

"You know what I heard about SADM?"

Suspicious silence.

Conspiratorially, Eddie glanced left and right and scooched a little closer. "I heard when you hit the timer, the fucker goes off…*boomo*!"

They looked at each other.

"Aw, bullshit."

"No, think about it. Higher is just going to let a nuke sit there? Not a chance…*boomo*!"

Now they really looked at each other.

"Bull-fuckin-shit."

"I'm just telling you, boys. I'm here to help. See ya around."

Eddie strolled off. Short dicking, ya gotta love it.

The headquarters for the exercise was an old World War II airbase outside a small town in East Anglia. There was an all-ranks club that stayed open around the clock. To liven things up, the local women were allowed to be escorted in. This was the English countryside, so the club was pretty much the only game around. The babes lined up at the main gate, and periodically a bus went down to pick them up. This was known as the cattle call. Country girls around the world are usually of a plain sort. Brit country girls, with an exception here and there, made "plain" a compliment. These were some rough babes. No matter, Special Forces was used to going native.

There was a young lad on one of the teams who, oddly enough, was still virgo intacto. Not even close to the image on the recruiting posters, he was likely to remain so for a while. And then, wondrous to relate, while nursing a beer in the club one night, he gets picked up by a hottie. The negotiations were minimal, and in record time she orders a taxi and they rocket into town. Dropped off at a no-tell hotel, she propels Junior up the stairs into a room.

"If ya don't mind," says she, "I like it a little rough."

Don't mind? Junior was not just going to get his cork popped, it was going to be weird shit too. Tootsie pulls out a rope she just happened to have in her bag and ties Junior to the bed. Bombs away, baby! Dazed in anticipation, Junior fails to notice that Tootsie has tied him to the bed face down.

"Nice and secure, luv?"

"Oh, yeah. Can't move an inch."

"Righto, enjoy it," says she, smacks him on the ass and pisses off. Then the closet door swings open, and a guy in a mask, a cape, and a hardon jumps out. Junior gets his cork popped alright.

Later, he manages to untie himself. Tootsie had snagged all his money, so he had to walk back to the base. Sorely in need of sympathy, he finds his team sergeant.

"Sergeant Bazatz, something terrible has happened, but if I tell you, ya gotta keep it to yourself."

"Sure, kid. What's the problem?"

Junior unloads, Bazatz tells him to go lie down, and the kid isn't gone a minute when Bazatz goes running down the hall.

"Hey, listen to this shit!"

So, Junior gets his cork popped twice in one night.

The next day, Eddie and the boys are in the club. Now the short dicking reached Homeric proportions.

"Are you shitting me? You sorry fuckers are just going to sit here and do nothing?"

"Aw, for Christ's sake. Sure, it sucks for the kid, but what can we do?"

"Do? You can go into that faggot town and burn the fuckin' place to the ground, that's what you can do."

"Easy for you to say."

"Well, isn't this a historic moment. This is the day they let women into Special Forces, cuz I don't see anyone here with a dick."

"Fuck you, Brandt."

"Can't happen. You got no dick."

That's entertainment.

It was a little over ten years since Eddie had been in combat and he was still trying to sort it all out. It was becoming more and more apparent to him that the organizing principle was horseshit, horseshit on almost everything relating to the military. He had received massive amounts of horseshit before combat, stunning amounts during combat, and even now, after combat, the horseshit kept coming.

One day on the exercise, Eddie ran into a staff sergeant wearing a 173rd patch on his right shoulder.

"You in the Herd, Sergeant?"

"Yes, sir."

"Which batt?"

"Fifth batt, sir."

"No kidding, so was I. Which company?"

"Foxtrot, sir."

"Me too. When were you there?"

"'69, sir."

"Jesus, that's when I was there!"

Eddie looked at his nametag. Didn't ring a bell. They compared notes. Company Commander? No match. Platoon Leaders? No match. First Sergeant? No match. *Well, there's a puzzler*, thought Eddie. That night in the club, he ran it by the boys. One of them, a Toledo cop in real life, started laughing.

"What's so funny?"

"It's simple."

"What's simple?"

"One of you fuckers is lying."

"What?"

"Same time, same unit, no matches, right?"

"Not a one."

"Yep, one of you guys is lying his balls off, never there."

Years later, they would call this behavior "stolen valor." To Eddie, it was just horseshit, pure and simple.

Eddie got back to the States and the marriage was over. Opposites might attract initially, but fascination wears thin quickly. At some point, there has to be common ground, and he and Connie had none. They went through the usual talking and arguing and fighting, but it was over. He hated his job, he hated Arizona, and he hated confrontation.

"Aren't you ever going to be happy?"

He hated that shit too. He reached out to the only life preserver he knew, the fuckin' Army. It was like a big brother who beat the shit out of you when you were a kid, and now is the one you turn to when you're in trouble. He called his personnel manager at Reserve Components in St. Louis.

"Got any long-term assignments?"

"Starting when?"

"Now."

"Where?"

"Don't care."

"Call me back in an hour."

An hour later, he accepted an assignment as an instructor at the Reserve Intelligence School at Ft. Devens, Massachusetts. Adios Arizona, job, and marriage.

Devens was a bandage for the cuts and scrapes Eddie had received in the last few years. Back in uniform, he got the respect so absent in his recent experience. The CIB worked its magic, particularly in a class full of intel pukes. It felt good. And he was instructing. And he met a babe. Dolly was from Thailand. She had just unloaded her NCO husband and was working as a waitress in the club. She needed a ride home one night. Bingo. All she knew about America was the Army. Eddie was in the Army; swap the old for the new. He understood all that and didn't care. Thai nookie, numba one boom boom.

Life was good, and in the blink of an eye, his tour was over. His wife let him use the condo, so that's where he went. He'd saved enough money to live on for two months. Two months to get a job, any fuckin' job, he didn't care. He put together a resume, a ream of typing paper, a stack of envelopes, and a roll of stamps. Every morning he'd buy a paper, make coffee, and go through the want ads. He circled anything that sounded even remotely possible and followed up with a cover letter and a resume. Most were a blackhole with no response. Some responded with a form letter. Now and then, he even got an interview. Finally, with about two weeks of money left, he interviewed with a company that had just won a contract to provide training materials for several army schools. He lied about having experience with most of them, and that, coupled with his experience as an instructor at the Infantry School, got him the job. And just like that, Eddie became a management consultant.

1981-2000

At this point in his life, Eddie had had lots of experience with horseshit. Consulting just took it to a new level. There was an old joke about consulting that pretty much summed it up:

A senior manager is looking to hire a consulting firm. He has representatives from three firms in the waiting room. He calls in the first one and asks him a question.

"How much is two and two?"

"Four."

"Thank you, please wait outside."

He calls in the second one.

"How much is two and two?"

"Well, depending on how you look at it, if you add them up, it's four. If you put them side-by-side, it's twenty-two."

"Thank you, please wait outside."

He calls in the third.

"How much is two and two?"

The rep jumps up, runs to the window, shuts the blinds, runs to the door, and locks it, then goes to the boss and whispers in his ear, "How much do you want it to be, boss?"

For the next thirty-three years, Eddie told clients what they wanted to hear. Army, civilian...boocoo dinky dau.

Having pissed away ten years, Eddie found he was older than most of his business peers. And then there was his horseshit meter. The Army turned it on and it stayed on. His civilian career gave it a workout. From the time he first walked into the office, it started beeping.

Gee, he thought, *there's some serious horseshit here.*

The work itself bored the crap out of him, but it was easy and they soon made him a manager. The work wasn't the problem, it was the people. The

Army had turned on his horseshit meter, but it had also turned on his flatpeter meter. That one was beeping too. Horseshit was one thing, but goddammit, Eddie hated a flatpeter, and consulting was Flatpeter City. What was new was that some of the flatpeters were women.

What they hell are they? he pondered *Flat pussies?*

No matter, in his mind they were all equally worthless. He realized if he were to make a go of this consulting stuff he would have to bury his contempt under a big old rock; couldn't let that monster out into the light of day. Nonetheless, he must have been sending out major wazoo waves, because after a while they all picked up on it. But that was the one advantage of the consulting racket: there were so many of them feeding at the government trough that if you laid a turd at one, you just picked up and moved to another. Eddie went through eight before he called it a career.

He was taking a night course at the local college. On a break one night he ran into Beanie. She had been one of the jumpers out at the drop zone. Eddie had thought she was hot stuff, but she was married, so hands off. They chatted. She told him she was divorced. He said he was separated. She told him her course was boring. He said his was too. Ten minutes later, they were sitting in a bar. While getting shitfaced, she mentioned when she was a checker in a grocery store, she had a special service for assholes. She had a ball point pen with the ball sharpened to a needle point. Any dickhead behavior and she innocently put the pen next to a carton of milk, clicked the pen, and, bingo, a pinpoint hole in the carton.

"Have a nice day." Smile, chuckle, and when dickhead got home, a soaking wet bag of groceries. Eddie recognized a kindred soul. Two weeks later, she moved in.

Life should have been good for Eddie. Beanie checked all the boxes: smart, pretty, tough, funny, and fun. But, somehow, somewhere, something wasn't quite right. Things were just a little…off. His life wasn't really broken, it just wasn't smooth like it was supposed to be. It was like an engine low on oil; sure, it ran okay, it just squeaked and smoked a little.

Like talking to people. They never seemed quite to get what he was saying. He got a lot of funny looks. Jesus, it was annoying. Didn't anyone understand plain fuckin' English?

Like working on a team. He hated teams, and he was a manager for Christ's sake. He was in charge of all these flatpeter pukes, always whining, always coming to him with their flatpeter problems. So, he always selected some doofus on the team for "professional development" to handle personnel issues. "It's a growth opportunity," he would tell doofus, all the while thinking, "just keep these sorry fuckers away from me."

Like buying into organizational horseshit. All organizations, from the corner social club to General Motors, exist for one reason, to support and extend their own existence. They all pay lip service to supporting their members, but if it ever comes down to choosing between the welfare of the individual member or the welfare of the organization, they will always choose the welfare of the organization. Always. The big humma humma about the importance of the members is self-serving crapola, horseshit pure and simple. The Army taught him that and he never bought into it again.

Like processes and procedures and rules. "Rules are made for the obedience of fools and the guidance of wise men." He believed that implicitly. Any time he could break the rules without getting his jimmy smacked he did so.

Like heroes. There weren't any. The Army taught him that too. Every so often someone would do something "heroic." But other than that isolated blip they were just flawed guys like everyone else. He knew a medal of honor winner. He lied about how many parachute jumps he had. He knew a double DSC winner. He was a loud mouth and a braggart. The bravest person he ever met was Beanie, and she had never been in uniform.

Like lying. Everybody lied. Especially guys. They lied about how many women they had stupped, how many guys they had beat the piss out of, how much money they made. And they really lied about the war. At first, Eddie lied about the war too. His war wasn't like the movies, so, goddammit, he made it sound like it was. Funny thing, he always felt bad about doing that. Nothing to do with morals. Lying about the war just made him feel like shit physically. So, he just stopped. He didn't just stop lying about the war, he stopped talking about it all together. That worked, no more feeling bad. Then he stopped being around lying guys. That really worked but it cost him some of his best friends, like Fritzie and Wacky Willie and Beast and just about every Marine he knew…cut 'em all off. Later, they called it stolen valor. Eddie knew it as the Short Pecker Syndrome and his peace of mind demanded that he avoid anyone who had it. Sure, he was lonely, but lonely didn't make him feel bad.

Then there was dealing with assholes. Assholes were all around him. He just tuned 'em out, no sweaty da. Assholes getting in his face was another matter. It flipped a primal switch and there was no tuning out that. There is a reptilian part of the human brain, it's the part that controls the primitive drives related to thirst, hunger, sexuality, as well as habits and procedural memory (like putting your keys in the same place every day without thinking about it or riding a bike). Everyone has it. It runs automatically in the background, benevolent and unnoticed. But there's another part of the brain, also unnoticed, just as automatic, but fearsomely malevolent. Science is still exploring it, so it has no name. Eddie called it "the Dragon Brain." Fortunately, for society, most people live their lives with their Dragon Brain dormant and unknown. And then there is the unlucky few that suffer trauma. Trauma is the siren call to the Dragon. Like a lightning bolt, trauma sizzles through the normal brain, striking ground in the primordial darkness of "Dragon Land." The dragon rages to life, and just like that, ten million years of human development disappear. When the dragon roars, all you can do is hang on.

The first time Eddie rode the dragon was right after Beanie had moved into the apartment. To save money, the builder had skimped on insulation so there was no soundproofing. You could hear the guy next door take a piss. One night, they were jolted awake by hammering and banging from the unit above. Eddie gave it a while, and when there was no let up, he called upstairs. The guy said it was a plumber fixing his bathroom and it wouldn't be too much longer. "Fair enough," said Eddie and hung up. A few minutes later, someone started pounding on the front door. Eddie pulled on his pants, went to the door, and opened. It was the plumber, yelling about minding his own fuckin' business, and fuckin' this and fuckin' that and, and…and *bam*, Eddie hit him. Well, it was Eddie's fist, but the dragon was doing the hitting. Eddie remembered nothing of the fight. Somehow, it stopped and he went inside. Beanie looked at him wild-eyed. He was covered in blood. "Not mine," he said, "his." She cleaned him up and true, he wasn't cut, but his right hand hurt like hell. He went to the hospital; yep, broken. Riding the dragon wasn't fun.

The second time Eddie rode the dragon was about a year later. Two young punks had moved in upstairs and Eddie knew right off there was going to be a problem with noise. The punks liked their music loud. The first time, he went up and asked them politely to turn it down. They did. The second time, it was a little less polite. The third time it wasn't polite at all. The following Saturday night, they came home shitfaced. The music blasted. Then they started stomping on the floor. Eddie got dressed. Beanie tried to stop him, but the dragon was driving. He went upstairs and pounded on the door. Punk one opened. Again, Eddie couldn't remember much. They were fighting, he remembered that. Then, out of nowhere, Beanie jumped on punk one. He turned around and slugged her. Fire roared out of the dragon. It had Eddie throw the best punch of his life. Punk one went down and out. Eddie went to Beanie. She had taken the smack full on the cheek but didn't go down. Tough, tough cookie. The dragon turned and saw punk one sprawled out on the floor. The fire roared again. Eddie went over to beat him to death. Then punk two tackled him, the dragon slid back into his den, and just like that Eddie didn't have to spend the next ten years in prison. He did file charges and they went to trial. With a veteran's dark knowledge of bureaucratic worthlessness, he was sure they were going to get fucked. Surprise, surprise, punk one was convicted. You don't have to be smart if you're lucky.

The third time he rode the dragon happened while he and Beanie were driving home from a restaurant one night. Something triggered another driver, who pulled up next to Eddie and began yelling at him. The dragon pulled Eddie out of the car and had him pound on asshole's window. It rolled down, and for the first time in twenty years, Eddie had a weapon pointed at him. Survival instincts ran the dragon back to his hole and Eddie didn't die that day.

Eddie had done his share of stupid shit, but nothing came close to El Salvador. Beast opened the door, but Eddie went in all on his own. After getting back from Rhodesia, Beast hooked up with the guy who published *Mercenary Magazine*. It was a shit rag aimed for the most part at wannabes, but the honcho did have connections with the government in El Salvador. Periodically, he sent down mobile training teams to support the Salvo Army. He did it at no charge, so the price was right. Beast had done a bunch of 'em, and pumped Eddie and the boys full of the usual horseshit. Of course, Eddie knew better, but when Beast invited the gang to participate, the dumb shit in him said, "Why not?" He was in his forties, out of shape, and in a job he hated. Besides, Wacky Willy and Fritzie were going. Yeah, "Why the hell not?" So, he took personal leave from work, packed his shit, jungle fatigues and pistol, and went to El Salvador.

The civil war was going strong and the government had just formed the "Ronald Reagan Battalion," no less, to fight the guerrillas in Morazán province. The boys were there to help in the training. They flew out to a shithole called San Francisco Gotera, the battalion base camp. Eddie taught the infantrymen care and cleaning of the M-16 rifle. Beast, Fritzie, and Willie did 81 mm mortar training for the heavy weapons group. The rifle training was uneventful; Eddie could do that one in his sleep. The mortar training was different. They actually killed some people. The designated live fire range was an open field with a small house in the middle. The mortarmen needed something to shoot at, so the little house was a natural. Willy demonstrated, putting a round on it, dead center. Then the troops took their turn. A short while later, a guy on a burro came riding up. One of the officers exchanged a few words, gave him a smack and a kick, and drove him off. The boys didn't take any notice. Later, they found out that Willy's round had gone through the roof and killed the guy's son. The officer hit the guy because it was a restricted area, no civilians allowed. Eddie recognized it immediately: Sin Loi, Malloy. They finished up the training, and on the way back to San Salvador stopped off at a place that had a club for the US Army advisors. It was empty and the boys were having a drink when two regular army guys came in. They got pissed because the boys were armed. Regular army couldn't carry weapons. One thing led to another and, true to form, Willy Boy got into it with one of the Army dicks. It really wasn't a big deal, just a small fight in a small bar in a small country far from home. But Beast never got to go on another *Mercenary Magazine* trip.

2001 - 2013

Eddie's final employer was one of the biggies. Founded in 1914, it claimed to have invented management consulting. Its motto was "results that endure." Its attitude was "We Be Consulting." This was the major league: thousands of employees, offices worldwide, highly developed corporate culture, and a gold-plated reputation. He didn't buy any of it. No matter how you packaged it, it was still a mug's game and Eddie saw it for what it was, an effective mechanism for making the partners rich and everyone else miserable. Everything else was just self-serving horseshit, "polishing a turd," as he had so profoundly experienced in the Army. He didn't buy any of it.

"Say, Ed. Were you ever in the service?"

"Yeah."

"Which one?"

"Army."

"How was that?"

"It sucked."

"Why?"

"Vietnam."

"No kidding? You were in Vietnam? We've worked together for three years and I never knew that. So, what was that like?"

"Private, Mel. It's a private memory. But I will tell you what it taught me."

"What's that, Ed?"

"Never trust an organization."

"Come again?"

"Organizations, Mel. Can't trust 'em."

"I'm not with you, Ed."

"It's like this, Mel. The world is full of assholes and they're in charge of everything."

"Huh?"

"Assholes run the world, Mel. Politics, the military, religion, all run by assholes. This company, Mel. Run by assholes."

"Oh, I don't believe that, Ed. This is a great company. Look at all the benefits they give us—health insurance, a 401-matching plan, training."

"Cost of doing business, buddy. They don't give you that stuff, you go with someone who does."

"That's a pretty grim outlook, Ed."

"Realistic. Mel. Business is a bottom-line deal. If it saves them money, the assholes will shitcan you, me, the whole division. Bet on it."

"I can't believe that, Ed."

"Well, son, welcome to Vietnam."

Eddie had three company commanders in Vietnam. The third one went on to be a famous general. In retirement, he wrote a book. One of the chapters covered his time as a company commander, his time as Eddie's commander. Eddie went to the bookstore and leafed through it. It mentioned the platoon leaders; Eddie never heard of them. It mentioned the first sergeant; never heard of him. It mentioned some battles; never happened. It mentioned close air support; at that time free fire was over, it was pacification, close air was verboten. And so, and so, and so. Innocent Eddie went into Amazon, clicked on the book, and gave a review. It wasn't the usual armchair stuff, this was an "I was there and it wasn't like that." The response was brutal. He was attacked for disparaging an American hero. Eddie pulled his review. Don't fart in church, sonny.

The secret to success in We Be Consulting was top cover. Sure, there was a lot of corporate humma humma about meritocracy, but the reality was if you didn't have a partner looking out for you, you weren't going anywhere. It was a snake pit and the partners kept the vipers away from their chosen few. The rest lasted two to three years and then moved on. The chosen were chosen not just on brains and talent. Just about everyone in the firm was smart. Every now and then, a dumb shit managed to get through the hiring process, but they lasted even less time than the non-chosen. No, the partners looked for a special something, brains to be sure, but more importantly, that intangible set of qualities that together added up to an aura. In the Army, Eddie heard more than once if you lined up ten officers, you could pick out the OCS grads just by the way they looked. It was the same in We Be Consulting: if it looked good it was good. Appearance trumped everything else. Same shit, different game. Jesus, he hated it.

Eddie was chosen by Doris, a partner and the most senior woman in the firm. For whatever reason, she liked him and within a year he was a senior manager. It was money and prestige and he still hated it. But he got to travel, and he liked that...Saudi Arabia, Rumania, Jordan, Germany, Canada...a real road warrior. And then the firm went public, the partners got even richer, and Doris was out. No more top cover. Oops.

With the end of Communism, Yugoslavia broke up into seven little countries. We Be Consulting got the contract to help one of them get into NATO. The request for proposal stipulated the team leader had to be a retired general, so the firm hired a former Marine Corps brigadier. The guy's name was Dirk, and Eddie interviewed him.

"Dirk, the secret to success on this one is that you have to take your stars off. Low profile. Can you do that?"

"Hell, yes."

Hell, no. Dirk wore his stars in the shower. So did Mrs. Dirk. Eddie was put in as his deputy. Bon voyage, Titanic.

Eddie considered himself well-versed in most forms of assholery. With fifty-plus years of firsthand experience of parents, religion, school, the army, the media, and business, he thought he knew the phenomenon head-to-foot. Then two things happened to complete his education: Bush initiated the Forever Wars in Iraq and Afghanistan and Eddie went to Eastern Europe on this military support contract. Eddie quickly realized his concept of assholery was strictly small time. Here was assholery on a worldwide scale: Bush wanted to show the world invading Iraq was an international coalition against the "axis of evil." That meant get as many countries as possible to send troops to Iraq. So, the drug deal went down. The US funds a get-'em-into-NATO contract and the teeny-weeny former Yugoslav republic sends troops to Iraq. Truth of the matter was Bush didn't give a shit if Teeny-Weeny got into NATO or not. He just wanted their warm bodies in the war. So, the US dropped a few million on the contract, Teeny-Weeny sent twenty-six men to Iraq, and Bush proclaimed to the world that "...We have a coalition of twenty-six nations..." And so Eddie extended his Asshole Awareness Program. The thunderous subtlety of this horseshit diplomacy whizzed over Dirk's head like a salvo of friendly fire.

Dirk wasn't exactly stupid; he was just...well, Marine-like. One thing Eddie had noted about a lot of Marines, they believed their own press. They didn't understand that propaganda is designed to fool the enemy, not yourself. As the farmer boy said to the city boy, "Don't eat that, son, that's horseshit." Dirk didn't just eat it up, he went back for seconds. The tipoff was his rank, brigadier general. For the most part, BG is the waiting room for entrance to the club of the real generals. Some armies don't even consider it a general; it's "Brigadier," pure and simple. The club takes a close look and if the BG passes muster, they let him in. If not, it's brigadier general (retired). Dirk never made it beyond the waiting room.

Dirk had another problem: this was an Army contract. The client wasn't Teeny Weeny, it was the US Army Office of Defense Cooperation, Lieutenant Colonel Benda in charge. Benda didn't buy any of that hero stuff. Although an armor officer, he had skillfully steered his career out of harm's way, avoiding combat for every one of his seventeen years of service. He was that rarest of birds, an unapologetic flatpeter, loud and proud. Up yer butt with a CIB. He didn't even seem to like being in uniform, most days coming to the office in tweeds and pastel-colored shirts. Like most Marines, Dirk had a semper fi stiffy for the Army to begin with. But reporting to a non-combat tweedy lieutenant colonel was, well, let's just say he'd sooner piss in his mess kit.

The cherry on top of this shit sundae was Dirk's personnel evaluation system. He measured everyone against the yardstick of infantry combat: in his Marine mind, it was simple, if you'd been shot at you were a hard dick, if you hadn't, you were worthless. Hence his hasty estimate of the situation was quick and irrevocable: LTC Benda – worthless; the Defense Attaché – worthless; the Ambassador – worthless. Subtlety is not a Marine virtue and Dirk hid his contempt about as well as a fart in church. In no time at all, the battlelines were drawn.

"Why is Dirk such a dick?" Benda queried Eddie. It was a fair question.

The solution was simple, take your stars off, Marine. Move off to stage left and let the client get the spotlight. That wasn't going to happen. Dirk had spent thirty years building a monument to himself, and nothing, particularly a dorky little contract in a dorky little country run by a bunch of dorky little non-combatants, was going to change that. Hey diddle diddle, straight up the middle, damn the torpedoes. In no time at all, Dirk was to all involved, "the dickhead." Mrs. Dirk didn't help.

Officially, Mrs. Dirk was a non-combatant, but twenty years with Dickhead was enough to give anyone honorary veteran status, so he tolerated her. If occasionally she cried in the lady's room or made incoherent phone calls after a few drinks, what of it? She had worked hard to become "the General's Lady," and, goddammit, she could act as she pleased. Problem was a consultant's spouse had to be even more invisible than the consultant. Not going to happen. Her ironclad sense of entitlement trod heavily on sensitive diplomatic toes, and in no time at all she was "Nutroll." Dickhead and Nutroll leading Teeny Weeny into NATO. Jesus.

Eddie knew a ship in peril when he saw it. Sure, you try to steer it around the rocks at first, but when you hear them grinding into the hull it's time to head for the lifeboats. Too bad, he really liked Teeny Weeny.

Back home, it was the same old shit, now without Doris for top cover. Eddie's ability, more to the point his willingness, to put up with it was pretty much gone by now. He asked for the unheard of, a demotion. After some big humma humma, a flummoxed Human Resources okayed it and Eddie wasn't a senior manager anymore. He also put in for a teaching slot and, ironic though it might sound, wound up presenting the Intro to We Be Consulting to all new hires. He enjoyed being on the platform and if they had kept him on that everything would have been peachy. But they wanted him to work on projects as well, and he just couldn't do it. His horseshit shield was broken. So, for the first time in his consulting career, he fucked off. Leveraging his disability to work from home, when he wasn't teaching, he basically just fucked off. He didn't even try to hide it. He didn't go to meetings, he didn't review deliverables, he didn't do projects, he just fucked off. Even Beanie noticed.

"Are you still employed?"

"Well, I'm still getting paid. Employed would be a stretch."

Of course, the wheels began to turn to unload him, but once again he played the Disabled Veteran card, and that slowed it down. Finally, inevitably, thankfully, they dropped the hammer, and just like that, after thirty-three years and eight firms, Eddie was retired.

2013-2014

Eddie didn't have many pals. His best ones had been killed off in the war or had died quietly in the peace. When he realized he now knew more dead people than live ones, he figured that was just part of getting old. He was having a beer with John, one of the few remaining.

"They just upped my disability."

"No shit? What for?"

"PTSD."

"PTSD? You gotta be kiddin'."

"That's a firm titty. I'm now certifiably fucked up. Got the paper to prove it."

"Ahh."

"You ought to put in for it."

"Ahh. Not that faggot shit."

"Sure. You're fucked up worse than me."

"Ahh."

"Here's the card of the American Legion rep. She'll do it all for you."

"Ahh."

"Why not?"

Eddie thought about it for a few days. Yeah, why the hell not? He went to see her, gave her power of attorney, and filled out a few forms. A month later. he was interviewed by a shrink. A few months later, he got a letter from the Veteran's Administration:

"We have determined that you have post-traumatic stress disorder based on the following demonstrated behavior:

Unprovoked irritability with periods of violence

Occupational and social impairment, with deficiencies in most areas, such as work, school, family relations, judgement, thinking, or mood

Suspiciousness

Depressed mood

Impaired judgement
Retention of only highly learned material
Mild memory loss
Impaired impulse control
Chronic sleep impairment
Forgetting to complete tasks
Difficulty in understanding complex commands
Difficulty in adapting to stressful circumstances
Difficulty in adapting to work
Inability to establish and maintain effective relationships
Impairment of short- and long-term memory
Difficulty in adapting to a work like setting
Difficulty in establishing and maintaining effective work and social relationships
Forgetting directions."

"This is me they're talking about?"

Yes, in the eyes of the Veterans Administration, Edward Brandt is severely disabled.

"Well, fuck me sideways."

So, PTSD? PTSD was for pussies. That was the message Eddie had received loud and clear, lima charlie. Real men shook off the effects of combat like nothing more than a bad hangover…a cold shower, a change of clothes, head down, drive on, no sweat. None of that faggy therapy shit.

It took Eddie a lifetime to understand PTSD wasn't human weakness, it was just human. It was the way human beings handle stress, combat or otherwise. Sure, combat stress was more extreme, but life had lots of extreme stress: you got bullied in the third grade, your parents had a messy divorce, you were in a bad accident, you saw a loved one get hurt…you got PTSD. Welcome to the human race. This was a big step for Eddie. It wasn't a cure, but it was a pencil light in what had for years been a dark room.

With new insight, Eddie turned a hard eye to his journey. He reflected on his first fire fight, not what happened, that was almost predictable and that he could handle. More to the point, he remembered what he felt, what he sensed, the smell of it. They smelled terrible, not the dead ones, the living.

They stank…bad breath, bad sweat, just plain bad odor. He had read somewhere you could smell fear, but none of the war movies, war books, or war stories ever touched on that. Heroes don't stink. But Eddie realized this was how real people reacted when faced with the terrifying possibility of their own violent and messy death in the next few seconds. Nothing had prepared him for this. Years later, sitting next to an old lady on a plane that hit rough weather, he smelled it on her, the stink of fear. He wondered if anyone else sensed it. Probably not. It spooked him for weeks.

Eddie had nightmares. The worst was in the hospital right after he got hit. It was always some variation of the same shit – the platoon was in contact but he couldn't react: The radio didn't work; the radio worked but he couldn't remember the call signs; the radio worked, he remembered the call signs but no one answered. That lasted about a month. Then the nightmares stopped and the bad dreams started and that lasted the rest of his life. The bad dreams weren't terrifying, they were just annoying. Their relentless theme was that nothing ever worked. The setting varied. Sometimes it was military, sometimes it was business, and sometimes even school. He had a mission, a project, an assignment, and he couldn't get it done. He didn't have enough time or the proper resources or the required information. Every so often it would be a fist fight and he couldn't throw a punch. He was helpless, and just as it all began to crash and burn, he would wake up. The bad dreams weren't scary, but goddammit they were frustrating. And for fifty years he never had a good night's sleep. He would have paid a thousand dollars to have one night with a sweet dream.

Of course, there was the physical part: his wounds and his injuries. As always, nothing in the popular culture prepared him for these. The books and movies and stories about war didn't come close. They didn't tell you the body never forgets. If you're young and in good shape when you get hit, your body gives you a temporary pass. It masks the permanent damage. Eddie figured it was biological, that 200,000 years ago a young homo sapiens had to cope with serious injury all on his own, cope or die, fool the other predators that the boogered up caveman was vigorous, fool them into giving him a wide berth. Still works that way today. Youth will infuse a damaged body with seemingly miraculous recuperative powers. Eddie saw that first hand in the Intensive Care Ward. They'd wheel a guy in awash with shrapnel wounds and within a day or two he'd be talking. Sure, there was some medical science involved, but youth was the secret ingredient. Youth created the illusion of healing. But it was wasn't a gift, it was a loan. You paid it off with interest for the rest of your life. Again, Eddie saw that firsthand. After nineteen days in intensive care, he was up and about. He was a little shaky, but goddammit he was up and about. After a thirty-day convalescent leave, he was returned to active duty. Full recovery, just like the movies. Well, not really.

The first thing Eddie realized was that he now had a very different relationship with his body. He had been born with the gifts of an athlete: timing, coordination, and strength. He hated team sports, so the accolades that normally followed along with being athletic never happened. There were rewards, but they were subtle and he never realized what they were until his wounds took them away. Before he got hit everything worked, and worked really well. He never dropped anything, he was never off balance, he could lift pretty much anything that needed lifting, he rarely was out of breath, and, the greatest and most unacknowledged gift of all, nothing fuckin' hurt. His body did what he wanted and never complained.

All that changed after 9 July 1969. At that moment, his body switched sides. At that moment, it went from the home team to the opposition. At that moment, and for the rest of his life, his body went from being a trusted silent partner to an implacable enemy. At that moment, the pain started and never stopped.

To address the sucking chest wound the harried surgeons, pressed for time, simply hacked into him, cutting across his right side from spinal cord to sternum. It saved two of the three lobes, but killed everything below the incision. After Eddie "healed up," the result was bizarre: the left side of his lower torso was, as it always had been, well-muscled; the right, smooth as a mannikin. In addition, all that surgical futzing around left his right shoulder an inch lower than his left. As if in protest against all this abuse, what was left of his stomach muscles would periodically cramp up, doubling him over in pain. Over the years it eased up, but it never went away.

The gunshot wound to his left hand had similar odd consequences. The bullet had cleanly snipped off Eddie's ring finger and he was pretty sure that wasn't ever going to grow back. The nasty surprise, however, was the effect it had on the rest of his hand. Though visibly untouched, the middle finger and pinky somehow suffered some loss: Eddie couldn't fully bend them. They contracted just so far and that was it. He couldn't make a proper fist...

lots of fun when he got into subsequent fights. And then there was the phantom pain. The missing finger hurt, annoying, but not unexpected. The surprise was it also itched. That was maddening, an itch he couldn't scratch. The doctors said that too was normal and would eventually go away. Well, it did diminish over time, but it never completely stopped. The movies didn't cover that shit either.

As the years passed, something else began to bother Eddie: the older he got, the more alone he felt. It seemed like his life was a marathon. The race began with a crowd of other runners, but the longer he ran, the fewer the others, until as he got closer to the end he was all alone. Where the hell were the other people? Where the hell were the people like him? And why in the hell did he always feel like he was running a shitty course? School was shit, the Army was shit, business was shit, government was shit, the movies were shit, religion was shit, history was shit, the community was shit. And then came the PTSD evaluation:

Occupational and social impairment, with deficiencies in most areas, such as work, school, family relations, judgement, thinking, or mood.

Son, you just can't adjust.

Can't adjust? Can't adjust to what? Can't adjust to a shitty world? That made him 100% disabled? Sounded to Eddie like just more shit. He needed answers. Where to find them? The Veteran's Administration pointed him to group therapy.

By this time, Eddie was an old fucker. Almost everyone in the group was from the wars in Iraq or Afghanistan, some young enough to be his grandchildren, some women. No matter. By this time, he was used to being the odd man out. Two things quickly became apparent. First, most were support pukes. Every so often there would be a grunt, but for the most part Eddie was it. He tried to have an open mind, but goddammit, how could all these flatpeters have PTSD? Were papercuts giving them nightmares? But what really amazed him was the number who had thought about or even attempted suicide. It came up in almost every session. Once the shrinker asked Eddie if he had every thought about killing himself.

"Not ever, but I sure felt like killing an asshole here and there."

It was an eye-opener. For Eddie, and many of the other Vietnam vets, he knew the rage was directed at other people. For the Iraq and Afghan vets, the rage seemed to be directed inward. Let someone with a Ph.D. behind their name figure that one out. So, the group stuff had some interest, but, try as he might, Eddie couldn't make a connection. Once again, he was running the marathon alone.

Eddie had always been a reader. Over the years he had collected books, lots of 'em. Now retired, he had as much time to read as he felt like. His approach was deliciously unstructured, a reaction to the tightly organized life he had suffered in the army and business. He wandered pleasantly through history, fiction, biography, poetry, the arts, and memoirs. It was nice. One of the really nice things about it was actually NOT reading. If a book didn't grab him in the first fifty pages, he deep-sixed it. He kept a cardboard box handy to collect the discards… shitty book and *patoom!* …a three pointer. Not only did it free up shelf space, but it worked on his hand-eye coordination; win-win all around. He developed a handy-dandy triage system: boring, bullshit, or tits. Fifty pages in and boring… *patoom!* This included most of the stuff on the best seller list. Fifty pages in and bullshit…*patoom!* This included most of the war novels, memoirs, and histories. Fifty pages in and a gripper…tits! A keeper! Yeah, the titskis were way outnumbered by boring and bullshit. But that wasn't just books, that was life.

Eddie developed a taste for opera. Well, the sound of opera, really. He never read the libretto. If he liked what he heard, he just made up his own story. It was a hell of a lot easier than looking up all those dumb foreign words. More fun, too.

Something interesting began to emerge. The voices from the keepers sounded, well, they sounded just like Eddie. So, from German novelist, Erich Kaestner:

"The world is full of idiots and they are in charge of everything." *Check.*

From Indian writer, Krishnamurti:

"It is no measure of health to be well adjusted to a profoundly sick society." *Check.*

From adventure novelist, Raphael Sabatini:

"He was born with a gift of laughter and a sense that the world was mad." *Check, check.*

From Groucho Marks:

"Whatever it is, I'm against it." *Check.*

From crime novelist, Raymond Chandler:

"Down these mean streets a man must go who is not himself mean, who is neither tarnished nor afraid." *Ditto.*

And:

"There are days like that. Everybody you meet is a dope. You begin to look at yourself in the glass and wonder." *Yup.*

From poet W.H. Auden:

"Our earth in 1969

Is not the planet I call mine,

The world, I mean, that gives me strength

To hold off Chaos at arm's-length." *No shit.*

From science fiction writer, Theodore Sturgeon:

"90% of everything is crap." *Right.*

Reading led to other things. Auden wrote a poem about Breughel's painting *Landscape with the Fall of Icarus*:

> In Breughel's Icarus, for instance: how everything turns away
> Quite leisurely from the disaster; the ploughman may
> Have heard the splash, the forsaken cry,
> But for him it was not an important failure; the sun shone
> As it had to on the white legs disappearing into the green
> Water, and the expensive delicate ship that must have seen
> Something amazing, a boy falling out of the sky,
> Had somewhere to get to and sailed calmly on.

Eddie looked it up.

Painting, *The Fall of Icarus*

This painting is presented with the permission of the Royal Museum of Fine Arts, Belgium.

He was stunned. It exactly captured his Vietnam experience. It nailed Vietnam and its aftereffects better than any of the books, movies, or war stories hawked as portraying the "real" war. It got the aloneness Eddie had always felt. He was that tiny little boy falling unnoticed, as the rest of the world went about its business unconcerned and unaware:

> *...everything turns away*
> *Quite leisurely from the disaster.*

Eddie had faced the world's horseshit alone. It took a 400-year-old Dutch guy to make him finally understand that was nothing unique to Eddie Brandt, that was the human condition. Life was a marathon affair. Friends and loved ones might hand you water along the way, but you ran the race alone. And when you finally went in the drink, the angels didn't sing, the world just "sailed calmly on." Sin loi, Malloy. Live with it.

Okay, a lonely long-distance runner. How DO you live with it? Without knowing it, Eddie had already begun. Refusing to fit in was the first step. He had been doing that most of his life. "You've got a bad attitude" followed him for years. Discovering keepers was the next. Without knowing it, Eddie had been building his fellow travelers. He wasn't sure where they all were going, he just knew these were his kind of guys and being around them made him feel better. Finally, he discovered George Carlin:

"The decay and disintegration of this culture is astonishingly amusing if you are emotionally detached from it. I have always viewed it from a safe distance, knowing I don't belong; it doesn't include me, and it never has. No matter how you care to define it, I do not identify with the local group, planet, species, race, nation, state, religion, party, union, club, association, neighborhood improvement committee; I have no interest in any of it. I love and treasure individuals as I meet them, I loathe and despise the groups they identify with and belong to...

"I don't like ass-kissers, flag-wavers or team players. I like people who buck the system. Individualists. I often warn people: 'Somewhere along the way, someone is going to tell you, 'There is no 'I' in team.' What you should tell them is, 'Maybe not. But there is an 'I' in independence, individuality and integrity.'"

And so, the seemingly disparate pieces of Eddie's bumpy life fell into place. He didn't have PTSD, he had 20/20 vision. He didn't have attention deficit disorder, he had attention surplus disorder.

Carlin again:

"The longer you live, the more you look around, the more you realize, something is fucked up."

"When you're born into this world, you're given a ticket to the freak show. If you're born in America, you get a front row seat."

"And what should you do in the front row seat? Laugh often, long, and loud. Laugh until you gasp for breath."

2015

"What can I do for you, Dave?"

"Oh, nothing, Ed. I'm just observing."

"Observing what, Dave?"

"Well, as president of the woodturning club, I'm observing your technique to see how I can help you improve."

"That's nice, Dave, only I don't want to be observed and I have no interest in improving."

"I'm here to help, Ed."

"Like I said, Dave. Don't need it, don't want it. Please move on."

"No need to get testy, Ed."

"Testy, huh? You want testy, here's testy: Move the fuck out, asshole."

A short time later, Eddie quit the club.

Carlin: "Avoid teams at all cost. Keep your circle small. Never join a group that has a name. If they say, 'We're the So-and-Sos,' take a walk. And if, somehow, you must join, if it's unavoidable, such as a union or a trade association, go ahead and join. But don't participate; it will be your death. And if they tell you you're not a team player, congratulate them on being observant."

"Heh, heh, heh."

"What is it, sweetums?"

"It's recycling day."

"And have you put out the recycle bin?"

"Have I ever."

"I don't think I'm going to like this."

"I recycled the shit out of it."

"Oh, dear."

"You know that list of stuff they don't want you to put in there?"

"Oh, dear."

"Like Styrofoam."

"Oh, dear."

"That's right, baby. Right in the middle where they can't see it. Styrofoam city."

"Oh, God."

"He's got nothing to do with it. Been MIA for centuries. This is all me."

"Oh, joy."

"Recycle? Who do they think they're kidding? They don't recycle dick. It all goes into the same big hole."

"And your source for this insight?"

"Deductive reasoning, toots. Lying lungwarts lie. It's just that simple."

"The lungwarts in question would be the managers of the recycle program?"

"You're cooking with gas, sweetcakes. Those fuckwads are playing their malignant tune and I ain't dancing."

"Your own little guerrilla warfare, is it?"

"You know it. A small step for mankind."

"And this is why we have no friends."

Carlin: "Don't confuse me with those who cling to hope. I enjoy describing how things are, I have no interest in how they 'ought to be.' And I certainly have no interest in fixing them. I sincerely believe that if you think there's a solution, you're part of the problem. My motto: Fuck Hope!"

2016

"Happy Thanksgiving, folks. Come on in."

"Hi, Johnny. Happy Thanksgiving to you too."

"Great, Patty. Eddie, get yourself a beer. Everyone's in the lounge."

"Hi, there, Ed. How's it going?"

"'Lo."

"Here, grab a seat over there."

"Um."

"Boy, that was a swell dinner, Marge. You really outdid yourself this year."

"Thank you, kind sir. We'll leave you boys to solve the world's problems. Come on, girls."

"Thanks, Marge."

"Hey, John. Did you read that new book on General Patton?"

"I sure did. What a guy!"

"Yeah, old 'Blood and Guts.'"

"How about you, Ed? You like history. I think you'll get a kick out of this one."

(Whaddya nuts, John? Don't ask Ed something like that. You know what he's like.)

(Ah, he's fine.) "Ed?"

"Not a chance."

"You're missing a good one."

"I'm not 'missing' anything. Patton was a phony."

"Say what?"

"A phony. A four-star, phony-baloney, bullshitter."

"Whoa, there, partner. You're talking about one of the greatest combat leaders this country ever produced."

"Combat? What the hell did Patton know about combat?"

"He was just one of the fightingest leaders we ever had. Blood and Guts!"

"Izzat so? Okay, here's a little quiz. How much time did he actually spend in combat? And I'm not counting his time as a general. Generals don't fight. So, how much time in combat?

Three days?

Three weeks?

Three months?

Three years?"

"Easy, gotta be three years."

"Negatron. Three days."

"Ah, no way, Ed."

"Yep, three little days. One as a lieutenant in the Punitive Expedition in Mexico and two as a major in two tank battles in World War I."

"That can't be right, Ed. We're talking about old 'Blood and Guts.'"

"A four-star, phony-baloney, bullshitter."

"What am I going to do with you? Can't you just give it a rest?"

"PTSD, baby. Loud and proud."

Carlin: "It's all bullshit, folks and it's bad for ya."

"I am not a crook!"

"What's with the Nixon imitation, sweetums?"

"You remember him saying that to the press? Think I nailed it, huh, toots?"

"If you mean by nailing it, truly annoying the piss out of me, then yes."

"I am not a crook!"

"Eddie-poo, love-of-my-life, please shine some light on this latest dark shadow of yours. Why on earth are you talking like Nixon?"

"Tricky-Dicky, kiddo. The world heavyweight champion of lying weasels. All politicians bullshit the people, but they at least give a half-hearted attempt to dress up their bullshit with a cloak of sincerity. Not so Tricky-Dicky. He was completely full of shit and everyone knew it… I am not a crook!"

"You are aware that he's dead, right?"

"Dead, yes, but still useful."

"To whom, might one reluctantly ask?"

"Nothing less than Western civilization itself. You see, my dear, lesser minds are often confused if not completely overwhelmed by the depth, breadth, and sheer volume of the bullshit thrown at them literally every waking hour of the day. Wouldn't it be great, I said to myself, if the language had a built-in horseshit meter?"

"Tricky-Dicky?"

"There you go! Every time you hear the Tricky-Dicky voice, you know you're in for some major horseshit. Kinda like that furschlugginer red light thingy on the car instrument panel. Nice, huh?"

"You thought of this all by yourself, did you?"

"Yep. You know me, I'm here to help."

"No, honey. You're here to shit in the Wheaties."

"I am not a crook!"

"We're doomed."

Carlin: "Bullshit is the glue that binds us as a nation."

2017

"I'm going to pants Wellington."

"What's that, sweetie?"

"You know, pants him: tippy-toe up behind him and zippo, pull the pants down to his ankles."

"What on earth for?"

"For being a dickhead."

"He's not really a dickhead. He's just our next-door neighbor."

"Hah, that's what you know."

"I'm not with you, tuddy-wuddy."

"It's simple. There's too much shit in his front yard. It's dragging down the whole tone of the neighborhood."

"But you don't give a shit about the tone of the neighborhood."

"Balls to the neighborhood! My concern is dickhead behavior. Dickheads need to know there's no free lunch. Not around Big Mamoo. Play the dickhead, pay the piper."

"Play the dickhead, lose the pants?"

"Exactamundo, muchacha."

"I really need to talk to your PTSD counsellor."

"Hey, you know that sci-fi movie we saw last night? The bit where they space the guy?"

"You mean where they put him in the airlock and whiz him out into space?"

"That's the one. Boy, would I like to space someone."

"Oh, God."

Carlin: "People who see life as anything more than pure entertainment are missing the point... It's important if you don't give a shit. It can help you a lot."

"Morning, Ed. Well, garbage day again."

"Yeah, every Wednesday."

"Looks like you've got a full load there."

"Yeah, lotta garbage."

"You vote yesterday?"

"Yessiree, I'm a good American."

"Well, I won't ask who for."

"Not a problem, Harry. The same two I always vote for."

"Eh, how's that?"

"Always vote for the same two guys: Mickey Mouse for president and Donald Duck for vice president."

"Huh?"

"Yep, Mickey and Donald. If they get in, they can't fuck things up any more than the other assholes."

"You know, Ed, I just realized I've got something really important to do."

"Okey dokey. Do the shit out of it, Harry."

Carlin: "I have solved this political dilemma in a very direct way: I don't vote. On Election Day, I stay home. I firmly believe that if you vote, you have no right to complain. Now, some people like to twist that around. They say, 'If you don't vote, you have no right to complain,' but where's the logic in that? If you vote, and you elect dishonest, incompetent politicians, and they get into office and screw everything up, you are responsible for what they have done. You voted them in. You caused the problem. You have no right to complain. I, on the other hand, who did not vote – who did not even leave the house on Election Day – am in no way responsible for what these politicians have done and have every right to complain about the mess that you created."

2018

"Try to behave, sweetie, just for me."

"I hate Christmas."

"I know, but it's my sisters-in-law. They're good people, so be nice, okay? Here we are."

"Patty! Eddie! Merry Christmas! Come on in. Let me take your coats."

"And a Merry Christmas to you, Johnny. Eddie, why don't you go with Johnny and sit with the fellas?"

(Mmmrrrr)

"Merry Christmas, Ed. Grab a beer and have a seat."

(Mmmrrrr)

"…and that's a fact. Hey, Eddie. Merry Christmas."

(Mmmrrrr)

"So, like I was saying, I'm reading this new biography on Washington and it's super. I mean it really gets down to the nitty gritty, you know, what a great man he was and all."

(Mmmrrrr)

"Yup, father of the country."

(Mmmrrrr)

"Yup, told the Brits where to get off."

(Mmmrrrr)

"Yup, and a military genius to boot. Don't you think so, Eddie?"

(Mmmrrrr)

"What's that, Ed?"

"He's overrated."

"What?"

"Overrated. Big time."

"Ed, we're talking George Washington here."

"Yeah, George Washington. Let me tell you about George friggin' Washington. He was a dud."

"A dud? What are you saying, Eddie?"

"I'm saying he fought sixteen battles in the war. Guess how many he won. Six. Six out of sixteen. That's not the guy I want leading me in battle. Gimme the one with sixteen and oh."

"Jesus, Ed. You're talking about the father of the country."

"A dud. A big fuckin' dud."

"Well, I hope you're proud of yourself."

"Heh, heh, heh."

"You just couldn't put a lid on it, could you? Just for a few goddamn hours. Just for me. You just had to stick to them."

"Ah, it's good for 'em."

"You're really carrying this PTSD stuff too far."

"Ah, it's fun."

Carlin: "Think of how it all started: America was founded by slaveowners who informed us, 'All men are created equal.' All 'men,' except Indians, niggers, and women. Remember, the founders were a small group of unelected, white, male, land-holding slaveowners who also, by the way, suggested their class be the only one allowed to vote. To my mind, that is what's known as being stunningly—and embarrassingly—full of shit."

"I hate Halloween."

"Yes, dear, I know you do."

"I hate those little shits coming around grubbing for candy."

"Yes, dear, I know you do."

"Well, none of that this year. I'm going to get some barbed wire and wire up the driveway. That'll keep the little fuckers away."

"You don't have to do that, sweetie. They won't come anyway."

"Whaddya mean, they won't come?"

"They won't come because they all think you're a crabby old fuck."

"Crabby old fuck! Who's a crabby old fuck?"

"You are, honeybun."

"Yeah, well maybe I'll throw in a few boobytraps just for shits and giggles."

"That's nice, dear."

"Listen, I went down a long hard road to reach crabby-old-fuckness. I earned it, I deserve it, and goddammit, I'm not hiding under a bush. Old, crabby, and proud of it."

"That's nice, dear. More coffee?"

Carlin: "Sometimes a little brain damage can help...fuck rational thought."

There were two more steps that tied a bow on the whole process. The first was no rules. Eddie had spent his whole life in a world constricted by rules, rules invented, imposed, and enforced by people whose ideas of acceptable behavior fit him like a cheap suit. Sure, he had for the most part ignored them, or simply bent them a little. But it was still someone playing a shitty tune and yelling at him to get in step. No more. Retirement was his world and his rules. He never read instructions. If he bought something that needed assembly, he just figured it out. No can do, patoom, shitcan. He never followed procedures. He had a dozen fruit trees planted. Some of them called for specific fertilizing and insect spraying. He never did it. Shitty fruit or even no fruit, tough titty. It was his goddamn orchard and he'd grow fruit his goddamn way, end of story. He never planned anything. If he had a project, he just did it. There was no Gantt chart, no spreadsheet, no cost estimate; he'd done that shit for thirty-three years. And, you know what? Without planning, most of his projects worked out fine. If they didn't, he just laughed because it really didn't matter. He read somewhere that rules were made for the obedience of fools and the guidance of wise men. Roger dodger, over and out.

The final part of the "Eddie Program" was furnishing the house. It wasn't "Home Beautiful;" it was "Home Eddie." His approach was simple: no matter where you go, you see something interesting. So, the place was full of stuff. According to standard guidelines of décor, it looked junky. According to Beanie, it looked like a ransom note. According to Eddie, it looked cool. To his way of thinking, it told the human story. He had carvings from Africa, statues from Thailand, Art Deco figurines, Norman Rockwell prints, great master prints, airplane stuff from the first world war, heads from Egypt, sculptures from Weimar Germany, stuffed heads from the Serengeti, and porcelain from where ever. Junky? Maybe. Interesting? You know it. Just walking through home made him feel good, and that was the goal of the Eddie Program. It was his favorite place in the world.

2019-?

Eddie had travelled far in seventy-four years. It felt like far. He was missing several of his original body parts and much of what remained either hurt periodically or sometimes just plain didn't work. But he had read Hunter Thompson:

"Life should not be a journey to the grave with the intention of arriving safely in a pretty and well-preserved body, but rather to skid in broadside in a cloud of smoke, thoroughly used up, totally worn out, and loudly proclaiming, 'Wow! What a Ride!'"

Wow, indeed. So, he crawled forwards, laughing often, long, and loud, laughing until he gasped for breath. He couldn't see the finish line, but he knew he was close. Another challenge…

One more river to cross
One more river to cross
One more river to cross.

CPSIA information can be obtained
at www.ICGtesting.com
Printed in the USA
LVHW071105040522
717863LV00001B/1

* 9 7 8 1 6 3 9 3 7 2 1 6 4 *